Regression

Regression

The Strange Journey of
Thomas J Martin

Paul L Moorcraft

MILLSTREAM PRESS

Distributed by Gardners Books, 1 Whittle Drive, Eastbourne, East Sussex,
BN23 6QH
Tel: +44(0)1323 521555 | Fax: +44(0)1323 521666

All the characters in this book are fictitious and any resemblance to actual
people, living or dead, is purely imaginary.

British Library Cataloguing in Publication Data
A catalogue record for this book is available from the British Library.

ISBN 978-0-9537977-4-5

Typeset by Amolibros, Milverton, Somerset
www.amolibros.com
This book production has been managed by Amolibros
Printed and bound by T J International Ltd, Padstow, Cornwall, UK

ABOUT THE AUTHOR Paul Moorcraft has been a professor, paramilitary policeman, film producer and political pundit as well as a Whitehall warrior and a war correspondent. The author of over twenty books of fiction and non-fiction, his auto-biographical *Inside the Danger Zones: Travels to Arresting Places* (2010) is available in paperback and in e-book.

Editor's note

"Eternity is a terrible thought. I mean, where's it going to end?" *Tom Stoppard*

*M*any famous diaries have turned out to be bogus. Hitler's diaries, for example, were soon proved a fake. I am sure, however, that the journal of Dr Thomas J Martin, an American psychiatrist living in London, is genuine. It recounts a tale which defies logic but not belief.

I have dealt in hard facts, the standard fare of over thirty years of frontline journalism. This is what happened. I received the diaries in May 2007 and spent over a year checking out their provenance and historical detail as well as police evidence. I've also conducted interviews with the doctor's friends in London and family in Washington. Dr Martin disappeared on or about 17 February 2007. No trace of him has ever been discovered.

I have occasionally edited the diary for grammatical consistency and removed or translated a sprinkling of Americanisms which might have confused a wider audience; I have also excised a few repetitive historical details. A handful of archaic Surrey dialect words or expressions were updated or sometimes taken out. In addition, one or two small deletions were suggested by lawyers and, in one case, there was a possible slight bowdlerization of the text before I received it. These minor issues have been footnoted. Also, I have added, corrected or enhanced occasional sections of dialogue, based on the facts or later interviews. Sometimes the original text was a bald, rushed journal; in most cases Tom Martin tried to write in a more literary style. He was, after all, a Rhodes Scholar, though a man under considerable emotional pressure, as the story makes clear. I have ventured to standardise the work. Except for this editing, the account is as true to the intentions of the final text left by Tom Martin as I could make it.

The original typed diary, plus a few handwritten notes, were given to me by his closest friend in London, Dr Jane McCarthy, to whom it is partially addressed. Tom Martin's family has given me permission to edit and publish it as a book, in the hope that it might stimulate a public awareness that could resolve the mystery of the disappearance of a very promising physician.

Dr Paul Moorcraft
Gomshall,
Surrey
England
8 August 2011

The Journal

of

Dr Thomas J Martin

One

February 2007

I have loved her all my life, though it has taken a lifetime to appreciate it. Perhaps it has taken many lifetimes.

Jane, you will see this as a betrayal. But I love you, and I also love her. And I know that she must come first. This sounds bizarre, I know. But this is what I feel, and this is the absolute truth, the only truth that matters.

This is my story, written not just for my friend Jane McCarthy but for anyone else who wants to understand my strange journey.

I was trained as a scientist and, before this happened, I believed in only what I could see, or what other scientists had seen, and tested, in a laboratory or a hospital ward. But now I know better. I am describing what I saw, even though it defies all the science in the world. Although I had always been an agnostic, it does seem that modern science has left little space for the soul in the body or for God in the universe.

I am writing this almost without stopping; "a stream of consciousness" writers call it, though I am staking no literary claims. I am a doctor not a writer. I need to get it all down in case it is all a dream, in case I have gone mad. I need to explain it all to myself, and to Jane, and to my family. I have to tell this story now, while it is pulsating through my brain. My body feels in the grip of a fever. I am immensely thirsty, but I cannot easily drink, or eat. My brain is utterly clear, though. It's as if I have been blind my whole life and now, suddenly, I can see the intricate mechanics of the universe. As if I can savour to the full all the perfumes in existence. I'm utterly alive for the first time, but perhaps I'm not…that is the central question I ask myself.

I shall lock myself away until I have finished, though I'm not sure exactly how it started. Perhaps it was that night in the Dolce Vita restaurant in Southwark, south London…

England is all that matters now. Sure, I'm an American and I love my country, right or wrong: whoever its president may be; whatever its foreign policy. I believe that America is trying to do its best in the world. It makes mistakes, but if there wasn't the USA sticking its nose into other people's lives a hell of a lot more tyrants and megalomaniacs would be making their countries more miserable. I'm not a political geek, however, I'm a doctor. And, I'd like to think, a bloody good one. Yes, I say "bloody", because I like the English way of saying things and sometimes the English way of doing things. And, despite England's fixation with class, I admire its heritage and culture. I've learned a lot about its history, a little bit by reading, but more by living it, particularly the 1790s. England in the eighteenth century was a tough place: grime, sickness and hard, short lives for the vast majority of the people, the poor. But it made them live for the day, and − in my case − love for eternity.

At best that must sound banal, or confusing.

But I must tell my story as I experienced it.

So I suppose I should tell you a little about myself before I discovered my passion for an England of long ago.

I was born in Washington DC on January 11th in 1961. A good middle-class suburb is where I lived. My father was a reasonably successful dentist and my mother had "taught school" − I shall try to write the Queen's English in this story − my mother had been a school teacher for about ten years, before concentrating on raising me and my brother, Mike. My brother was two years older than me. I guess I always played freshman to his junior, at least when we were younger. He went into sports administration, which disappointed my father. My father wanted Mike to be a doctor. But Mike didn't want that − he loved baseball and football.

Therefore my father worked on me instead. I definitely got the curveball there. Maybe he thought I was more malleable. I was reluctant at first, but he went on and on, telling me how, if only he had his time over again, he would have been a real doctor, not just someone filling teeth. I managed to keep up my grades at school and was not great at sport, but I had a feel for science, secured high marks and was accepted into Harvard Medical School. The morning in 1980 when we received the letter was the happiest day of my father's life.

So that was it. I passed my exams and did well as an intern. Then I was awarded the opportunity to study psychiatry at Oxford, a Rhodes scholarship. That made my father really happy. He said to me, "Tom, you've got to learn to play rugby. Get a Blue − that's what they call it, if you play for the university against their old rivals, Cambridge."

I went to England in 1987 and, except for occasional visits home, I just sort of stayed. I didn't get the hang of rugby. I also tried, and failed, to decipher cricket. It was just unbelievably tedious. I did, however, play squash for my college, but not for the university, so I didn't achieve a Full Blue. I loved the place and the people, the sense of history, and the feeling of being at home, especially when I walked in the countryside. I had that deep feeling in my gut of somehow belonging, even then... I just felt at peace in England, though initially I found London rather intimidating.

I studied and then worked at Warneford and John Radcliffe hospitals in Oxford, which were affiliated to the Department of Psychiatry at the University. I ended up as a consultant psychiatrist at both St Thomas' Hospital, in central London, in a special unit for sleep disorders, and at Guy's. That was in 1999. Although I had a comfortable apartment in Kensington, just around the corner from Notting Hill tube, I enjoyed exploring south of the River Thames, especially Southwark. So much history enveloped me. Some of it was ersatz – the London Dungeon for example: much too touristy, even for my American taste. Much more attractive was Shakespeare's Globe theatre, a re-creation, true, but a fine one financed by a compatriot. Almost next door stood an ancient pub, the Blue Anchor. And not far away, one of my favourites, an old coaching inn, the George, with its impressive wooden balconies.

In some of the less tourist-infested pubs you could find real people. I thoroughly enjoyed talking to ordinary British men and women. They didn't talk to me as a doctor; that was always stilted, despite my alleged professional skills of making people relax. But, in public houses, people say the most amazing things. Some of it I dubbed "pub bullshit", but I got into the way they thought, and talked. Soon I lost most of my Washington twang.

I managed to practise a lot in pubs, despite my long hours in work. I persevered because it was a way around the constricting rules of class. I soon appreciated that a bar counter is one of the few places in England where it's socially acceptable to make conversation with a complete stranger.

Americans find it hard to swallow the no-waiter system, but I soon understood that it was designed to promote sociability.

I used to go to Southwark Cathedral for lunch-time concerts, and, next door, a real old-fashioned piece of London – Borough Market, especially on Fridays. I always bought some of the country cheeses. I was busy, but I did try to take a proper lunch break at least once or twice a week. Some of the old passages recalled Charles Dickens. Now I understand why the blackened walls of the alleyways, with their hidden secrets, so attracted me: they were my secrets too. The roads were clogged and public transport was equally Dickensian, but I grew to love London.

Southwark was especially appealing because so much of the eighteenth century survived, even into the twenty-first century. It's working class, while Kensington is one of the most up-market suburbs in London. You can survive in the city only if you treat the area where you live or work as your village, otherwise you become overwhelmed by the size, the bumper-to-bumper traffic, the throng of people. In short, I became acclimatized, almost naturalized.

I found it challenging to work for that decaying miracle of English socialism – the National Health System, the NHS. Well, at first of course I talked about "English" socialism, but I soon learned differently; that many of the leading early socialists were Scottish, and that robust Welshman, Aneurin Bevan, had steered the National Health Act through Parliament after the Second World War. One of the first things I understood about Britain is that it is made up of four nations at least – England, Wales, Scotland and Ireland.

Besides its four native nations, London is also teeming with other races. The cosmopolitanism appealed to my inquisitive and restless spirit, although some of the racism of the native British was often downright offensive. It reminded me sometimes of the American Deep South. A few of my black NHS patients reported blatant incidents of racism to me.

Maybe, because I was American, they thought they could complain about the Brits.

It was different in Harley Street. Compared with America, NHS consultants were paid a pittance so we needed to top up our salaries with private work. On some evenings, on Fridays and some Saturday mornings, I held court in my own rooms. My patients were mainly uptight middle-class whites, largely women. Perhaps I was a good doctor, but I possessed sufficient self-awareness to know that many of my wealthy female patients came because I had an undeserved reputation for being popular with celebrities. It's true that I did have a number of minor TV personalities and a few starlets as my patients.

The social calibre of my practice was improved by occasional mentions in the gossip columns and showbiz sections of the *Evening Standard* and magazines such as the *Tatler*. Dr Jane McCarthy was described as "my frequent companion" though I think she failed to see the funny side when I was once described, very inaccurately, as "one of London's most eligible bachelors". I can see that must have been hurtful now, but it raised my profile, and my bank balance.

I was professionally committed to the sick, but I didn't have to go around in rags just to prove my commitment. The good things in life were welcome. I worked hard and played hard, squash and even a little golf. I drove a Mercedes convertible, an old one, partly because Jane would have accused me, in her inimitable Yorkshire way, of being "too flashy". I found it amusing that Yorkshire people relished breaking the English taboo on talking about money. "Where there's muck, there's brass" was the leitmotif of their unique rejection of the English reluctance to discuss money even in business, which so astounded my compatriots in the City.

Life was good. I enjoyed Britain, my work and Jane. Maybe it was too good to last.

Then life wacked me over the head with a baseball bat.

The epiphany came to me, as I mentioned, in the Dolce

Vita, a small Italian restaurant around the corner from Borough Market. I can remember so many things – especially what people said and did on my later "adventure" – but some things about London in the twenty-first century now elude me. Though I do recall clearly that Jane and I had had a good meal: simple pasta – spaghetti carbonara – I think it was – with straightforward Italian wine, a pinot grigio. We'd shared a bottle, just the one. I wasn't drunk.

Jane was talking about her work as a hospital registrar, and how she hated the indignities of cramped mixed-sex wards. Then she started going on about having to put patients on trolleys in the hospital corridors. Sometimes for more than twenty-four hours. Although it happened only occasionally, Jane – rightly – saw this as a personal affront as well as an assault on her profession.

"Bloody bureaucrats," I remember Jane proclaiming very passionately about her pet hate, NHS managers. "They wouldn't like their wives or mothers lying in corridors at night, with people knocking against their drips. They get paid a fortune, more than specialists some of them, and they can't organize a piss-up in a brewery.

"The golden rule is pass the buck: never do today what will become someone else's responsibility tomorrow."

I always admired the fact that Jane had never forgotten her northern roots; she inevitably called a spade a bloody shovel. She went on in the same vein for a while and my mind started to drift, just a tad.

That's when it happened.

I couldn't tell Jane. She would have thought I was "off my trolley" – one of her favourite phrases.

One moment I'm looking at Jane. I'm sitting in front of a slim blonde in her mid-thirties, the woman I love. She's dressed in a tan-coloured linen suit.

The next second she isn't there anymore.

An entirely different female is sitting in front of me: a

slightly larger, dark-haired woman is right smack there, in a blue dress that was tucked in under her bust. "Empire line" I think it's called.

I felt as if I had been kicked in the stomach by a mule and I thought I would retch…

And then in another second the apparition was gone.

And Jane was there saying, more in exasperation than irritation, "Tom, what's wrong? You look like you swallowed something really awful. Whatever it is, you're not listening. You men are all the same. You can't listen…"

What could I say? Luckily Jane stopped short because it wasn't a fair comment – generally. She often said that I am a good listener, professionally and personally.

Jane did seem a little alarmed now.

I was too.

Jane had been sitting a few feet from me, across a small table. Then she morphed into someone else.

It was just a flash, but it was very real.

To me.

I couldn't tell Jane what I had seen, or imagined I had seen. I made some lame excuse about overwork and stress, and Jane let it pass. But that night, after I went home alone, in my mind I replayed the flash over and over again. Somehow, I managed to slow down that momentary vision. The "other woman" – that's how I put it to myself – was slightly dark-skinned, perhaps Italian.

From another time.

It wasn't just the dark-blue empire-line dress, made, I think, out of coarse cotton. No, it was her diffidence, a shyness that was quite old fashioned. She had a mole on her left cheek, and a blue ribbon around her neck, with a kind of brooch.

Where had this vision come from? Whatever it was, I became an instant, if temporary, hypochondriac. Was it transference from my patients? I asked myself. Had I succumbed to Mûnchausen's Syndrome? I must be sane, I argued, otherwise I would not have considered, even briefly such various options. I was a little concerned at the involuntary brain activity, but I was also curious. I soon put it behind, though. Psychiatrists are trained to do that.

Two

$\mathcal{T}$he next memorable incident in my story was not a vision but a real-live alpha male: a rather unsavoury businessman from the East End of London.

I met him at 42a Harley Street.

I have two small rooms on the third floor, and a part-time receptionist, who is a retired nurse. Mary Duncan is the best sort. She could have become a successful matron in the days when they ruled the roost in British hospitals. But she had quit her career to bring up her two children. Now the children, as well as her husband, had left home, and she doted on me. She worked for two and a half days a week officially, but I reckoned that – with extra administration and paperwork – she put in a lot more time. She mothered me, which I liked, but there was also that hint of flirtation, even though she was at least twelve years older than me.

So it was with the normal degree of polite informality that she entered my main consulting room one Friday afternoon in April 2006.

"Jim Crozier to see you, Tom."

It had taken me two years to get her to stop calling me "Dr Martin" or "Mr Martin" when we were on our own.

"He's quite well known," she said conspiratorially. She turned around to make sure the door was closed.

"Connections," she said, tapping the side of her nose with her outstretched index finger. "No convictions since he was a kid, I understand.[1] ... Smart lawyers now of course. Often in the papers. He looks a lot like a younger version of Bob Hoskins, the actor. Well, I think so anyway. Usually he has on his arm Nichole Sandman, the actress – one of your former patients, you will no doubt recall – though it was some time ago. The papers say she's spent more time looking up at ceilings than Michelangelo."

Her tittle-tattle was usually delivered in a slightly ironic style which belied her generally professional manner.

I initially indulged, then slightly encouraged, her penchant for gossip, not least because it gave me occasional insights which I missed as a foreigner who didn't read the tabloids or glossy society magazines. She enjoyed meeting the minor celebrities who came to see me. And it sometimes saved my having to read up – and read between the lines of – all my case notes, which she would type up. Mary also had an encyclopaedic memory.

Strictly speaking, I was already breaking rules. A good psychiatrist should start with a clean slate, and not prejudice a professional opinion by prior knowledge. But I sometimes found the extra data rounded off the profiles I created from my therapy sessions. Nor was it a good idea to deal with couples, unless they came in together to be treated. Otherwise I could get sucked into what we called "a drama triangle". I hadn't treated Crozier's partner for some years so I brushed aside that warning signal. God knows why, but I felt curious about this man. I was relying on instinct not scientific analysis, a pattern which would soon repeat itself, I later realised.

"Show Mr Crozier in, please," I said when the door was open.

James Crozier walked in, with a practised air of both nonchalance and aggression. He was in his mid-forties and rather overdressed. The suit was Armani, I guessed, and the tie and shirt matched, but the white contrast collar was a touch too flamboyant. His style smacked of conspicuous consumption: a signal that James Crozier had money, new money, and he wanted the rest of the world to know. I came to the front of my desk and managed to survive his crushing handshake. He wasn't tall, but he was very strong. I sensed that he carried his mind as some men carry their heads – a little to one side; the kind of man who brings a gun to a knife fight. I disliked him on sight.

"Mr Crozier, please sit down." I gestured to what I called a reclining armchair; a psychiatrist's couch was a cliché. "How would you like to be addressed – what should I call you?"

"Call me Jim – everybody does."

"Fine, er, Jim," I said a little self-consciously, though I usually tried to avoid calling my patients by their first names. Another rule broken.

"How can I help?"

"Well, Dr Martin, I didn't really want to come, but my Nichole is always singin' your praises. You helped a lot in the past…with her…little excesses. She nagged me into making an appointment…She sleeps too much now, but that isn't my problem. I have trouble gettin' into the Land of Nod. And when I finally fall asleep, I get awful nightmares. Nichole says my shoutin' is drivin' her nuts."

"Er, before we get down to details, would you like my receptionist to bring you some bottled water?" I rarely offered tea, in fact any stimulant, to my patients. The English tea ritual was too time-consuming, and it encouraged pointless small talk.

"No, thank you. I don't want to be here longer than I have to. Just need some advice and maybe you can give me somethin' *special*." The emphasis implied that he deserved and expected VIP treatment all round.

"Your GP, who has referred you, says in his notes that you have already tried most of the conventional sleeping remedies.

And I see that you have spent some time with that excellent clinical psychologist in Cobham, Dr Wendy Hamilton. You will be aware that she deployed cognitive behavioural therapy, but you were, apparently, somewhat, er, resistant to her approach."

"Yes, she's a foxy lady, but I found her bleedin' irritating. That's why I'm here to see you, to find out if I have what they call 'neurological problems'."

"That's possible, but I will need to do some more standard medical checks, blood tests an so on. So I can prepare a proper treatment plan. And I can see that previous clinicians have discussed 'sleep hygiene' with you."

"It was all bollocks. I want someone to fix me properly. I need my sleep."

It was obvious that Mr Crozier was going to be a demanding patient.

"OK, let's discuss what you believe the issue to be. What are your sleep patterns at the moment?"

Crozier fiddled with his tie knot for a few seconds, then he said, "I can eventually get to sleep – especially if I've been drinkin' – but it's the bloody nightmares I get. I can't ever get back to sleep after one of 'em."

"Would you describe the nightmares?"

"It's usually the same one, though sometimes there's a slight variation."

Crozier paused, and I waited for him to continue. He looked down at his expensive Italian shoes, as though he were weighing up whether he should trust me or not.

"It's like this, Doctor. I'm nearly always in some sort of hut. And it's freezing cold. This geezer – dressed in very old-fashioned gear – is comin' towards me with a knife. No matter how hard I fight – and I've been in a few scraps in my time – I can't beat him off. He keeps comin' at me, no matter how hard I hit him. He keeps comin' at me, like some kind of mad bear, keeps runnin' at me... and he then tries to cut my throat with a dirty great knife...then I feel a terrible choking sensation, and I can't breathe at all, then I usually wake up. Often in a real sweat. Nichole says it's drivin' her mad. And I need some sleep. It's affecting my work."

"May I ask what your work is?"

"I used to be a footballer, professional, some top clubs, until I had a bad knee injury. Now, I'm what I would describe as 'an entrepreneur'. I run a number of clubs and restaurants. High-class establishments. Nothin' sordid. So don't ask me whether I recognize the man from any of my 'associates'," he said pointedly. "'Cos I don't. He's a complete stranger."

After taking some blood samples, and checking his general health, I spent about forty minutes creating a case history of Crozier. I asked about his work, his relationships and a little about his upbringing. He was cagey, so I didn't press him too much on this first meeting.

I outlined some of the basic causes of sleep disruption, explaining it is often anxiety-related, and also that it's quite common. It's possible to bring back essential restorative sleep, I said. I was trying to build up a rapport with him at which I feel I was partially successful as, towards the end of our session, he did seem more relaxed.

I suggested that he spent a night in the sleep disorder clinic at St Thomas' where we could monitor his sleep patterns precisely. I explained that I worked there for some of my time.

Crozier seemed agitated at the mention of St Thomas'.

"It's state of the art, very modern, the leading unit in the UK, with excellent staff who get impressive results." I tried to reassure him.

His eyes narrowed to slits as he said, "I don't do bleedin' NHS, and I hate hospitals, any institutions for that matter, that's why I came to see you privately here in Harley Street. And I certainly don't fancy spendin' a whole night with electrodes stuck to my bonce, with people gawking at me."

I managed to pacify him.

Again he asked for "something fancy to get off to sleep".

"Let's hold off for a little while, I don't want to prescribe anything until I know more about what we are dealing with here. If you feel it will be helpful, I suggest that you come to see me again."

I suggested once a week. Crozier was reluctant, however.

"Look, Doctor, I appreciate your help, but can I come maybe twice a month? My life is very hectic at the moment – I'm opening up a new club in Piccadilly."

"That's fine. Please make an appointment with Mrs Duncan on the way out. Two weeks' time. I shall see you then. And we'll see how it works out."

He shook my hand, slightly less forcefully this time, and left.

After a few minutes, my receptionist came in with a tea tray, with some of my favourite cookies. She knew I would never discuss my patients with her, but she always looked for signs of special interest, especially if the patient were a minor celebrity.

"He's booked for two weeks today – three-thirty p.m.," she said, placing the tray on my desk and hovering for a few seconds.

I said nothing, but a thank you. Something about Crozier certainly did interest me, and I think the canny Mary Duncan had noticed this.

"Do you want me to get the files on Nichole Sandman?"

This was rather intrusive and perhaps unethical of Mary, I thought, so I smiled and said no. Nevertheless, I did stay after Mary left and examined Ms Sandman's file on my own, and at length.

Crozier came to see me regularly over the next six months. It was more a confessional than therapy, though I reckoned they often amounted to the same. Initially he was reluctant to talk, but soon I had trouble getting a word in during our sessions. He talked about his life, his work and his occasional brushes with the law when he was younger. Crozier claimed that he was sleeping better and that his nightmares were less frequent, but I was not sure that I believed him. He seemed almost to be justifying – to himself – a return on the fairly large fees he was paying me. Eventually, he conceded that, although he "quite" liked talking to me, his nightmares, though less frequent, were still afflicting him.

I surprised myself when I heard myself saying, "Perhaps we should try a different approach. What do you feel about hypnotherapy?"

I had spoken informally over a few drinks to an American friend, an experienced hypnotherapist, about his techniques, and I had dabbled in it a little bit before during my post-graduate research. But I hadn't in any way made up my mind to try it.

Crozier was as surprised as me, though he didn't hide his feelings. "You mean you want to dangle a pocket watch and hypnotize me?"

"It's not like that…let's say it's a deep-relaxation technique, a form of meditation, if you like, and then, when you are suitably relaxed, I'll try to take you back to your early childhood. Sometimes early trauma, even a single incident which you have probably repressed, can affect adult behaviour, especially sleep patterns. Dreams, and nightmares, can sometimes shape our waking hours."

"I'm not keen, Doctor. I wasn't sexually abused, and my old man – though he wasn't around much – didn't belt me more than I deserved. I thought that you people had given up on that sort of thing, anyway. Went out with Freud."

I laughed. "Psychiatry has come a long way since Dr Freud. He got some things right and a lot wrong, but science has progressed. As I said, I don't often use deep-relaxation techniques, hypnotherapy – or hypnosis, if you insist. But some of my colleagues have found it to be very useful in treating sleep disorders. Why don't we try it? It could well help you."

Crozier reluctantly agreed. And I explained what I would do.

"I will tape your responses, for you to listen to later, if you wish. This is standard practice. Then I will use the word 'alpha' as the signal to relax you. The word will not affect you at other times, only when I use it in your treatment.

"Make yourself comfortable in the armchair and close your eyes. Relax. Try to put all thoughts – of business, your personal life – out of your mind… Are you relaxed?"

"As much as I ever am. But carry on. I'm pretty sure you won't be able to hypnotize me. I suspect I'm too bloody-minded to respond in the way you want."

"I am not trying to hypnotize you. I want to relax you, and to get your mind to be at peace with itself, and to open up a little. OK, just relax. I shall count down from twenty. When I reach 1 you should be in a very relaxed state. Ready? 20 alpha. 19 alpha. 18 alpha."

I continued gradually lowering the tone of my voice. My voice grew stronger, more resonant, more insistent.

"10 alpha. 9 alpha…"

Crozier seemed to have fallen asleep.

When I reached 1 alpha, he seemed to be soundly asleep or very deeply relaxed. I wondered whether my patient was simulating a hypnotic state.

"Can you hear me?"

"Yes," he said hesitantly, almost in a childish voice. Crozier's answer seemed to come from a long way off. He was either a talented actor, though he had had no reason to pretend, or he had indeed fallen into a deep hypnotic trance. I had never imagined I could have induced a deep trance state so quickly;

it was certainly not a speciality of mine. It was as if Crozier's psyche had overcome his external bluffness and welcomed this entry into his hidden mind.

"Relax: time is running backwards. I want you to go back in your mind to when you were a little boy. Let's try when you were five or six. Alright? Try to picture yourself then."

I asked again, "Can you hear me?"

A pause. Then, in a small voice, "Yes."

"What do you see?"

"I am in school. In the playground. I am with a gang of my mates. We are pushin' Henry Williams around. I never liked him. He is cryin' and we are laughin'."

"How do you feel?"

"Good. I like makin' Henry cry. He is a twat."

"OK. Go back a little further. What is your earliest memory?"

"Of where?"

"Anywhere. Perhaps at home. Think of a time when you were most happy."

"What do you mean by 'happy'?"

"When everything was good in your life… when there was no hurt or anger."

My patient was silent for nearly a minute.

Then he spoke in slightly excited, very breathy, tones: "It's near a caravan. I think I'm three. It's at the seaside. I'm sitting on the sand. And my mother is next to me. She is helping me to build sandcastles. I can see my mother laughing. She's so happy."

"And how do you feel?"

"I don't know."

"Can you see yourself on the beach?"

"Yes, sitting next to my mummy."

"Good, try to move around the back of the little boy that you say is you."

"How?"

"Just walk towards his back"

20

"I'm doing that," he said in a frightened voice.

"Just move towards him, reach out your arms, as though you are putting on a large dressing gown."

"I don't know what you mean."

"Just reach out to him and you will merge into him."

Crozier paused, then blurted out, "Yes, I can see my legs, and mummy's right next to me, and I can touch her green dress."

"Are you happy doing this?"

"I feel warm. Everyone is happy." And Crozier sighed with contentment.

"How do you feel towards your mother?"

"I love her."

"And your father?"

"I don't know. He isn't here. It's just my mummy, and some other kid I don't know. We're making sandcastles."

"So you like building sandcastles?"

"Yes, but the other kid kicks them over when my mummy isn't lookin'. I am hitting him and he's startin' to cry."

"Do you feel better for hitting him?"

"Yes. I like hitting people when they hurt me." Crozier started to pant.

"Shall we go back a little further?"

"Er, OK."

"What do you see, now?"

Silence hung in the room for about twenty seconds.

"I just see a blank screen, fuzzy, like a black-and-white TV that isn't working." His voice seemed small.

"Alright, concentrate on this…screen. Can you see any shapes emerging from the fuzziness?"

"No, I can't see anything. It's just like, er, static." The adult word "static" seemed strange in the little voice.

"Keep looking."

"I'm trying, sir."

"Sir" also seemed out of place. He had become like an utterly submissive child.

Crozier was silent for another minute or two. Suddenly his voice became much deeper, the child had gone. "I'm falling...falling. It's dark. Now it's like swimming in black treacle. I can't breathe..."

I was about to bring him out of his trance, when Crozier suddenly spoke in a growl, in a strange accent. It was English, but a rural archaic dialect expressed with theatrical intensity.

For a while he seemed to be a little drunk. He seemed to be celebrating. "She's a double bagger[2]," he shouted with a bit of laughter in his voice, "but look'ee at them Cupid's kettle drums. A lot them women from Peaselake and the Hurtwood be like that, so they say."

Then the tone suddenly changed. He seemed to sober up quickly and move into a fight mode.

"Bastard. I warns thee, scum. Keep away from me. Stand back or I'll kill thee. Put that knife back. We can share this. Don't create this bedlam. Think, man...There's all this money. Enough for the two of us ...There's silver here to make a king happy. Don't, I warn thee again."

As I tried to make sense of what was happening, Crozier let out a scream and struggled violently in his chair. He clutched his throat with both his hands, as he fell back against the armchair.

He started to gurgle and cough, but more words came out of his contorted mouth: "I curse thee, for eternity...for betrayal...an eternal curse...forever."

Crozier's whole body seemed to shake with a strong electric current, his legs and arms jerked around; suddenly he slumped motionless in the deep chair.

I was stunned by the dramatic intensity of my patient's experience, but I knew that I had to bring him back to full consciousness, and quickly.

"Alpha 1," I said, trying to control the panic in my voice. I needed to sound confident. "You will slowly come back. Alpha 2. Alpha 3." I counted back up to 20. "Alpha 20," I repeated.

"You will now return to your normal state. You will come back out of your deep relaxation. Alpha 20."

I grew very anxious. After what seemed a long time, but was probably merely seconds, Crozier opened his eyes wide and looked utterly confused and vulnerable. Spittle flecked the edge of his lips.

"What happened?" he spluttered.

"You went into a deep trance. I took you into your early childhood."

"Fuck me, Doctor, that wasn't my childhood. I went right back into my nightmare. I was facing up to that murdering swine with the knife. It seemed as real as you are." He stared at me in a strange knowing way, and somehow I felt guilty, as though I had been accused of attacking him.

I was surprised that he had such a detailed recollection of his experience – any recollection in fact. I didn't mention that he had spoken in a rural dialect of what appeared to be a few hundred years ago. I did say that he could listen to the tape at his leisure. "I have two copies. It might help if you replayed one at home."

"Experiencing this once is quite enough, thank you. Keep the damn tapes. I saw the man who wanted to murder me. It was as clear as day. We were arguin' over a fortune we could have shared. But he wasn't open to reason."

"This must have been very disturbing, but we seem to be getting to the roots of your nightmare. I'm sure this is very useful in overcoming your problems. The next time you come, I think we should be able to address the real issues."

"I'm not sure I want to be threatened with murder again, especially in daylight hours."

"Later, you will feel better about it. I'm sure. When you come back in two weeks, I will be very interested to find out if you're sleeping better. I suspect that the answer will be yes."

"I hope you're right, Doctor. Nightmares at night are one thing. But" – he looked at his watch – "at three-fifty-five in the afternoon, that's something else. Wouldn't you agree?" He cocked his head, almost daring me to disagree with him.

"Let's discuss this in the next session."

I was worried, though, that I might not see my patient again. I feared that the innate bully in him had been terminally frightened. He had tasted his own medicine.

After he had gone, I said to Mary, "We might not be seeing him again. Pity. I think we were actually getting somewhere."

❖✺❖

I was wrong. A fortnight later I found Jim Crozier in my office again. Immediately, I asked him whether he was sleeping better.

He smiled. It struck me that I had not seen him smile before. "Yes," he said. "Definitely. I've slept like a baby for two weeks, and no nightmares."

"I'm pleased. It looks like we're making real progress, don't you think? Why don't you relax, and we'll build on the last successful session? I can understand that it was unpleasant. There's no reason for it to happen again. Continuing could reinforce your progress."

"Look, do we have to go back there again? It was pretty dramatic. And if it's done the trick, let sleeping dogs lie."

"Obviously I can't force you to have further treatment or that particular treatment, but this remission might just be temporary. Let's build on it and try to make it permanent."

I could see that Crozier was itching to get out of my consulting room. Most people like to get their full session's worth.

Something indefinable inside me wanted Crozier to stay. It wasn't just a professional concern. His regression to a previous persona, his use of archaic English and a rural dialect – they all intrigued me. I had re-read my notes and listened to some of the tapes again. I had understood a number of the dialect words. I had to look up one or two on the internet, but phrases such as "Cupid's kettle drums" – breasts – I seemed to understand. I don't know why. I also checked on Peaselake and one or two other place-names he had mentioned in the Surrey Hills, near Guildford, once famous for its smuggling. I wondered whether deep in my DNA I had family connections with the area, perhaps before my forebears emigrated to the New World. Fanciful thoughts for a scientist, I realise. The researcher in me wanted to know more. But I could hardly tell Crozier I wanted to satisfy my scientific, indeed personal, curiosity, could I? In retrospect, I can see that I was transgressing all sorts of ethical boundaries.

"Let's go back to your early days. If you suffer any anxiety, I will bring you straight back to your normal state of consciousness. Would you like some bottled spring water?"

This time he accepted – he had always refused before, as if he didn't want to be obligated a fraction more than he had to be. We made small talk about his new club, while we waited for Mary to bring in some water.

Five minutes later, we prepared for another session of deep relaxation therapy. I counted down and I took him back to the beach when he was three and asked again about his father. He said very little about him. Then I asked him to describe the sea.

"I can see it, smell and hear it," he said forcefully. "I can see the headland. I can see men in the bushes looking out to sea…"

I sat bolt upright as his voice started to deepen again, and he slipped once more into a long-dead dialect…

"There are spotmen on the headland, with their spout lanterns. The tubmen, the lander, and the batmen they're getting ready. When night falls, the lugger will come in. Ah, a night for us free traders, and to hell with the Preventers. Tonight there'll be tea and brandy aplenty. And baccy for us all. Our gang will be rich for a month or more, and nought for the King's men. The farmers have lent their carts and the felt has been put on the horseshoes, and the leather washers on the wheels to stop the noise. A profit for us all. From the sea…"

Crozier then slipped into a deeper dialect, full of oaths, and slurred as though drunk. He read out a sign he said he saw on a public house, "Drunk for a penny, dead drunk for two pence, straw for nothing."

Then he said something about "our great friends in France…our *amis* in Calais and Bologne".

He gurgled and then seemed to sleep for a while, but – after a minute or two – came to, still speaking in his strange dialect.

"Best night we had. We done well. More than enough to share…What's with thee, why are your bleedin' eyes narrowing on me, old mate? …Put that knife away, cully[3]. It's not the time for jest…I be no whiddler[4]."

Crozier shot his right arm in the air as if to protect himself from a blow. Then he put two hands around his neck and screamed. He jerked his tie loose and practically ripped open the top buttons of his shirt.

I was surprised to see an unusual birthmark, a thin red streak, about six inches long, at the base of his neck. It looked a little like a scar, but the pigmentation suggested he was born with it. But I had no time to speculate upon that – I had to bring him back as quickly as possible.

His face was ashen. He struggled to speak, with little success. And he was angry – at the phantoms, at me perhaps, or even himself.

He quickly did up his shirt and straightened his tie, as though he were self-conscious about his birth defect.

Crozier stared at me aggressively.

"In my nightmares, my attacker never actually stabbed me. This time, I felt the knife cut clean across my throat. It was terrible. Your sessions are worse than my nightmares. I've had enough of your mumbo-jumbo. Thank you for helping so far – I reckon I'll do better on my own," he said sharply.

I was rather taken aback. What I had witnessed, perhaps something hidden deep in his psyche or possibly even a regression to a previous life, was utterly bewildering…and fascinating. As a practitioner I had never experienced it, although I had read about such episodes under hypnosis. The scientist in me rejected any notion of re-living a past life experience, but the same scientist also wanted to know more, to experiment…and I was helping Crozier. I firmly believed that.

"Jim, you have a deep-seated trauma, and we need to work on it. Sometimes it may not be easy, but I am convinced we can – together – improve your condition, and perhaps even cure it. I know you say you are sleeping better, but you mustn't stop the treatment at this crucial stage – you could go back to where you were before. Or it could even get worse."

"Nothing could be much worse than reliving gettin' my throat cut. I've had enough of your fuckin' with my brain. Doctor Martin, I've had a gut full."

I didn't argue any more; I knew that perhaps my curiosity had got the better of my professionalism. I should have consulted with colleagues about my unusual flirtation with hypnosis. I was slightly worried that the aggressive Crozier might make an official complaint. I was now glad that he had always refused to take any of the tapes home with him.

So I backed off as gracefully as I could: "Jim, we've made a lot of progress. If you want to come back at any time, please get in touch. I wish you well."

I offered my hand and he grudgingly shook it, and left, without saying any more.

Mary rushed in without any pretence of propriety, and said, "What happened to Mr Crozier? He just flounced out without a word to me."

"Well, it looks like I've just lost a customer. The truth can be too hard for some people to handle."

I was feeling a little guilty about indulging my own curiosity, though I would never admit that to Mary.

She put her hand gently on my arm. "I think he's a dangerous man, and a criminal. We don't need that kind of patient here, Tom. Come on, I'll make you some tea. And I have a few of your favourite biscuits."

Ah, the sovereign British remedy for all ills, I thought. I knew instinctively that the Crozier story was just beginning. I absolutely had to know more about what had happened to him.

Three

It was the run-up to Christmas; Jane and I had been pre-occupied with other things, not our relationship nor my flashback. We had managed a number of social engagements together in London, we hadn't really talked. Crozier was on my mind and I wanted to share the experience with someone I could trust and who had a good medical mind. A doctor who was also my lover and personal adviser fitted the bill. We needed to talk over a good meal.

We decided on Maggiore's in Covent Garden. In the winter evenings, the foliage and lighting created the illusion of Aladdin's cave. Though often a little crowded with people rushing off to the theatre, it had an intimacy which we liked.

We had already consumed a quick glass of chardonnay in Gordon's wine bar on the Embankment. It was dark, crowded and louche, but popular with artists, the occasional stray spook or Ministry of Defence official from Whitehall and the more adventurous business types. The cellars recalled the London of Hogarth. Because Jane didn't want to stay in the smoky bar for long, we quickly moved on to Maggiore's, and the reserved table with the respectful and efficient foreign waiters.

I remember Jane commenting on the quality of the staff. "We have a service economy without service. Why is it that the British regard waiting as a third-rate occupation, while the continentals consider it as almost an art form?"

"True, the Brits have good table manners, but generally poor cuisine, and the service is even worse. Maybe it's the curse of their loveless marriage with food. More likely, though, it's your damn class system, Jane. Service equals servility. Shame you didn't have a proper revolution like the French."

She quipped back, "Ah, so your famous American revolution brought equality, did it? For all the crap we get in the NHS, at least it's technically free for everyone, for all classes."

I didn't rise to that bait. I knew she never quite approved of my private practice. And I wanted her advice, not prolonged debate. I made do with some half-baked comment on the fact that "the Brits do satire, not revolutions. Even when the English – sorry, the Brits – fought over the principle of monarchy versus parliament in the civil war, what happened? You ended up with both!"

On the third glass of wine, I decided to take the plunge. I told her pretty much what had happened to my patient, but did not stress my own fascination with the case. She listened intently, with no substantive interruptions, apart from the occasional request for factual clarification.

"So what do you think?"

She was deep in thought for a while. "Well, I know that some people believe that regression to childhood can achieve insights into psychological problems, in the same way that dream therapy is often deployed by psychotherapists. I remember reading about a psychiatrist who had dealt with this and he jokingly said that he would like to put all the Napoleons and Josephines and Churchills and Messiahs in the same room and just observe what happened."

She took a large mouthful of wine, and looked at me intently. "To be serious, Tom, it's not my area at all, although I am instinctively dubious about any past-life regression theory."

"So am I, but his abrupt change of personality is weird. I can't find any evidence of multiple personality or bi-polar disorder. And his historical accent – apparently it's from Surrey around the late 1700s. I gave a very small section of the tape – with no personal disclosure on it – to a sound archivist who's an expert on dialects and that's what he told me it was."

Jane was quiet for a few seconds. "You're hooked, aren't you? It's odd that you go to such lengths with the tape, and yet you haven't discussed this with any of your colleagues in your esteemed sleep disorder unit. You don't normally do hypnosis…"

"Deep relaxation, Jane."

"Don't patronize me, Tom. You have described somebody in a deep hypnotic trance. For all your brilliance, Doctor," – she smiled and squeezed my hand – "you are not the world authority on this subject."

"But it is working. Crozier is now sleeping well." I knew that sounded defensive and lame as soon as I said it. I tried to recover. "I will discuss the case with one or two of my senior colleagues, I promise. And I will do some homework on the subject."

"What's the point," Jane asked, "if he's walked out on you?"

"Research, my dear, is never wasted," I replied with the most pompous BBC accent I could muster. I also had some other research in mind, but I did not want to make her think I had become more than just a touch obsessive.

"And I have heard from him again," I wanted to say definitively. "I have an invitation for two to attend a charity opera event at Covent Garden. *Madame Butterfly*. God knows how he found out you are an opera buff. The tickets are worth nearly £150 each."

And I should have added, "Maybe he feels guilty about storming out and wants to make some sort of amends."

That's what I should have said, because that was the truth. But I had to can that version. If I had told Jane, she would have torn me to shreds – you never accept such gifts from patients.

Instead I felt compelled to lie.

"I got them from Dave Waterman, my master fixer at St Thomas'. He assured me they aren't nicked even though I paid only half-price for them. I thought I would surprise you. And I showed the tickets to Mary, my source of all wisdom, and she informed me that Mr Crozier was holding a charity reception that night for the same event. A coincidence indeed."

Jane looked at me a touch suspiciously for a second. But I did not make a habit of lying to her, and she absolutely adored opera.

"Well, I'd never look a gift horse in the mouth, so thank you, kind sir, for the tickets. Besides, I am mildly curious to meet him – I presume there will be some sort of drinks do as well?"

"I guess so. It's a few weeks' time – and I know a Yorkshire lass won't allow two good tickets to go to waste. Let's double-check later to see if we are both free."

I poured another glass and suggested we stop talking shop in general and about my patient in particular.

⋯⋯

Jane brought up the subject of our forthcoming Christmas together. We needed to relax, especially as we both had the following day off, a rarely shared experience. Even though it was only just after ten, we had drunk two bottles of wine by the time we left Maggiore's. I was eager to get back to my flat in Kensington and its large bed. Despite the pre-Christmas rush, I managed to hail a taxi on the Strand and, within twenty-five minutes, I was tugging her clothes off on my sofa.

"Down, tiger," she said teasingly. "Let's first have a shower together."

Like most men, when fired up, I wanted to get on with

love-making, but I figured I could wait five or ten minutes. And I had long ago worked out that I should be more measured, thoughtful, perhaps "loving" was the word I needed, when I made love to Jane.

She adored the power shower in my large bathroom. Jane went ahead, lit two candles on the window sill near the sink, and ran the shower to make sure it was exactly the right temperature.

"C'mon," she said coquettishly, "let's see what the American revolution has done for your servicing ability. Let's see what a Harvard man can do for a working–class Yorkshire girl."

Normally, I would carefully hang up my clothes – she used to regard me as rather anally retentive, I think – but that night I ostentatiously threw them over a chair and walked into the spacious glass cubicle.

She had her back to me. In the candlelight, she was more than tempting, her unblemished skin seemed to shine, and her figure was lean but also voluptuous at the same time. Though I regret to recall now that I examined her rather clinically: thirty-five and she'd had no children, her five-feet-eight frame carried very little fat. And despite her long hours at work, Jane somehow found time to cycle back and forth to the hospital from her small house in Battersea. "You take care of yourself," was my cold medical assessment, if I recall correctly.

I hadn't really noticed before how toned her figure was. Maybe it was my puritanical upbringing, but I was shocked when I estimated that this was only the second or third time I had shared a shower with her. No wonder she thought me inhibited despite my medical training, though that night I intended to disabuse her of that impression.

Jane turned towards me with the lathered soap, and I pulled her towards me with mock aggression.

She retreated a little and then slyly cupped her hands under my balls.

I coughed dutifully and whispered in her ear, "Kiss me."

Instead, she gave me a playful bite on my shoulder.

She put the soap back in the dish and held me firmly, as she eased us both under the jet of water. She was leading, as ever – so much for my intended caveman display.

The perfectly hot water caressed us both.

She reached back towards a small raised shelf which held the shower gel, and squeezed a generous quantity into her hands, and massaged my back, then my thighs, as I licked her nipples. They tasted of almonds.

I lifted her and eased myself into her, while bracing her against the shower wall. My head started to spin a little – from the passion or the alcohol – and I gripped my feet on the ridged floor tiles as best I could.

Though I had vowed to become more physically involved with Jane, I knew that she was always more serious about sex. I confess I had often been detached and occasionally saw the funny side of copulation, but this time I began to lose myself in her beauty and her passion.

She leaned her back ostentatiously against the cubicle wall, thus freeing both her hands. Her nails pressed painfully into my back. I felt my knees begin to weaken. But I pressed harder and harder into her. Jane's mouth was swollen and open, and driving forcefully against my defensive lips.

We moved together in harmony, rising faster and faster.

"Come," she said. "Come with me. Open your eyes, and let me see you come as well."

Normally, I don't respond well to such instructions, but this time I was swept up in the moment.

I said, "I love you."

This was almost the first time I had admitted to such an emotion – to Jane or any woman. I had said it and I meant it. But a corrosive detachment niggled in my soul, and I suspected it then, and I absolutely know it now.

"I'm coming too. Hold me," I moaned.

She kissed me passionately and arched even closer towards

me. She sighed, so deeply, as though every hope, regret, and desire were condensed into that one sad sound, and then she slumped onto my chest. I held her gently and stroked her dripping blond hair.

Jane cried a little, but I didn't ask why. Perhaps I was afraid of hearing the truth about our relationship.

She just said, "I hope we will always be like this…but even better."

I couldn't help myself. "Honey, I'm not sure I can manage love-making in the shower when I'm a good ole boy… Maybe I can buy me a rustproof Zimmer…with some jet skis attached," I said in a broad mock-Texan accent.

Jane half-laughed and reached out for a large blue towel hanging on the rail near the cubicle exit. I thought for a second she was going to flick me hard with the end of it.

I recognized instantly I had spoiled the moment by my buffoonish comment. I knew our love-making was wrong, despite the intensity I felt. It was the emotion I wanted, but almost without Jane as part of it. I knew that I had always disappointed her in physical terms, and even now I was not reaching her. Nor was she reaching me.

"Do you fancy a vintage port?" she asked, as if joining in my conspiracy to change the mood.

"Depends where you want to pour it," I replied, catching her strained attempt to match my off-key playfulness.

We sipped port in bed, and I held her as closely and as lovingly as I could. Soon I was in a deep sleep, even though I suspect she would have stayed awake thinking for a long time.

As I held her, I noticed the slight padding of fat around her hips. Her dark hair was tied into two long pigtails. The smell of wood smoke in her hair was strong, but it was not offensive. It seemed welcoming. Our log fire blazed away. A thick tallow candle flickered and cast strange shadows on the beams across the open roof. A bat fluttered in the under eaves of the thatch. I could smell the roast pork left over from our evening meal downstairs. It was warm in the bed, and from the mattress just a little straw protruded. Her nightshirt had ridden up above her generous breasts, and I could see the thin licks of scar tissue around the back of her left thigh, scourge marks where the whips had left their life-long legacy. She snored gently, and shivered a little. I pulled the rough sheepskin over her. She was my woman, and I wanted her, now. I leaned over on top of her, ready to mount her while she was asleep. Perhaps she would think it was a dream. More probably, she would wake up and guide me into her.

Suddenly, a horse whinnied outside. Cursing, I jumped up out of the bed, and grabbed my knife. I tugged the wooden shutter a few inches into my bedroom, to see what was afoot. It was a full moon, and I could see a little into the line of trees outside. Then I felt two strong rough hands around my waist, pulling me backwards, backwards, down, down into the darkness…

◁⧓∞⧓▷

Where the fuck was I? In heaven or hell? England or America? Was I awake or asleep?

Jane was standing over the side of the bed with a cup of tea in her hand.

"You were restless last night, Tom. You don't normally groan in your sleep. Must be something on your conscience."

"God, I feel strange. How much did we drink last night?"

"Not that much, buddy. And certainly not enough to slow you down in the shower."

"I had a strange dream…"

"Ah, psychiatrists and their dreams. Tell me about it over breakfast. If you really had too much to drink, I'm sure you'll have a Texan-size appetite. Finish your tea and then I'll make you some breakfast. Bacon and eggs?"

I didn't feel like a cooked breakfast, but I said, "Yes, please." Nor did I feel like talking about the dream. It seemed too vivid; and far too dangerous to discuss. Jane would be sure to say I was obsessing in my sleep as well in my waking hours. Maybe I was behaving strangely. But it was the same woman — the "Italian woman" I had dubbed her — whom I had experienced in that flashback. I thought that was a one-off. Now I was dreaming about the same woman. And getting fixated on a patient as well. Technically, I was indulging in what my medical colleagues would call "projective identification" — if I had risked consulting them. Maybe I needed a long holiday. Well, at least I'll get a few days off over Christmas, I told myself.

I managed to avoid the subject of dreams over breakfast. Jane was soon off to do some Christmas shopping in Knightsbridge. I said I would meet her in the afternoon in the bustling coffee shop in Harvey Nichols.

I wanted to do some internet research and then make a few phone calls. Allowing for the time difference, I could soon ring an aunt in Boston. She was an early riser. I wanted to find out more about my sudden obsession with an English past I didn't know about.

"Aunt Martha. How are you? And Merry Christmas to you. Sorry to call you so early."

After a round of small talk, I got to the point. "Aunt, you're the family's unofficial historian, right? Tell me, do we have any roots in Surrey or southern England in general?"

"You've passed up psychiatry and taken up genealogy, Tom? You'll have far fewer dollars in your billfold."

"No, not all. You know what it's like, living here in Merrie

Olde England, you begin to think more about history. Some of our family hail from Ireland, I know."

"Yes, some on your mother's side shipped over in the 1840s, after the Famine."

"But do we have any English roots at all? Most of my father's side came from Eastern Europe, but I wondered whether there were any English connections."

"Sorry, Tom, can't make an Englishman out of you. What I have traced from the British Isles is nearly all Irish, proud to say. A little bit of Welsh in you as well. But I ain't that smart on the internet yet, so I'm still working on the extended family tree. Here's the deal: if I find anything English I'll email you. What's your email address again?"

I gave it to her and wished her Merry Christmas again and said I would see her when I next went Stateside. "Maybe Easter time," I promised more in hope than expectation. "But definitely in the Fall."

"And give my love to your young lady. Jane, isn't it?"

I sighed with resignation. "Mom's been trying to marry me off for years. Jane's very cute, but there's absolutely no talk of weddings. But don't say anything to Mom. She'll be straight on the phone and nagging me to settle down."

"OK. Bye, Tom."

❦

I was late meeting Jane, because I had spent too long in the Central Library on Kensington High Street looking up books on the history of Surrey. The internet had not been very helpful except to direct me to the Surrey History Centre in Woking. No time to go there, though. Jane was slightly miffed at my being ten minutes late.

"Busy trying to find the right presents, darling," I said, hoping that she would assume I meant presents for her. She gave me one of her most graceful but slightly distant smiles.

I didn't usually lie to Jane, yet this was the second time in just a few days. I just didn't want her to question me about Crozier. I was behaving like a guilty man. I had enough sense to realise that I could self-diagnose some psychotic elements about my own behaviour. I brushed my concerns aside. After all, it was Christmas and I certainly didn't want any arguments. And I loved Jane, I said to myself. So why was I dreaming of somebody else? Somebody whom I didn't even know?

While Jane was in the ladies' room, I checked for messages on my mobile. There was one from Mary Duncan. She apologized for ringing me on my day off but Jim Crozier's girlfriend had rung. Could I see him as soon as possible in the New Year? she had asked. I rang Mary back and told her to book Crozier in for my first free appointment. I could have offered to see him before, but that might have been difficult administratively, and it would have made me look far too anxious. I was, however, very curious.

So was Jane when she saw me furtively pocketing my cell phone. "Thought you always put that thing in your office drawer on your days off."

"Expecting a call from my Aunt Martha in Boston." A half-truth. "I was talking to her about you. Got the family excited."

Again, Jane was not particularly assuaged. She said dispassionately, "I'd like to meet your family some time…Fancy another cappuccino, Tom?"

Four

The Christmas we spent with Jane's family in Barnsley went well. Her parents are completely down-to-earth and very friendly. Even though it was only the second time I had met her father – as a token of his acceptance – he took me to his workingmen's club and taught me the basics of snooker. He seemed impressed by my rapid progress, especially as I hadn't told him that I'd played pool in the US. Although he was a little embarrassed when I called him "sir" in front of his friends, he forgave me and insisted that I call him "Fred". We drank Guinness and celebrated our new relationship.

Jane was obviously pleased that I was such a hit with her family, even her frail but feisty aunt, Doris. The aunt immediately introduced herself as a "devout communist" and told me straight off, "I distrust all Americans."

Jane's mother shot back a rapid retort: "You didn't show much distrust to that GI you had a fling with in 1944. You didn't get all those stockings and chocolates for nought, dearie."

She turned and winked at me and said, *sotto voce*, "Don't worry, Tom, one more sherry and she'll be all over you."

Jane's mother was right, and it was the only sexual attention I received in Barnsley. I even played the dutiful male guest and slept on the sofa downstairs, while Jane occupied the single bed in her old room, still adorned with her teddy bears and dolls.

It was a side of my tough-minded doctor that I hadn't imagined.

When we got back to our own homes in London, on December 28th, 2006, Jane was in fine spirits. We'd had enough of other people's company and she was keen to cook for me à deux in her small house in Battersea. I arrived on time for once, and with a bunch of roses, from a florist, not a gas station.

Even now I remember the smell of garlic, as she took the fresh ribbons of pasta from the fridge and boiled them lightly, and added single cream and the herbs she had carefully dissected. I gulped down the cheapish but acceptable pinot grigio. I drank too much, perhaps because her lodger, a nurse, was out for the night and I was asked to stay over – something I rarely did. I didn't have to worry about a taxi and continued to drink. I don't remember Jane consuming more than a few glasses, not that she was ever a drunk.

So she caught me a little off-guard when she asked me, out of the blue, "Have you seen *Sixth Sense*?"

"No, but I like Bruce Willis. Have you got the DVD here?"

Jane was standing over the sink in the kitchen and I was perched on one of the two pine stools in the narrow galley.

"Do you want to watch a film?"

"Not really. I'd rather talk to you." I pulled Jane on to my lap and gave her a gentle kiss on the cheek.

God knows how we got on to it but she led me on to the subject of ghosts, and then finally re-incarnation. In retrospect, perhaps it was her indirect way of approaching the subject of Crozier. Maybe I was being a touch paranoid. Perhaps it was the wine, but I compounded the situation by spouting a little of what I thought and what I'd learned from my recent reading.

Despite the booze, I recall the conversation went something like this. I started pompously, "Reincarnation is consistent with the law of physics. Energy – the life force if you like – cannot be either created or destroyed. It can only be changed."

I expected her to deploy a frank Yorkshire put-down such as "bollocks", but Jane went with the flow and compared ancient religions. "Why do we accept all the historical and archaeological evidence that ancient civilizations, such as the Greek and Egyptian, were intellectually and culturally sophisticated yet we decry their religions as primitive?" she asked with an incisiveness that I had rarely seen in her – beyond professional medical matters.

"Conventional Christianity," she continued, "decrees that one lifetime can determine a man or woman's destiny for eternity...especially if you are a Catholic. But theosophists, for example, believe that one life is merely a single day in the passage of the soul."

Like Jane, I didn't usually engage in religious or even intellectual debate, outside of medicine. I thought a lot, but my table talk – as she kept teasing me – was mundane, even if I dressed it up with what I termed wit and whimsical asides on current affairs. On this occasion, however, I was keen to indulge her; perhaps indulge myself as well.

I still couldn't help being flippant, however. "You know what Henry Miller said, 'Sex is one of the nine reasons for re-incarnation...The other eight are unimportant.' But the best argument for reincarnation is a simple question – why is it necessary to nail or screw down coffin lids?"

She gave me a slightly indulgent smile, and said, "If you are going to be your usual smart arse..." But she stayed with the subject until we moved on to her medical opinion on near-death experiences – all the usual neurological explanations. "The similarity of numerous examples, throughout history and across cultures, could mean more than just the evolutionary similarity of the human nervous system," Jane suggested.

She mentioned that she had heard of a researcher who had put a number of cards with large dots on top of a tall cabinet in an intensive-care unit. "The researcher found that two out of the seven people who claimed a near-death experience during the five years of research in that unit had recalled seeing the cards and recounted the precise number of dots. The patients, lying on the bed, could not have seen the dots. No one except the researcher and two specialists knew of the cards' existence, yet two patients recalled seeing the cards when they claimed they had floated to the ceiling, before 'being drawn to the light'. They all say that about light, I know, but it is interesting."

Jane was now in full flight: "What is also interesting is that all those who have endured a near-death experience say they feel a sense of peace, of warmth. That could be explained by the body's systems closing down. What I find challenging is the almost universal claim to feel a sense of timelessness."

I interjected: "Yes, I understand that even if a patient has been brought back to life within minutes, even seconds, they often say they've been through a series of events which take hours or days or, occasionally, months. Perhaps it's not time that changes but our experience – or interpretation – of time. I don't say it's possible, but I do say it could be true." I heard myself say that, and it didn't sound like me.

I was still suspicious of her approach: was she really engaging me, or perhaps probing me on my interest in Crozier? Despite the drink inside me, I still wondered whether she was trying to prod me into being more open about my experience with my patient. Nevertheless, I took her intellectual engagement at face value, and dismissed, for the time being, any ulterior motives. Clearly, some trust was missing in our relationship, and I knew it was my fault.

Just before we went to bed, she mentioned an invitation she'd received from an old college friend, who lived near Shere in the Surrey Hills.

"You've expressed an interest in the local history so you might enjoy a weekend visit to the country. Get you away from the city."

I accepted happily, but again I wondered whether she was trying to make a subtle point. Maybe she was right — I was a touch too paranoid about everything. Maybe she was trying to be supportive, and trying to understand a curiosity which I was doing my best to hide — obviously I was not succeeding very well. Maybe I should have been more direct and asked her straightforwardly, but I didn't. And I couldn't just blame my training as a psychiatrist. I had to consider the flaws in my own personality. The Crozier business had me doubting all sorts of things about myself.

Five

Ten days later, at three-fifteen in the afternoon, Jane picked me up from my Harley Street rooms. Mary was as pleased to see her as ever; she thoroughly approved of my long-term relationship with someone who was "good, kind and well-grounded", as my receptionist said regularly. "The right kind of qualities for a wife and mother," she would add.

"You sound like my mother," I had responded, with mock harshness in my voice when she repeated her views.

She frowned – the flirt in her disliked my making the uncomplimentary age comparison.

Mary and Jane chatted, while I finished off a few things. I wanted to clear the decks to give me some peace of mind during a free weekend.

"Don't call me – no emergencies this weekend, please," was my parting shot to Mary.

I squeezed my six-foot-two-inch frame into her dark blue MGB two-seater, of which she was so proud – she had owned it for only a few months. Despite being slightly cramped, I needed to relax. The heavy traffic out of central London en route to the A3 didn't help. The traffic lightened as we approached Esher, and so did my mood. We crossed over London's biggest car park – the M25 motorway – and slipped off the highway to drop into the pretty part of old Surrey:

Ripley, then through West Clandon, and its stately home, and up the hill to Newlands Corner, one of the highest points of Surrey. I had been here just once before, on a cloudless sunny afternoon, and had marvelled at the expanse of forest which lay below me. Now in the mid-winter dusk I couldn't see much but the twinkling of lights, yet the memory of the forests and downs came back to me.

Shere nestled gently in the Tillingbourne valley about three miles further on. It was my first visit to the picturesque village, although I felt a chill down my spine as we drove slowly past the half-timbered houses. Too much history – much of it dark – seemed to permeate the place. The village had no public lighting: the main illumination was the single village grocery shop and external lights from the two pubs around the square. Despite the darkness, I felt engulfed by the omnipresent history and the brooding charm of Shere. I was anxious to explore its exquisite character in daylight.

Jane's friends, Nathan and Margaret, lived in a small farmhouse about a mile outside the village. I hadn't met them before, but warmed to Nathan when he suggested almost immediately that we should go on a quick tour of the local pubs before the women joined us later.

Nathan's conversation in the Prince of Wales was a mite forced until I figured out that he was happiest talking about his job as a stock-broker. The nuances of the market were explained to me over a pint of tepid so-called "real ale" – I continued to have a problem with warm beer, for all my anglophilia. What I really wanted was a glass of ice-cold Bud. I drank the ale, and ignored two large wet dogs that were running around the bar.

I was also rather up-front in the American fashion. Until I learned better, I used to say, "Hi, I'm Tom from Washington."

But the Brits seemed to find personal information somehow painful. I soon worked out they gave their names out only at the end of a long conversation, and then as an embarrassed afterthought.

The Brits still struck me as friendly but altogether too uptight, too closed, except when it came to their pets: the most repressed people in the world love indulging the most badly behaved animals on the planet. From a psychiatrist's point of view perhaps their pets represented their wild side, allowing them to break all their rigidly imposed, class-bound rules, if only by proxy. I learned that pets were even more a class marker than language. But it took me longer for my social GPS to work out which class preferred which dogs. I did, however, realize in the pub that an upper-class Labrador was playing with a working-class Rottweiler, before their masters separated them and took them to separate bars.

Nathan was more than friendly, and we chatted inconsequentially, starting inevitably with the weather. I had long appreciated that weather talk was simply a means of gauging education, class and income via subtle nuances of transport and work place. The Brits would be extremely self-deprecating about their alleged lack of national sexual prowess, but pathetically over-defensive if foreigners dared to criticize their weather.

After the weather, Nathan had talked again of the City and the budget, but he struck me as a man who was trying a little too hard. So I was somewhat relieved when we met up with our partners in the White Horse, fifty yards from the Prince of Wales. The White Horse stood right on the square. Its mock Tudor frontage was appealing and the interior had the right ambience, despite being part of a brewery chain, piped music et al. A light sprinkling of snow on the roof made the log fire inside even more welcome. Jane and I had recently seen the Hollywood movie *The Holiday*, which was partly shot in Shere and featured this old pub.

We ate in the White Horse, despite Margaret's warning: "The food isn't terribly good here, but it's a great place for a visitor to soak up the atmosphere."

I found myself agreeing on both points.

We managed to grab a table near the open log fire as Nathan gave me a short history lesson on the place, and I listened intently. He went a little too far when he threw in a ghost story presumably guaranteed to entertain an American country cousin. He outlined the story of a former female hermit who was walled up alive in the church opposite the pub.

"The anchoress, as she was called, was immured in 1329, but some of the locals who live in Lower Street, where she grew up, claim that they quite often see a ghostly figure dressed in medieval garb. She walks through the walls of the old house there, which is now subdivided into two cottages. Apparently, she's very friendly. There is no sense of dread, or so Mrs Edmundson tells me. She's seventy-five and she's seen the ghost many times."

We ate steak except for Margaret who proclaimed her vegetarianism. We all drank too much Rioja.

Margaret declared herself not only a vegetarian, but "a Buddhist mixed with Hindu" to boot. And she was dressed like an ageing hippie. I thought, "Here we go: we're going to have crystals under the bed, astrology, *Guardian* politics and back-of-a-matchbox-style philosophy."

She also added. "I am not religious, but that doesn't mean I'm not a spiritual person."

That kind of sentence usually meant that I was about to bored witless. When Americans say I'm not religious they mean they are deeply gullible about all sorts of New Age fads, and always terribly picky about what they eat. What they also often mean is that they will deify the Earth as a Goddess or bow down to Native American folklore. Well, that was perhaps more '60s or '80s. I guess now they are into meditation, yoga, mantras and still Eastern religions. For these folk, spirituality usually means believing anything rather than nothing.

I determined to grit my teeth and be non-committal. As it happens, I was wrong about Margaret.

After another bottle of wine, I think it was at my prompting that she explained her definition of karma. Probably I was trying to humour her, but she turned out to be very well informed.

She explained that she felt aware of her previous re-incarnations. One phrase stuck out: "I found it hard to be a child," she said. "I just didn't relate fully to the inconsequential things that other children seemed to find important. I had dolls and so on, but they were casual playthings; they weren't important. I always felt that there were things I had already done, and would do in the future, which were more important. I've always had a sense of unfinished business – my whole life."

I remember butting in and saying that "a lot of highly intelligent people" – a bit patronizing that, I suppose – "have this sense of destiny: it propels great artists and, of course, great dictators."

Margaret practised what she preached: she did have a sense of peace about her and was not about to be riled by my capricious comments.

I tacked into less choppy waters: "Many religions do not have a concept of karma, fate, destiny, whatever you want to call it – that actions in one life dictate the terms of the next."

"I'm not Jewish," interrupted Nathan, "but I like their idea of trying to do good in this life, without waiting for rewards in the next, although they have a concept of some kind of after-life, I believe." He stroked his goatee board with a hint of smugness.

"Yes, they call damnation *sheol* in Hebrew," Margaret added. She displayed just a scintilla of frustration with her husband's lack of intellectual precision. I wondered too whether she subconsciously resented the fact that, despite her mysticism and professed non-materialism, she was totally dependent upon her husband's apparent skills in the halls of Mammon.

Nathan persisted: "And I like Jewish humour. I think it was Woody Allen who said that 'If I believed in reincarnation, I'd come back as Warren Beatty's fingers.'"

We politely laughed, which served only to encourage him. "I had a friend," he said, "who did some astral travelling, but packed it in because there were no air miles."

Margaret ignored this. "To go back to what I was saying about Buddhism," she continued with obvious determination. "Death in the West is seen as a tragic medical failure rather than as a necessary culmination of a good life. It depends on what kind of death, however. What partly explains our pacifism is the idea that a violent death will almost certainly damn the person to a traumatic subsequent life. There is no time to prepare for the next; that's why the death rituals – the chanting and so on – are so important. A number of cultures believe, however, that only a violent death can induce a reincarnation."

"I suppose that may be tied into Christian ghost stories – our ghost in Shere, for example," Nathan joined in, again at a slight tangent to the main conversation.

Margaret nodded but again refused to take up her husband's remark. "Philosophically, I like the notion that we have many chances to improve, to strive for an ideal of perfection. That souls are like uncut diamonds; each life can fashion a facet of that jewel. Each time we incarnate, we grow spiritually. Or should do. A lot of politicians, especially the warmongers among them, might be a little more responsible if there were a more widespread concept that even death does not release us from moral responsibilities."

"Ah, the Catholic guilt trip that I was brought up on – not sure that it's helped, even in Italian or Irish politics," Jane said. She took a big sip of wine and leaned back in her chair – I think she wanted to lighten the mood.

Margaret chose to ignore the signal. "Of course some

religions believe," she said, "that an individual, whatever they do, whether they succeed or fail in a particular life – however you define success – has no influence on the next life."

Over cheese, we turned briefly to house prices, a subject which absorbed the English middle class, but bored me. I did venture, however, that I thought the housing bubble would have to burst soon.

"Let's not be boring and talk about house prices," Jane said. "I get enough of that in London. Since we are in Shere I want to hear more about the local ghosts."

Our hosts did not respond immediately to the challenge, so Jane filled the silence: "Is there any kind of proof of an afterlife? So far, we have mentioned only the sightings of ghosts, which could all be explained by scientific means. We need proof of afterlife or a pre-natal existence – a past-life existence? Is there any hard evidence?"

"It is hard to prove," Margaret conceded, "as opposed to belief and faith, although people such as the infamous Madame Blavatsky made a career out of it. According to her, it took hundreds or even thousands of years to reincarnate."

"That long?" Jane asked. "I thought the death of someone – according to the theory – led the soul to migrate quite soon to a new-born baby. And do you reincarnate within the same family, clan or gender?"

"It depends," said Margaret. "Often souls do seem to group in various reincarnations, even if they change class, profession or even gender and race."

"So two souls could come back as father and daughter in one existence and then mother and son, with roles reversed, in the next?" Jane asked.

"Possibly."

"I still would like some proof," I said.

One of the waitresses cleared up the plates and asked whether we wanted coffee. It was a natural conversation break.

"Where's the John?" I drawled mischievously, because

Nathan had clearly cast me in the role of naïve US tourist while he was the urbane Brit expounding on the country's noble heritage in the correct version of Shakespeare's English.

Nathan pointed, but missed my point.

On my return, I expected the conversation to have turned to the terrors of commuting or sallied back to the secret joys of booming house prices, but the table talk appeared to have stalled.

⋘⋙

I looked into the fire, pretending to be distracted…and I almost jumped out of my chair. An electric shock ran like a wildfire up my spine. I felt like vomiting on the spot.

In the fire I saw – very distinctly – the face of "the Italian woman" staring at me.

Her eyes were wide in horror as though she were burning in hell. She was begging me to save her. I could not see her hands reaching out to implore me, but her eyes spoke of her utter agony.

Somehow I stopped myself from using the small fire extinguisher near the log stack to rescue the lady from the grip of the flames.

It was just a second, and I struggled manfully to compose myself and persuade myself it was too much booze, not another flash of insanity.

Jane and Nathan were looking the other way, but Margaret saw my savage, if momentary, panic attack. "Looks like you saw a ghost," she said softly.

I didn't even try to dissemble. "Yeah, I saw a face in the fire – must be all the talk of ghosts. Maybe it was your anchoress coming to say hello to an American visitor."

I forced a very unconvincing smile.

Margaret was generous enough not to press me, especially as she saw me cast my eyes nervously to Jane, who was engrossed in a separate conversation with Nathan. She waited for a few moments for them to re-join the group discussion. Then Margaret looked me directly in the eyes, and asked, "So what is your scientific explanation for any existence beyond our biblical three score and ten? Especially my comment that seemed to have piqued your interest, that I have always felt aware of a previous existence?"

I hesitated, not least because I had not fully composed myself. Again I looked at Jane, perhaps intuitively seeking her permission. She smiled and raised her eyebrows, as if to say: your call. "Well, it's not my area of expertise…" and I paused. I sensed my cheeks were flushed. I thought of her face in the flames, and I remembered my childhood stammer, now long gone. I feared I would start stammering again.

"Jane, may I have a swig of your water?…Thanks."

"Excuse me. Where was I? Ah, yes, there is…there is… a theory of the collective unconscious. Sensitive, perhaps introspective and intelligent types could tap unwittingly into the collective pool of genetic information at their disposal and assume it belongs to their own individual past…Another theory is called cryptomnesia – the idea that the brain can record everything we have seen, felt, heard – even in the womb. It also refers to when a forgotten, hidden memory returns without its being recognized as such by the subject, who believes it is something new and original. In a deep trance, or perhaps after a traumatic event, access to such memories is possible. That's sort of the untapped-powers-of-the-brain theory. That could also explain the sense of déjà vu.

"Poets of course have an explanation. Wordsworth talked about 'trailing clouds of glory' – that children can tap in to an innocent pre-natal universe. Their imagination is less sullied by adult conditioning …Children might simply be more psychic."

I looked around and my audience seemed attentive, in one or two cases even rapt. But Margaret clearly wanted to add something, so I gave way to her.

"There is a frequently told story, so forgive my repeating it," she said. "A young family was blessed with a beautiful baby girl. A few weeks after she came into this world, her five-year-old brother asked to speak to her alone. Intrigued, their parents said yes, but listened in on the baby monitor in the next room. They heard the son say, 'Can you please tell me what God looks like? I am starting to forget.'"

We all smiled at the sweet story.

"Margaret, you mentioned your childhood instincts – perhaps they were stronger then, your feelings of seriousness about past and future events. Some experts have also speculated that intelligent children, especially if they have a somewhat isolated childhood, could be much more telepathic than adults. It has been suggested that they recall, or rather receive, memories – other people's memories – via telepathy."

I knew I was in danger of becoming an intellectual bore, but Margaret was driving me on, despite the fact that Nathan would rather have been watching football on television. I was also being fairly cogent, I convinced myself, despite excessive red wine.

I would have one last stab at a coherent explanation: "Inherited memories genetically transferred may have some plausibility. Take the stories about people with transplants developing the habits of their dead donors. Sci-fi, possibly, but there are some good yarns out there.

"Collective memories – collective unconscious – they all suggest a personal experience for those who believe in a past-life, but genetics could dictate a somewhat impersonal interpretation. I must say science seems to be pushing us more towards genetic explanations – nature not nurture."

I resisted the impulse to look directly at Margaret, but I did take a sip of wine, to let someone else take the floor. But they waited, so I supposed I was making some kind of sense, or was at least being mildly persuasive. "Possession could be another explanation, especially if you're an ardent Catholic, or Hammer horror buff. That's unacceptable to modern psychologists, outside the Vatican. But multiple personality disorder is not. Or, cynically, it could just be mostly fraud, false memory or fantasy."

A bell clanged loudly, and the barman shouted, "Time, ladies and gentlemen, please."

I used to get annoyed sometimes at Britain's crazy and restricted drinking laws – I found France, Spain and Italy much more to my taste when it came to eating out with friends; you could talk and drink, sensibly, for as a long as you wanted. But on this occasion the laws originally invented to cut down on the tippling of armaments workers during the Great War made sense for stopping this American obsessive. It was time to go home.

I thought that my poor rendition of a few Duran Duran songs on the way home, with Nathan on air guitar, would have brought an obvious end to our serious discussion, especially when, back in Margaret and Nathan's farmhouse, I had a straight bourbon, while Jane had a port along with our hosts.

Jane returned, however, to the previous theme when she said, "Margaret, if she doesn't mind my mentioning it, is an expert at reading Tarot cards. She has done a few readings for me – but a long while back. In college, wasn't it?"

Margaret modestly demurred. "Not an expert, Jane, but I do occasionally produce results which time and events have vindicated. I don't know if you would agree with me after your previous readings?"

"I never tried, but I am open to it," I said butting in.

"Maybe, tomorrow. I do take it seriously so I wouldn't do it now, not after all the booze. Perhaps tomorrow, if you really want to." Margaret assumed a half-smiling, half-frowning expression.

⟨⟩∞⟨⟩

Nathan was yawning, and making no pretence that he wasn't desperate to get to bed. This time Jane took the cue to ask whether we could retire. The day, and the discussion, had been long. I normally specialized in being deeply superficial in intellectual debate, but Crozier had not only diverted me, he had also turned me into a pub bore. Well, that was my excuse, and I choose to stick to it.

Margaret led us to the far end of the house and to a small, but very luxurious, room converted from the former stables.

"You can make as much noise as you like here. Thick walls in them there days," she said with twinkle in her eye. "And we're down the far end of the farmhouse. I won't wake you in the morning — stroll into the kitchen when you want some coffee."

As soon as Margaret walked out of the door, Jane launched herself across the room and pulled me onto the bed. She kissed me so passionately, and I must confess I responded a little coldly. I don't know if I was surprised or just being my usual slow-burn self.

"Don't get into your undressing rituals, you buttoned-up Yank. Make love to me now."

I started to protest. "Don't give me any nonsense either — about cleaning your teeth first."

"Hell, the country air must have turned you on."

"No, darling, it was your mind. I don't often see it in action — even when you were humouring Margaret a little. In fact that was sweet of you. Now shut up and kiss me."

She gave me a quick hard kiss, then turned me over on my stomach, and started to tug down my trousers. Perhaps because I didn't assist very much, she whipped off my new silk tie, the one she had given me for Christmas, and firmly tied my wrists together.

Then she rolled me over, hitched up her skirt, rapidly pulled her top off and started stroking my emerging erection with her breasts. She seemed to want to control me – she none-too-gently mounted me, while forcing my tied hands over my head and down onto the bed. Then she slid back off my full erection, and instead she adopted a crouching position and reinserted herself. Slowly but firmly she started to rise up and down using her leg muscles like a piston. Her internal muscles squeezed and then relaxed their grip on my penis. I'd never experienced this kind of muscle control before.

Jane started to groan and then scratched my ribs as she maintained her leverage and momentum. She started to utter a muted scream from deep inside her throat, as she reached her orgasm, but she continued moving up and down, knowing that I hadn't reached mine. A warm wet shower seeped down over my groin. Soon she gave another throaty yelp and came again, as more liquid oozed over me. It was the first time she had been multi-orgasmic with me and it made me excited. I shouted too when I reached my own climax a few seconds afterwards.

She collapsed by my side.

"I love you and that's what makes our love-making so wonderful," she said eventually.

"We have a special love, Jane," was my lame rejoinder.

I even managed to stay awake and to hold and caress her for a few minutes, before falling into a deep sleep.

Six

We breakfasted late: full English style – eggs, lots of slices of bacon, tomatoes and toast, along with baked beans, another local delicacy that I've never quite got the hang of. But I was very hungry after the sex and drink.

I also needed some fresh air. Despite the winter chill, it wasn't raining for a change, so Nathan promised to take us for a nature ramble combined with a history lecture. Margaret excused herself – she had to pick up her daughter from her private school, Marlborough.

Nathan drove Jane and me the mile into the square.

"I thought we were walking," Jane said.

"We are, later, but I want to show you around different areas of historical interest."

Nathan started to explain the age of some of the houses around the square, and then led us towards the churchyard of St James's. The architectural harmony of the houses was deeply alluring. I was entranced as I gazed around me. In the dark of the previous night, I was a little spooked by Shere, but now, strangely, I felt as though I had come home.

"This church was mentioned in the Domesday Book in the 1080s – a few years before the US Constitution," he said, taking on a rather schoolmasterly tone. "And the gateway was designed by Edwin Lutyens, the famous English architect –

much later of course. Lutyens fell in love with the daughter of the Lord of the Manor; the title still exists. It is a she now, and she owns the houses painted green and yellow – like those over there." He pointed out a row of pretty cottages opposite the church. "Lutyens hung around on and off for a few years, but it was an unrequited love affair."

"Yes, you can almost sense the sadness of some of his designs."

"How do you know that – you've only seen the gateway?"

"The lychgate? No, I've read a bit about Lutyens."

Nathan was a bit put out. "You tell us about him then."

"No, no, carry on. I am really interested in what you're saying."

Inside the church Nathan talked about the anchoress, the female hermit, and the story seemed familiar. As did his not-too-insightful history of the church. Somehow I seemed to know what he was talking about. Actually, I hadn't read much about Lutyens, because he was a late nineteenth-century figure. I had researched the late eighteenth century, but even some of the earlier medieval history seemed very accessible.

When we walked into the antique shop in the High Street, Nathan said that it was the oldest building still standing. "This goes back to 1420 or thereabouts," he said. Inside, the very low ceilings brought back an eerie sense of déjà vu. Yet I appreciated that this was just the proverbial tip of the iceberg. No amount of reading could have created that very definite sense of geographical affinity. No, it was more an emotional – personal – relationship. I belonged here.

It was the same when Nathan drove us to Gomshall. We walked around the mill and it seemed uncannily familiar as did the old packhorse bridge next to it, though I didn't emotionally relate to the traditional pub on the river, the Compasses, perhaps because Nathan explained it had been built in the nineteenth century.

He also showed us a second smaller packhorse bridge almost

hidden in riverside bushes. I glided my hands along the edge of the mossy stone rampart as though I was enveloping a long-lost artefact from my childhood. I wanted to touch it for hours, embrace it, love it, belong to it, because I knew that it was part of me. I looked at my companions to see if they had noticed the sudden onrush of my emotions, but they had walked on, deep in conversation.

Nathan was an impatient tour guide and quickly shooed us back to the car. He probably didn't notice my possessive – obsessive – response to the stone bridge; or, if he did, he might have dismissed my slightly eccentric behaviour as due to a hangover.

He drove us high up into the Hurtwood in the direction of Ewhurst, to the Windmill Inn, where we stood in its garden luxuriating in the glorious vista of the South Downs, a view only slightly marred by haze.

"There's always been a pub here called the Windmill," he said.

By now I had listened to his incorrect historical pontifications about the area for an hour and had resolved to shut up and not annoy my host. Yet I heard myself instinctively contradicting him. "Actually, I think it may once have been called the New Inn."

"Well, you can buy me a drink in the former New Inn," Nathan said a mite peevishly. I was reluctantly growing to like his honest annoyance – many Brits would tend to hide it under an urbane patina.

And Jane loyally defended me: "Don't take any notice of him, Nathan. Tom's a smart arse – he probably read up on the place in detail before he came. He was so excited about coming, you know."

Nathan wasn't obviously mollified by this comment, but he was happy about the rather early whisky.

"Hair of the dog is good for you, isn't that right, Doctor? Even though it's only twelve-thirty."

"Yes, but only one if you're driving, and adding to the intake from last night," Jane said with a laugh, but authoritatively nonetheless.

"Perhaps, Professor Martin, you can enlighten us as to how this place used to look like before its refurbishment," Jane said in her assumed authoritarian voice, but spiced now with a little light sarcasm.

"I can't 'cos I know bugger all except that it would make my day if Eric Clapton walked in. I do happen to know he lives nearby. These hills are full of ageing rock stars and retired models, or so my receptionist tells me. She knows this area well." I said this for Nathan's benefit.

"So she's your secret source – faithful Mary," Jane said.

We took in the view across the forests and downs. "Apparently, on a very clear day you can see all the way to Brighton coast – due south for maybe forty miles," Nathan claimed.

"This was on the smuggling run into London, I understand. Tea, tobacco, spirits. The gentlemen of the night were very active in this area."

"You're right," Nathan said. "In fact, the windmill itself and the pub were used as meeting places for the smugglers and a big punch-up erupted near here between the smugglers and the customs' men."

"A publican could lose his licence and be heavily fined – £50, a fortune in those days – if he were caught trying to bribe a customs and excise man. And collective fines were imposed on whole villages if someone was caught helping the 'free traders' as everyone except the authorities called them," I informed the company.

That was the sum total of information I had specifically gleaned about the area around Shere and its local history, plus a very little general reading on the period. I had absolutely no idea how I knew what the pub was once called. Or why I felt I had been in the area before. Or why the church seemed so familiar. Or why I was emotionally pole-axed by a simple old bridge.

Our host took us on the brief walk up to the four-storey brick windmill. Nathan said, "This is one of only two tower windmills left standing in Surrey."

I didn't feel drawn to the building.

Then Nathan explained that the original mill was built around the 1640s, but it was blown down, and the present one was much more modern. Perhaps my intuitive sense of history related only to a specific period.

Nathan drove us next to the old parish church in Albury Park

"Now where have you seen this church before?" Nathan asked and looked hard at Jane, as if to exclude "Mr Encyclopaedia Britannica", as she had called me in the Windmill pub.

"Not sure, but it *is* familiar," she said, "but, like Tom, I've not been here before."

I recognized it from somewhere as well, but I was definitely keeping my big mouth shut as I had to stay one more night under Nathan's roof. I had taken to his wife, despite myself, but he mildly irritated me, even though I knew it was partly my fault. If I were a medieval historian, it would make sense. Why should a psychiatrist feel so proprietorial about the history of a place he hardly knew, and had driven through only once before?

I was lost in my own thoughts, when Nathan announced, "You have both seen this church in a film."

Jane looked quizzical.

"No idea," she confessed.

"Me neither," I said.

Nathan was playing the showman and allowed for a dramatic pause: "It was used as an external shot in…one of the weddings in *Four Weddings and a Funeral*."

"Yes, I see what you mean," Jane said with a little relief in her voice. Not half as relieved as I felt.

That clean-cut piece of logical explanation helped a lot. I had been feeling rather strange – a mixture of personal disassociation yet instinctive sense of belonging to the area.

Nathan took me to his golf club for a quick look around the bar and Jane went shopping in Guildford. I managed to get back in time for a brief snooze and a long bath. The porcelain bathtub looked like a genuine antique, down to the clawed cast-iron pedestals. I luxuriated in the tub as I needed some down time. I was still shaken by the face in the fire, and the uncanny sense of widespread déjà vu I was experiencing, and I blamed it on my patient, Jim Crozier. I had to exorcise his evil spirit.

We were to re-assemble at seven-thirty p.m. for an evening meal in the farmhouse. Our hosts had invited an older couple from the village to join us.

Jane bustled in from shopping and demanded I surrender the bathroom to her. I got out quickly, grabbing one of the bathrobes behind the door, but was met with a slightly sharp comment – "Try not to be Mr America tonight, knowing everything about insignificant local tribes in these benighted islands. Even if you do know so bloody much, don't show it."

"Jane, that's not fair, you know how much I love Britain."

"I know you do, darling," she said gently patting my cheek, while she removed her bra and twirled it around for effect, "and I know you are interested in so many things, but it sometimes comes across – well, like your President's foreign policy[5] – teaching the world how to be American."

I smiled, but it hit home. I really didn't see myself as the ugly American abroad. Secretly, I thought I had assimilated pretty well with the Brits. I was even thinking of possibly marrying one, after all.

We were soon summoned to dinner. The extra guests were a retired farmer called Max and his wife, Marietta. He was a red-faced man and, as Jane said later, straight out of central casting for the role of gentleman-farmer. I didn't say a lot, I just drank moderately and listened to the conversation on local affairs. The headline was definitely about supporting the hunting lobby. Personally, I couldn't see the need to chase a fox around, but I dutifully kept my opinions to myself.

Certainly, I admired the sense of community which infused the gossip. How a disabled couple in the village had had their car stolen and in a week, after a communal collection, the money had been raised to buy them a new vehicle. Max talked passionately about his favourite rooster going AWOL and of how the scar on his face was healing nicely, thank you, after being whacked during an accident with a clay-pigeon machine. His wife teased him about chasing moles in the garden with a pitchfork, and being obsessed about a neighbour's cat crapping on his flower bed. Fifteen whole minutes were devoted to labradors, a conversation interrupted by Nathan insisting on playing loud CDs of Ferraris driving around a race-track. Fox hunting seemed far saner by comparison.

The overall impression I got from the evening's local gossip was the extent to which some of the traditional pillars of community, especially the Church, still supported a sense of cohesion. People cared, despite or because of the fact they lived in each other's pocket, except that the cohesion was stratified by a rigid class system.

I had learned to decipher some of class-specific words. Max and Marietta talked about "settees" not "sofas" and, of course, going to the "lavatory" – definitely not the working-class word "toilet". English class codes were baffling to outsiders, even one like me who tried hard to decipher them. The best guide to class etiquette is definitely *Alice Through the Looking Glass*, I concluded.

But, heck, I couldn't help liking the Brits – they fulfilled nearly all the clichés I had cherished before I came to live in the UK: that the Brits are tolerant (despite the media brouhaha about immigration and Muslim extremists) and that that they are courteous, reserved and moderate – by and large – despite the dispiriting yob culture among the young. And they like eccentrics. Above all, though, they are badly dressed. And the higher you go up the social scale the more you could get away with dressing down.

The rural chatter served to reinforce my affectionate prejudices about the Brits. I liked our hosts' guests, not least because they were so completely unlike Americans. The couple left early, at about ten, and their departure bestowed a sense of refreshed comity between the four residents of the farmhouse. None of us had drunk too much, partly because of the excesses of the night before, but also because I wanted to take up Margaret's offer of a Tarot reading.

I had checked with Jane whether it was alright to approach the subject again. Margaret agreed and we sat down for a reading. The candles from the dinner table added to the sense of mystical purpose.

I don't remember the precise details of the cards, because the concept was new to me, but Jane refreshed my memory on the drive back the next day, telling me a little of "the power and mystery" and minor and major arcana.

Margaret had spread out the cards and asked me what I wanted to know.

"Can I be specific?" I asked.

"As specific as you like – it makes it easier, in fact," she replied.

For once Nathan sat back in the settee and kept his own counsel. He stroked slightly dementedly a very scraggy brown fleece cardigan he was wearing – maybe he was hankering after his very own labrador.

I had been wondering about marriage to Jane, and whether I would need to settle in the UK, or perhaps take her back with me to the States. I hadn't seriously discussed any of this with her, but it was very much on my mind, so I asked, "Do I need to travel, perhaps one-way, to fulfil my destiny?"

Margaret spread the Tarot cards on the dining-room table, after moving the candlesticks to the side. "Choose five," she said.

I did.

The first was the six of swords – "reversed", as Margaret put it. The second was the two of swords, also reversed. Then came the knight of wands – "the right way up", Jane said, sitting on the edge of her seat – and the eight of wands. And finally the knight of pentacles.

"So what does it mean?" I asked with very genuine curiosity.

"Ah, Mr Sceptic seems to have undergone a conversion," Jane said quietly.

Margaret ignored her, and Nathan yawning on the sofa.

"The knight of wands is the strongest journey card. You will change residence, perhaps countries as well. The other cards strongly confirm this. This is a very balanced reading. Very definite."

"I am fated to travel?"

"Yes, it seems – from the cards – that you have no option but to undertake a major journey. You are very definitely a seeker and you have been given a specific answer. This is not entirely in the cards, but I personally sense danger in this journey as well. But also a great opportunity is offered – the chance of a lifetime perhaps."

I wanted to ask about the journey, but I sensed Margaret did not want to say any more. Clearly, a warning hovered behind this reticence. Jane seemed a trifle unsettled by it too. And Nathan, with his short attention span, was clearly agitating to wind up the session.

Jane and I soon went to bed and cuddled very perfunctorily before falling asleep.

Fairly early the next morning, after effusive thanks and a very light breakfast, we left the glorious village of Shere. We had been told that the name derived from "Essira": "a place of light". Something deep inside my brain told me that Shere meant "pure" or "clean" — because of the way the river water was filtered by the limestone hills and watercress beds. Yet I also felt uplifted, renewed, perhaps even enlightened by the so-called place of light. After meeting Margaret, I was almost tempted to say I had been "re-born" in Shere, though I hated the phrase as redolent of the worst red-neck Evangelicals in my home country's Bible belt.

I felt more than a touch of sadness at leaving, as we drove under the rickety wooden bridge on the hill that leads past the half-timbered houses, leaning way off the perpendicular, and then on to the main road.

On the journey back to London, I asked Jane what she thought about my Tarot reading, and I think she was a little evasive, frightened perhaps. Maybe anxious about my portended dangerous travels, or whether she guessed I was working out where we would live as a married couple. She had never expressed any enthusiasm about living in the US. Maybe she shared her Aunt Doris's bitter-sweet attitudes towards America. Jane just said, "Margaret knows what she's talking about."

I sensed very strongly that Jane was right. A journey clearly beckoned. I was thinking of the US, and I felt an almost tangible jab in my heart about leaving England. Hell, I loved the place — and Jane. I didn't sense an opportunity. It was a stark foreboding.

Seven

*J*ane may have hoped that the trip to the Surrey countryside, the history and our metaphysical chats would have sated whatever she thought was driving my distraction with Crozier. Being a typical shrink, I didn't discuss issues openly. I should have, but I kept my thoughts to myself. I rationalized that I couldn't explain them to myself, let alone to someone so important to me.

For a couple of days the Shere weekend seemed to have invigorated our emotional and sexual relationship, but then I knew that I was beginning to withdraw. I quite often did that when I was trying to resolve an important problem. Sometimes it might be personal and at other times it could be professional. I didn't share things. I always reckoned that I had to fix issues first and then perhaps discuss them in a semi-detached way as a former problem. It was selfish, but it wasn't aimed at Jane in any way.

She was generally patient with me. Except one evening we met briefly for a quick drink after work – she was working awkward hours at the time, so was I.

"You've become rather anti-social, Tom," she said with her usual Northern bluntness. "You used to be a bit of a social butterfly, now you're more like a bloody hermit. You've given up the gym – you don't mention squash any more. Some fancy woman?"

"Specialists don't have time for even one partner. Two would be impossible, darling." I stressed the last word with all the theatricality I could muster. "Even if I had all the time in the world, I would love only you," I said. Jane recognized and accepted the truth of what I had said, but there was something deep inside me which questioned my own statement. A fancy woman, as she had put it, would have been an easy matter to resolve: give the bitch up would be the simple solution. I really didn't want anybody except Jane. I was thinking more and more about marriage, and not just because Jane's biological clock was ticking away. Despite my gamophobic bachelor instincts, I know that Jane was nearly everything I wanted – after years of varying field trials.

And yet I had been making excuses about working late or being tired. I was exhausted, because I was spending a great deal of time researching past-life experiences. I also started to read more about Surrey in the late eighteenth century, the time and place – apparently – of Crozier's recall. I didn't discuss the case with my colleagues in any detail. I didn't want to seem unprofessionally obsessed. I talked a little to Professor Michael Hendrickson, a respected scientist who had done a great deal of work on suppressed and false memory syndromes. What he told me didn't fit into what Crozier was experiencing. I didn't talk to my immediate colleagues in the sleep disorder unit, however. Perhaps, looking back, I should have. But they wouldn't have understood my motivation. Now I know – after what happened to me – that they would have thought me a little deranged.

Of course, I asked myself: why bother so much with this one patient? Christ, I don't even like the fellow, I told myself repeatedly. Perhaps irrationally, I intensely disliked him. Yet somehow I knew I was connected to this man. Intuition? Maybe. Was intuition the enemy of science? Hunches, I knew, had inspired many scientific advances. I could not deny that it could be seen as irrational. But there was almost a palpable impulsion – deep within me – to follow up, investigate, resolve, discover…I wasn't quite sure how to describe it.

I wasn't thinking in mystical or religious terms at all. But I recalled what Thomas Jefferson advised his nephew about doubt and faith: "Question with boldness even the existence of a god; because, if there be one, he must approve the homage of reason rather than of blindfolded fear." I didn't regard myself as superstitious, but as a rational and scientific hunter chasing after truth.

What was most frustrating was Crozier's adamant refusal to return to his treatment. He had made that surprising request to see me urgently in the New Year, an appointment was made, and he just didn't show up. I wrote to him to suggest that he should continue with his consultation and of course offered to waive the fee for the missed appointment. No reply.

I did make a point of attending the Covent Garden performance of *Madame Butterfly* for which Crozier had previously sent two tickets. I assumed, correctly, that even he would not be gauche enough to mention his own generosity, the tickets he sent to me, but which I said I had obtained from a colleague. Jane and I spoke to Crozier at the reception and praised his contribution to the children's charity. He seemed very charming. I was distracted by a question from another guest, with whom I was slightly acquainted. I noticed that Jane and Crozier were apparently engaged in a deep though brief conversation.

At such a social function I could hardly bring up a medical issue – why had he refused to return to his treatment? Nor, of course, could I ask him about his birthmark, even though I knew that believers in reincarnation often see them as indications of how people died in a previous life. Nightmares about having one's throat cut, and then sporting a scar-like birthmark on the neck, was altogether far too pat. I wondered whether Crozier had been fed such superstitious nonsense when he was young, and he had psychologically embraced the explanation and then subconsciously this had fertilized his adult nightmares. Again, this was plausible but too simplistic.

I had so many unanswered questions that, on our way home, I couldn't resist asking Jane about her impressions of Crozier.

"Interesting bloke. Quite sane and rather smooth," she said later.

I wasn't going to quiz her in more detail, but Jane teased me by deliberately cutting short her account, and then pausing for a few moments, knowing that I was intrigued by the man. "He told me about his boxing club for young boys, one of the charities he supports. Sounded genuine to me. Maybe you have cured him, Doctor," she concluded with a lilt in her voice.

I could not let it rest. After a few weeks or so, I asked Mary to speak to him again about renewing his treatment. She said that Crozier had been abusive.

She relayed the brief phone conversation – minus some expletives: "You can tell that shrink to 'eff off. I'll report him to the medical council, if anyone tries to ring me again. And I've told my Nichole to keep away as well."

"Then he hung up," Mary told me.

"Some patients do react a little like this when they return to a traumatic experience," I replied. Though I didn't say the trauma might have happened a few hundred years ago. I also reflected on whether my dismissal of a bipolar disorder had been too premature. Why should he be so charming to Jane and yet so abusive to my receptionist?

I continued my research on historical Surrey, but I tried also to be more attentive to Jane. I attempted to revert to some of my old social rounds, the odd visit to my club, the Athenaeum, and even ventured again into the Frontline Club, where a handful of real foreign correspondents and a host of wannabees used to hang around. I went to the gym once or twice, but it seemed rather pointless – especially as an idea was forming in my mind.

I had decided to experiment.

"Physician, heal thyself," I told myself.

Besides, if I thought the therapy was right for Crozier, then why not? I still felt guilty about Jane's just accusations that I had not discussed the case with my colleagues. I talked again to Professor Hendrickson, but in deliberately vague terms over an informal drink. I also asked him, apparently en passant, about self-hypnosis techniques. Although he was rather dismissive, he mentioned one or two references which I did look up. I knew a few basics about psychosonic rhythm methods and various popular approaches such as the Jacobson progressive relaxation procedures, but I would do it my own way. I had dabbled for a while in meditation in my undergraduate days, though I had not talked to my friends about it. Mantras and my pretensions to be a jock didn't mix, I knew.

I vividly remember the date, the weather and my mood when I tried out my little personal experiment. It was 13 February 2007. Jane had just rung me and, with perhaps just a touch of mock-discretion, asked what I had planned for the next evening. I told her it was a secret. It was, even to me, because I had forgotten about Valentine's Day until she unsubtly prompted me. I knew I was pre-occupied. I convinced myself that my experiment might cure this increasing historical irritation in my psyche. I could then put it aside and concentrate on my career and Jane.

I was alone in my flat, and the doors were locked. It said seven-forty-five p.m. on the carriage clock on the mantelpiece of my marble fireplace. I sat in my favourite leather armchair and carefully placed a metronome on the coffee table in front of me. I nursed a small glass of Armagnac, but I was careful to take just a few sips to relax myself. I pressed the button on my tape recorder to record what I might say. I lowered the lights with an automatic dimmer control placed on the table. Mozart played softly in the background. I was almost ready.

I switched the metronome on and I placed a second tape recorder on the table. I pressed the "on" button. I had already recorded a wake-up message – timed to go off in twenty-two minutes. It would gradually talk me up and out of my deep relaxation, just in case it worked too well. I refused to admit that I was trying to hypnotize myself. It was not good practice for a well-known psychiatrist to do this to himself, on his own, with no trained minder – with nobody else there at all. I felt a little guilty and yet excited at the same time.

The metronome clicked away.

The second tape recorder went from a slight hiss to a message telling me to relax. It used my own voice and technique. The alpha countdown began. I did not wait for it to happen. If it happens, it happens, just like sleep, I said to myself. And I was, as usual, dog-tired.

The tape intoned: "Relax. Keep your eyes shut.

"Try to find the most peaceful part of your mind.

"You will remember everything when you are fully conscious."

I recall hearing my own voice starting again at alpha 20 and the less insistent click of the metronome. "Alpha 19. Alpha 18." The countdown went to alpha 1, I remember. And I thought my voice sounded powerful and a little strange. The sound of the clicking stopped.

Then I heard, I think, "Imagine you are going back in time. Time is running backwards and you are free to choose a character in the immensity of all times past." I didn't recall putting that on the tape. There was a blankness and I wondered whether I was asleep. I wanted to lift my eyelids, but I couldn't – they seemed very heavy. Perhaps I was asleep. Then I remember floating but I didn't feel any water. Then I seemed to be lighter than air, drifting through clouds. No voice urged me to remember my childhood or any specific historical period. There was just blackness, and then warmth and a detached floating – almost flying – sensation.

Again I heard the voice counting down. "Alpha 20, alpha 19…"

I seemed to have lost the ability to understand counting. I could comprehend sound, however. Mozart had been transformed into an amazing experience, like a low chant but, oh, so sweet and harmonic. Music filled my heart and my head, the whole planet – the whole expanding universe – seemed suffused with angelic harmonies. I saw lights, small like stars, then bigger and stronger. Gradually they all fused into one and I was sucked into the light, so willingly. I wanted it so much. At first I was drawn slowly, then faster and – suddenly, my God, I felt I was being propelled out of my body at the speed of light.

I remembered darkness again, a feeling of desertion. Utter, utter hellish darkness as though I was alone in a Black Hole far from the Earth's Milky Way. I had been abandoned by every particle in our universe. I had been forsaken by man, gravity and then by God and all his creation…No sound permeated this complete state of sensory banishment. Nothing existed. It was death…

Gradually, I awoke. It was still completely dark, but I could hear very muffled voices. Very, very faint, but somehow I knew they were friendly tones, though I couldn't understand the words or perhaps the language. Nevertheless, they were welcoming me, I was sure. A gentle tingle of pleasure ran through my body. I have no idea for how long I was in this state.

The next thing I knew someone had thrown me very hard against the floor. Pain coursed throughout my whole body: acute pain, catapulting me into unbearable agony.

Eight

Through the haze of pain I could see a large man bearing down on me with a dagger. I managed to get up on one knee and propel myself to the side as he lumbered towards me.

I knew I would have to fight for my life.

He took a few seconds to turn around and charge again. I had a chance in the gloom to work out that I was in some kind of forester's hut. Straw bales, work-benches and old pieces of wood lay around. I made out what looked like the wooden handle for an unfinished pick-axe or perhaps a hoe.

Whatever the hell it was, I grabbed it and swung it at my assailant who was by now charging again. I hit his left arm hard and he shouted in both anger and surprise. It slowed him a little but he swiftly transferred the knife from his left to right hand.

I jabbed my makeshift club very forcefully into his chest but he seized the end and held on to it as he moved in for the kill.

"It's over for you, Rich. A thief don't cheat a fellow thief and expect to live," he said, panting heavily.

He was almost twice my weight and I felt all the wind rushing from me as he fell on top of me. My club fell to the ground.

I didn't beg or try to persuade. This man was about to kill

me unless I killed him first. He pressed his great knees on to my shoulder and then sat back heavily on my stomach and deprived me again of air.

He put the dagger's tip under my chin and pushed hard enough to draw blood. My attacker seemed to delight in prolonging my agony.

"Steady yourself for heaven or hell," he said, staring at me manically. His scarred left cheek lifted into a rictal grin, displaying the greenest teeth I have ever seen. His breath smelled of cow dung and onions.

I wasn't ready to die. I instinctively felt for my belt with my right hand, and found a hard object – my own knife.

He leaned right over my face, his dagger still poised.

"Good bye, my old friend," he said with utter malice.

He arched his body upwards as he raised his hand to deliver the fatal blow.

It gave me a few inches to reach my knife and jerk it from its sheath. I had just enough time to thrust it into the back of his left calf. He squealed and I jerked my head aside as the downward movement of his dagger implanted in the hard earth. As he tugged to loosen it, I shifted sideways and scuttled to my feet, ready to face him.

I heard myself addressing the man by his name: "Jake, 'tis not my time yet, but it could be yours."

He was still struggling to remove his knife from the impacted earth floor of the hut.

I threw myself onto his back and swept my knife right across his throat – almost from ear to ear.

He uttered no cry, just a loud gurgling sound and a massive splaying of blood.

He slumped face down on the earth. In the enveloping darkness, a pool of crimson blood formed around his head. A strange rasping noise came from him and then silence.

In those few seconds, whoever I was and wherever I was, I knew that I had killed my first human being.

I staggered backwards and fell on to a straw bale. I dropped my knife and put my head into my outstretched blood-stained palms and howled with despair. I knew that I was Dr Thomas John Martin, yet I also knew that I was someone called Richard Bryant. For a few fleeting electric moments I had total awareness of both existences: I was simultaneously both Dr Jekyll and Mr Hyde. It was as if two different lives flashed through my fevered brain – Tom, a boy of eleven waiting at the bus stop for a yellow bus, then Richard, a grown man, walking past a gibbet clutching a dead highwayman, wearing just a tattered cloak, and swinging in the wind, as a coach and four horses jangled past.

I also knew that I was not now in London. I could sense the heart of the countryside and its twilight sounds and smells. I looked at my countryman's clothes – the worsted frock coat, brown waistcoat, corduroy breeches, linen cravat and ankle boots. I instinctively looked around for my hat – a man was not dressed without a hat. But it was gone.

This duality did not last long. Although I have blank spots in my recall of this time, from what I remember now as I write this account, the memory of a twenty-first-century psychiatrist lasted as long as it took Richard Bryant – me – to work out what to do. Within seconds I had become Richard Bryant – in language, culture and, above all, cunning...

I had to get rid of the body and move the silver hoard that we had fought over.

It was gloomy in the hut, but I managed to find two complete rush lights and use the tinderbox in Jake's pocket to light them. I found a dirty cloth to wrap around the dead man's neck to staunch the flow of blood. Using straw and some grease I lit a small fire around the heaviest blood stains. There was ample sawdust and I used that to soak up both blood and ash. I swept the used sawdust into a sack to take away. Thereafter, I dragged the body outside to my cart and covered it in sacks. I would pay Nathaniel the forester a few shillings, as agreed, to let his hut be used for free traders' meetings. He would never raise any questions as long as he got paid.

It was a moonlit August night, and I knew the woods well. The churchyard of St Luke's was one mile or so distance. There waited the altar tomb with part of the silver. Very few visited the deserted church any more. That's why we smugglers used it, and spread stories of the goblins which were said to haunt the place.

The small farm wagon was easily pulled by the single bay. The horse's name was Diamond, and he responded well to my voice. I didn't need the whip.

I felt burdened by Jake's death. I had not wanted it. I had never trusted the man completely, but we were both free-traders, man and boy. My God! We had stood shoulder to shoulder and then back to back when we were cornered by the King's men. It could have been the Tyburn jig for us, but our men help beat them back until the soldiers cut and ran. On two or perhaps even three occasions we owed each other a debt of life. And now, heavens, this…His greed had swallowed him. Until we fell out over the second part of the French silver…until he threatened to betray me, few harsh words had been uttered between us. Yes, sly he was, but he had stood by me for more than twenty-odd years. And yet, at the end, he would have killed me as readily as slicing up a hare. I would need to think on how it had all come to pass…once the body was gone.

St Luke's was largely abandoned and part of the roof was missing. The Hurtwood had almost enveloped the church in its ancient bosom. Twice a year, at Christmastide and Easter, services were held. But the irregular congregation at this church comprised we smugglers – honest men who were driven by the excess of taxes to trade with the French. Jake and I had joined the Abbotson gang when were both about sixteen. Now, God forgive me, I was putting him in his last resting place, our hidden smuggler's hole.

I stopped the horse near the gate of the church. With some effort, I dragged the dead weight of my departed companion. The altar stone seemed an appropriate place: holy ground and no one would come poking around. I looked around in the moonlight and then listened: just a small tired sigh from Diamond. I waited for a few minutes and heard no more than the hoot of an owl. And then I approached the stone monument, a few feet from the door of the church. I put all my weight against the top slab, and pushed hard. It slid across its base and left a triangular opening of three feet at its widest. I pushed again, but not too hard. I didn't want it to crash to the ground. I could never lift it again on my own. I knew where the small wooden trunk was, aligned exactly along the inside edge of the end nearest the church. Leaning over I could just lift it out. Flipping the trunk lid open, I let the moonlight caress the silver hoard inside: some of the finest candlesticks and platters from France, no doubt pillaged from the doomed aristocracy.

And they were all mine now. But possession of it would never have made me kill a man. Not with intent. Better to have shared it with Jake, but he wanted it all, and he was meaning to sink his knife deep into my flesh. No doubt there. No mercy would have been shown even if I had begged for it. I tried to cast aside the hurt, the guilt and, yes, even the loss I felt for my companion-in-arms. I had now to deal practically with the consequences.

Hoisting the trunk on to my shoulder I took it back to my cart. With some effort, I dragged Jake's body back up to the altar stone. Exhausted, I let it lie for a few moments. I remember quoting from the Bible – just a few jumbled lines. It was a long time since I had read the good book:

"Ashes to ashes – dust to dust…I am the resurrection, and the life: he that believeth in me, though he were dead, yet shall he live…Amen."

That was all I could think to say that was appropriate.

Maybe it wasn't even appropriate — I didn't want or expect such a blackguard to be resurrected. But I was a sinner myself even though I'd been brought up a believer. Jake needed a few words said over him, though he had tried to kill me.

That done, I lifted up his head and arms and hoisted them over the edge of the tomb. He looked as if he were drunk and vomiting into it. But he was stone dead and damned heavy. With some effort, I managed to lift the rest of his large frame over the edge. He was too big, and carefully I had to shift the top a little more, anxiously trying to prevent it falling off. Somebody would eventually notice that and peer in. Somehow I got the whole of Jake inside his new home, and I slid the stone top back over in three hefty shoves. I chalked a small triangle on each end of the tomb: the "Death to thee" sign. You would be cursed in heaven and stabbed on earth if anyone meddled. Few came to the haunted churchyard, and anyway they were free trading men who would recognize and honour the sign.

It was done.

It was three or more miles along rough tracks back to Peaslake. It took more than half an hour, even in the full moon. Peaslake was a safe place, a sprawling hamlet for those who wanted to avoid the law. It was isolated, and few of the King's men would dare venture, even in strength, though it was only thirty or so miles from London town. The high heath land and forest had little to offer farmers. The infertile sandy soil supported much birch and bracken and also the hurts, known by outsiders as bilberries or whortleberries, but the people of the heath, "the Heethers" as it was spoken, thrived — or at least survived — in the woods they called the Hurtwood. And many hurt people lived there, gypsies aplenty and good men broken by the city's hovels or crossed by some landlord over a shilling or two, or accused of poaching by a fat whore-hopping gamekeeper. Some were guilty men, prosperous and boasted of it, and some were desperate creatures — you could see the haunted looks and the filthy rags. The inhabitants of the more fertile Tillingbourne valley below, in Shere and Gomshall, looked down on those who built their squatters' cottages in the woods. True, it was full of poachers, free traders, hell-rakers and roisterers, especially after a successful run, but it was still a hard life, and honest by its own codes. There was no need for the condescending or sometimes downright fearful manner – if it were night – of the settled farming folk in the valley. That night I had no need of the valley – I stayed on the high ground and in the forest. Except for a frightened deer, nobody disturbed Diamond and me and the box that we carried.

I was making for Wheelwright Farm. It was a farm only in name and it was owned by Mrs Nye, an elderly widow. I had known her husband, Edward, in his last days as a free trader. He had taken to me when I was a lad and had been something of an uncle to me. Sometimes, after a tough run from the coast, I would stay at their cottage in an unused stable. She had always been kind to me, perhaps a replacement for her son who went to America and was never heard of again, and her daughter who had died when she was barely three days old. When old man Nye passed on, she encouraged me to stay whenever I had done some trading and needed to hide up for a few weeks. I gave her a few shillings and helped with some of the heavier chores, though I think it was the company she craved – though she was far too proud to say so. She always had a tear in the corner of her eye when I went off on a run to the coast.

Peaslake was a smugglers' haven, and Ma Nye I trusted, but still I needed to be careful. I dismounted from my cart a few hundred yards from the entrance to the farmyard and, dagger in hand, I led Diamond in. I freed him from the shafts and led him into the stable that I used to sleep in. Carrots were waiting for him, and some good hay – he had done me well. I carried my treasure into the house and up the stairs to the attic room which passed for home.

Home – sweet thought – now I could afford my own. Forty-three years on God's Earth and a chance to call something my own, but carefully and in good time. Ma Nye's room would do for the time being. I had to sell my wares in London, bit by bit, and build up my store of money. Good coins of mine were hidden in the thatch of Ma Nye's house, but the silver would bring me more, much more. First I had one more run to do. The silver was being brought in from France in two shipments. Some of the plate matched and would earn more as a set. Jake, though, had said one run was enough.

In this I was right, but it struck me hard how a big man's soul had gone to hell for a few bits of silver. I was glad, though, that Jake it was and not myself who lay beneath the slab. Not more than a few hours before we two had sat and argued across the oak board about the trade from France.

"Sell it quick," he said.

"And too cheap," I countered.

"And captured by the Preventers, too. I don't want to be wearing the Devil's neckerchief, dancing the hempen jig and be caged in a gibbet," Jake replied.

"Since when have you been afeared of the King's men – after all these years? Sending in the Dragoons here is like setting carthorses to catch eels."

"My gut tells me otherwise."

"All farts and Cousin Jack," said I.

"You knows cognac ain't my drink, Rich."

"The gibbet or transportation ain't my plans either, Jake, but we need to do one more run, and then slowly – slowly – deal with Solly in London. 'Tis the only way."

What I didn't say was that I suspected he wanted to do the second run on his own. Or, if he really thought his luck was running thin, then just one consignment – the whole of it – would be the same as sharing two.

He knew me too well, and fathomed what I was thinking.

That's what had caused our argument. That and too much booze in the New Inn, up Ewhurst way. He had been drinking like a horse, though it was rare for me get so much under my belt. We had finally agreed to move the silver from Nathaniel's hut together because the woodman would be at work there the next day. He didn't trust me to move it on my own, nor I him.

Sitting – just the two of us – around the small triangle table, Jake had become angry and kicked it over, with our beers. He hardly apologized, more sorry for the beer than my feelings, when he started to raise his voice.

"Hush, man. A thieves' den this may be, and no King's men. But good reason to still your tongue…"

"No betrayers here, Rich, except for the free trader I'm drinking here with…

"Don't call me false, Jake…after all these years. Let's be off to the hut. Fresh forest air may heal your temper…"

So that was it. We rode the three miles and argued all the way. As soon as we had entered the hut, he was upon me. The rest you know…

⋘∞⋙

And now a new journey lay ahead. I thought of Jake's great hands, all clenched to kill me, but still and useless now inside the tomb. I did not know if sleep would come, though for the moment I had nothing to fear.

I had just put the trunk in behind a hidden partition wall…when a gentle knock echoed around my room.

A second tap, even though it was three o'clock and the night was still as black as tar or "as white as midnight's arsehole", as Ma Nye used to say.. I felt for my dagger, now cleaned and back in my belt.

"Rich, sorry to be disturbing thee. I heard the noise of thy comin'. Needed to tell thee sumpin'. And I have some tea."

"Come in, Ma Nye," I said warmly.

She didn't ask what I had been doing. That was not the way of us free traders.

I thanked her for the tea, and then asked, "What's so pressing, Ma, that could not wait until the morrow?"

"Maybe it can, but I needs to tell thee that someone was askin' after a 'Mr Richard Bryant'."

"Who asked after me?"

"That's the mystery. A stranger in a hood, but he were no monk, no devil-dodger, though. Knew our ways, otherwise he would not have lasted the night here in these hills."

She explained that he went to the drinking den at Nance Rowland's and asked after me. Nine of the evening it was, or close. Nance's boy came over to tell Ma Nye.

"May be some bus'nes of your'n but I needed to tell thee – urgent, just in case."

Ma Nye knew I had been anxious of late. I had sensed that the affair with Jake was brewing, though I didn't know it would lead to killing.

"Did the stranger leave his name? Did Nance or anyone know of him?"

"No, slipped in like a ghost, she said, and spoke to Nance and just asked after thee. She didn't see his face – proper."

"Nought else, Nan?"

"Well, Nance's boy said that his mother told him to tell me that he had a Cockney speech, from London town. And that he were very pale. Like a ghost. That's what she said. Then he left. Maybe he'll be around in the morrow. Though I doubts it."

"A true mystery, Ma. But I'm off tomorrow, at cock's crow."

"To the sea, I guess?"

"Yes, Ma, to the sea."

And she smiled and tapped the side of her nose. "Many runs thee be doing, young Rich, but each one needs the care of the first time…I'll go to my bed an hour or more and then be up to make some victuals for thee."

"Thanks, Ma." I closed my door. I felt utterly drained of all my life blood but I doubted whether I would sleep. A partner killed by my own hand, and now a hooded stranger asking after me. My stomach was churning. Nevertheless, I needed to get some rest. It would be hard on the morrow, and even harder the day after.

Nine

I left Ma Nye's just after first light, around five-thirty a.m., according to the unpredictable but impressive timepiece in her kitchen. Her deceased husband had been so proud that he owned a smuggled French clock. "She" – Old Man Nye always addressed his clock thus – was certainly a grand piece: a tall clock with an eight-day movement. She had a plain panelled front and a richly moulded and gold-painted arched head, surmounted by brass ball-shaped finials. God knows how Edward Nye got his hands on her because she could hardly have come via the beach – it was just too big.

I used to admire her, though the clock often got me thinking of my life. That gilded treasure was the high point of Edward's life. I was now more than half of his age when he passed on, but I was still a smuggler and I was also now a murderer. Perhaps it was time to change, reform, improve: the second part of the silver consignment might do it. Once the silver was sold to Solly and his friends in London, I could start anew, become a man of substance, even buy a small house and – who knows? – take a wife. It was about time. I had married in my youth, Mathilde, because she was heavy with my child. Both died in childbirth, here in the Hurtwood. I took it as God's punishment for my fornication, but I soon strayed from His way. Twenty years on, and I was tired of dalliances with farm girls and sailors' widows. I wanted my own woman, to stay, to be mine, and perhaps bring up my children. I always felt that I would meet someone who would love me. I had no blood family to speak of and I felt alone.

But Ma was right: I had to concentrate on the job for the next few days, not think about the future. I had to think hard about the dangers of the present. It was a long run down to the coast. And Diamond wasn't right for this. "Black Harry" Risbridger met us in the central hollow in Peaslake with his pack ponies. There were seven Peaslake men and sixteen ponies, two spare for me. It was fitting that Black Harry rode a fine black gelding – he was our outrider. Armed with pistols, he was. If captured, the price of free trading with arms was hanging, but Black Harry swore he would die fighting and never swing in the gibbet, and I believed him. I had with me Nance's boy, as reward for his looking out for me earlier. He would tend the animals if we had to abandon them and deal with any of the Preventers. We hadn't encountered the King's men in a year or more, and even then we managed to evade them. Still, we had to be ready.

At first light and lightly laden, we made good progress along the few miles up to Pitch Hill. Night jars – puckridges we called them – gave us a chorus greeting. A sharp chill pierced the air, as we led our ponies up the steep tracks to the New Inn. In winter, wagons could be stuck in the clay and abandoned for months. The greensand soil would always be deeply rutted, even now, in the summer time.

Thomas Hall, the innkeeper, was wearing his striped apron, as he always did. He bade us welcome and had a good breakfast ready for us Peaslake men. The smell of bacon mingled with the fug of tobacco and wood smoke. Five Ewhurst lads with eight ponies and mules were set to join us. But this was time for resting, a little bargaining and waiting – for weather, and news from the "seamen". We were landsmen and that usually meant waiting – for good tides and no bad tidings about the Preventers.

We slept a little after breakfast, gave the ponies and horses hay, and took in five small barrels of local cider, and some woollen goods from Guildford; light stuff, more cover than trade – we usually exchanged the goods at a small profit or gave some out for favours, but a score or more ponies en route to the sea looked better with some goods rather than none. Few of the men in the New Inn drank more than one or two ales or cider – for they would need to stay awake for a long while. They also needed to be ready and able to fight as well as walk the many miles. Our Peaslake gang talked of the journey to come, while two of the Ewhurst men smoked their clay pipes and played dominoes with equal dedication.

We would leave at dusk – if no bad news came. We tried to relax but always a tension jangled in the air. Nance's boy – "Little Will" he was called [6]– came up to me and said in a whisper, "Mr Bryant, sir, ye knows this is my first run. I want to do good by thee."

"I have trust in you, boy. Just keep hold of the reins. No matter what – don't want to be chasing after runaways. And it'll keep you awake to mind the shillings for you and yours, especially the brandy for your Ma. She'll be proud of you, young 'un."

Gentle I was to him at first, then I became stern. "Turn around," I said. "And pull up your coat."

The lad did so reluctantly.

"Ah, I thought so. A knife. Give it me 'til we get back. No weapon, son. Just in case we meet the King's men. I don't want you fightin' for me, and – if caught – better to be without a knife."

"Sorry, sir. It were my father's."

"Good spirit, son, but await a year or more before you come to use it. I knew your father well, and he would not gainsay me on this. Be sure of that."

The young lad smiled and I felt the burden of his safety upon me.

I had not time to ponder on this as Tom Hall suddenly shouted to us all. "Men of the Hurtwood," he said, "news from Shoreham is good. The tides are fair, and you all be expected for the morrow." The miller, on lookout at the windmill – the highest point in the woods – had seen the beacon signal across the Sussex downs.

Immediately, our gang loaded up the ponies and mules with their light goods and set off just after dusk. We stayed in the "soft roads", the sandstone tracks through forest, heath land and bracken until Ellen's Green. Here, almost without a word, we split into three groups. Black Harry was still with us, mounted and in front, although sometimes, when the going was steep or uneven, he led his horse. There was little noise except for the thud of the hooves on thick sand. Sometimes in deep forest it was almost pitch black. The ripe aroma of damp foliage suffused the air. Little of the light from the full moon penetrated, but Harry had known these paths since childhood.

We met no one till the edge of St Leonard's Forest where we passed through a small hamlet. Three villagers must have heard us but had no time to hide. They turned their backs to us and faced the barn out of which they had just come. Poaching men, no doubt, to be abroad at this time of the night.

We exchanged a simple greeting – "Good evening, genl'men" was all that was said on both sides.

It was the custom to turn your back on us free traders. A sign of respect it was "to watch the wall". And in all God's truth they could tell the King's men that they had seen nought of smugglers or contraband.

Through the night we walked in woods and forest and hardly a village or hamlet did we see, though we glimpsed the occasional flicker of a lantern or rush light in a distant window. We kept to the wild tracks and stopped just twice, and briefly, to rest the horses and take some bread and cheese.

Soon after first light we arrived at a wood near Coombes, about seven miles from the headland above Shoreham by Sea.

Little Will had done well – no word of complaint and he had kept up, although he was just up to my waist in height. Here we waited in the barn of a farm owned by Black Harry's cousin. This is where we would meet up with the other Peaslake men.

They straggled in over the next hour – they had not been guided by a man like Black Harry. Arrogant was our Harry, but perhaps he merited some arrogance – he was tough, despite his slight limp, and where he led, men would follow.

The horses, mules and ponies were fed, watered and rested, all inside the big barn. Harry's cousin – I never knew his name – kept us all penned inside during daylight, except singly to use the privy across the yard. We drank some of the cider, but left two kegs for our host, as well as the rolls of cloth. We smoked our pipes, talked a little but the mood was expectant, though no man would dare show his fear.

Later, most of the men slept on straw bales. Little Will was too excited to sleep, I noticed, so I told him, "On a run, you sleep when you can. Otherwise you can't be a soldier of the night, which is our calling."

We waited till dusk, and then we led our animals through the woods behind the farm. Almost the whole of the rest of the journey was in good cover. We stopped less than a mile from the headland overlooking Shoreham; there we waited patiently, standing with our ponies' reins tight in our hands.

It was near midnight before we heard the whistle. It was Harry and he carried a small lantern, but it was not for the rocky path down to the beach. He had not yet lit his "spout" lamp.

"Cover up the horses," he ordered.

We quickly tied rags around the horses' hooves to muffle the clatter on the rocks. Harry led us almost soundlessly down to the steep path to the beach as a pale moon shed a faint glow across the sands. I welcomed the strong salt smell of the sea, and the gentle lapping of the waves, for – despite the dangers – it felt as though I were coming home.

Four men with horses and two with light wagons had joined us from the farm where we had hidden that day. On the beach, we all stood expectantly and silently, trying to see what was on the horizon. A sea mist had risen, despite the clear moon. I could just make out what looked like a lugger with short masts.

We stared at the shape for a few minutes until, suddenly, a blue flash came through the mists.

Harry lit his lantern and opened and closed the shutter to send out his "flink" – a response signal to say that the captain had found his "spot".

Out of the dark and soundlessly a team of men in harnesses joined us, as did five tall men with cudgels and pikes.

The lugger grew bigger as it came inshore, as close as her shallow keel, her broad beam and flat bottom would allow. Muffled oars we heard and two small tub-boats from the lugger came out of the mist to meet us in the surf, as we led the pack horses into the sea, just beyond the breaking waves. We waded out to our chests with the horses tight on the reins – sometimes they did panic in the sea.

One of the boats passed out a tub-line to one of the beach party led by a Shoreham man. Harry's cousin's men had taken up lookout positions and had supported the tub-men. The Shoreham foreman took the tub-line and hauled the line which held a pair of kegs tied at intervals, to be cut by the landing party. Each roped pair was quickly taken up by a tub-man, although in the Hurtwood we would call them "flaskers". But tub-men they were called here on the coast in West Sussex.

We Peaslake men took the two tied barrels straight over the backs of our pack animals. Sixteen of our animals had two kegs of brandy slung over them. A few extra packs in waterproof jackets containing tea and tightly packed tobacco were placed on top. I had taken a single keg. The last item due to come out of the tub-boat, which was unloading directly on to the horses, was a small trunk which I could see in the prow.

"That is for me," I said.

A sailor, whom I thought to be French, said in perfect English, "'Tis for a Mr Richard Bryant alone."

"I am the said gentleman," I said boldly, although my manner was spoiled by a small wave swamping my words. "And running with Black Harry," I spluttered.

"I was promised a guinea and a password, sir," said the sailor, with resolution in his voice.

Standing in the sea up to your waist, and our Hurtwood men rushing to leave the beach, was not a good position from which to barter. Besides, it was agreed, and in the same way that we had secured the first trunk.

"Calais," I said quickly, as I fished a guinea out of the top pocket of my soaking wet waistcoat.

I held it and the man could see the glimmer of gold in the moonlight, clearer now that the mist was lifting, and hence the need to be away was pressing on us. The sailor shifted the trunk to the side of the boat nearest me and he reached out a hand, as his companions started to lift the oars. I had no choice but to trust him, especially now that my companions had reached the beach. I reached out and placed the coin into his outstretched hand.

"*Merci, Monsieur* – and an agreement honoured – twice – between the English and the French. Were our masters as honourable as we smugglers," he said with a chuckle in his voice. With some effort, he lugged the trunk over on to my pony and helped it into a large basket-ware saddlebag on one side which balanced the brandy keg in a matching basket on the other.

The Frenchman, whom I suspected of being English, despite his clothes and flamboyant manner, rowed away. He even had the courtesy to wave an adieu.

I turned my head to the beach where Harry was acting as the lander, making sure that the tub-men, horses and wagons were off as quickly as possible. He gave a low whistle to hurry me along. I had no time to wave at the "Frenchman", but he had my guinea and no doubt another one from the other side of the Channel. Chilled and soaking up to my chest, I led my eager pony out of the water and onto the beach. Harry was gesticulating to me to make good speed.

No wonder. When I reached him he told me that two of the batmen had spotted a group of horsemen on the other headland. I needed no further urging from Harry.

We had hired five batmen to guard our little convoy to the Coombes. They each carried a steel-tipped quarter-staff known as a bat. They were protection for us against the King's men, if they were campaigning nearby, or, more important, they were paid well to ensure the Shoreham men didn't steal our contraband. Sometimes the locals would assemble a group of horsemen to make a noise and augment the payment of their batmen brethren.

Little Will was waiting at the tail of our horsemen at the bottom of the path. The flaskers had already moved quickly up the hill into the woods. It was backbreaking work for them, although the new flattened barrels – made in the Channel Islands especially for us free-traders – now made it easier. But the barrels, whatever the shape, linked by tarred ropes tied to a wire hoop to form a harness, were still heavy after the first few miles. They were paid five pence a night in advance and a shilling or two, plus perhaps a little tea or brandy, upon delivery. Labouring in the fields, their normal employment, the flaskers would earn – if they were lucky – just a shilling a week. So it was worth the risk. But I was glad we Hurtwood men had our pack animals, easier to be ridden down by the Preventers, true – but more gentle on the back for our more than thirty miles home.

Our men reached the Coombes farm two hours after midnight, and the batmen were paid off. Black Harry's cousin invited Harry and myself into the farm kitchen to dry off a little in front of the fire and share a noggin or two of brandy.

Little Will and the others were given some brandy and jugged hare in the barn. But it was a short stop – we needed to own as much of the night as we could.

Harry's cousin, however, wanted to know one piece of information: "They say that two Revenue men were killed near the White Horse in thy part of the Hurtwood. Is that true?" he asked in his strong West Sussex brogue.

"Romantic tales, they are," said Harry. "Like the twiddle-poop highwaymen who are going to be robbing us on the way home."

I noticed that Harry carefully didn't address his kin by name.

"No, Harry, I heard it from a sound man, who don't be telling old wives' tales. And their deaths are a day or two old, so thee might not have been informed. Be careful. If it be true, the King's men may dare to venture even into thy bless'd Hurtwood."

Harry laughed, but I could see he was calculating the odds. He paid his cousin in coin, and we soon moved off into the woods.

⋖⋗

About an hour into the journey home, Harry fell back from the vanguard, and said, "Be ready, Rich. I know I be the only man armed, but I have told the others to make sure their daggers and bludgeons are ready to hand."

I carried a dagger, two with Little Will's, and my bludgeon, which had a swinging loaded head, a little like a medieval mace.

Then out of nowhere, he asked, "What happened to that partner of your'n – Jake? He was on the last run."

This was the first time I had had chance to answer with my carefully crafted reply. Hurtwood men didn't ask too many questions, but Black Harry could and did. "He's half-Cockney, as you know, and he's busy in London with the polite end of our business," I replied.

"Ambitious man you'n becomin', Rich. Most of us stick to brandy, baccy and tea, the usual 'India goods'. What we've always done. But I knows that you'n dealing in lace, silks, snuff and other fancy stuff – in that locked trunk of your'n. Must turn a good profit in London town. Maybe we should talk somewhen – I could help."

Harry was a dangerous rogue, and a sly one. But I reckoned he was genuinely looking to expand his horizons, so I said, "Harry, I am thinking more of business in London rather than on the beach. Maybe I'm getting too old for this game. I don't have your dash, sir. So in time we could do business, I trust."

Harry laughed out loud, despite our rule of stealth and silence on the runs.

He leaned over me – even though everybody thought me a big man – and whispered in my ear. "Aye, Rich, thee and me could do some trade. I've had enough of these woods – London town might be the place for me, too. 'Piking to the start' be the game."[7]

I stood my ground and looked him in the eyes, his face a few inches above mine. "I shall make plans for that, Harry." I think I appeased his greed for a while, though careful I had to be with my trunk, which he eyed with some curiosity. We were a bigger gang going homewards, as most of our men preferred to follow Harry; only a few Ewhurst men had taken the longer, but safer, route through Horsham. A few of the men now with us might have backed me, if it came to a fight, but most would have sided with Harry. He was "the cock of the walk" in the Hurtwood.

But both Harry and I knew that our first duty was to get our goods back quickly to the New Inn. No sale, no profit; and better no dead men, for feuds ran deep in our forests. Innkeeper Thomas Hall would have checked with the miller to make sure that the sails on the windmill standing above the inn on Pitch Hill were set right. In an hour or so, at first light, Harry would use his spyglass to check the signals on the mill.

If the sails were locked in an X-position parallel to the ground, then it was safe to enter the Hurtwood and disembark our goods into the false roof of Landlord Hill's inn, as well as place a few barrels, on the morrow, in the secret cellar of the White Horse in Shere. The miller would also take some of the barrels, concealed beneath sacks of flour, to Guildford and Dorking.

We were all tired and hungry, but Little Will was still keeping up well, and we had about an hour to go before daylight. Provided we got to the Hurtwood before light we could trudge the last few miles under cover of our own territory. Harry pushed us hard to keep going – on our march we had stopped just once for a few minutes to water the animals. He didn't want to be out of his domain in broad daylight. We could have hidden the contraband and come back for it, though Harry was determined to do the run in one, a tradition he was proud of upholding. But the landing at Shoreham was a little late, we didn't normally stop off for hospitality in Coombes farm, and slow drizzle had dampened our spirits and made the going soggy in parts, especially in the Adur valley.

It was on the early cusp of dawn and we were a few miles short of the Hurtwood forest. There was still some cover – gorse, holly oak and fir, but it wasn't our territory and the covering was less than in our forest. A mile or two on and we were due to meet some riders from Peaslake – extra men to help and guard. We were tired but beginning to relax our minds, a successful run and Harry's spyglass had told him that the sails were correct on the windmill above Pitch Hill. If all went well, in an hour or so we would be sitting by the fire of the New Inn.

Little Will heard them first: horsemen riding fast. "Our men from Peaslake," he said excitedly.

But Harry pulled out his pistol, when he saw riders coming fast across a small patch of open heath land. Little Will knew all the men of Peaslake and, correcting himself, he shouted, "Strangers 'pon us."

"Soldiers," Harry yelled, as he pulled us back to a small but dense copse.

A shot rang out from a carbine – it crashed into a yew tree a few feet from me. Then more shots, too wide and too high.

The smell of gunpowder stung our nostrils, and all the thrashing in the small copse invited the leaves to discharge thousands of droplets.

Harry moved us back quickly into deeper cover and told three of our ten men to lead the horses back the way we came. Harry, me and five other sturdy Peaslake men stood our ground inside the small wood. Another shot rang out, but now a dozen riders – all King's men – Light Dragoons by the look of them, and two likely Revenue men in the rear, stumbled into the edge of the wood.

Harry shot one soldier at close range. I unhorsed another with my bludgeon. A third charged with his sabre drawn.

And then I saw what the cavalryman was doing – running Little Will to ground. I had thought my charge had gone off with the packhorses, but I was wrong.

The soldier's horse had slowed down to trot because of the enclosed wood, and I could see that the glinting curved sabre was raised to strike down Little Will. I couldn't run back in time, but instinctively I twisted my mace's head three or four times in the air like a sling and let it fly at the armed horseman. It would be a tremendously lucky shot over twenty yards in very poor light – but somehow, with God's grace, it did manage to hit the soldier a glancing blow on his side. It concerned him enough to rein in his horse and turn his attention to me, while Little Will threw himself into deep undergrowth.

Six of the Dragoons had stayed outside the dark wood,

trying to discern the situation. They kept shouting, "Surrender in the name of the King. Surrender and your lives will be spared."

With his dagger, Harry had meanwhile wounded another soldier, who staggered out of the wood. Harry shouted, "A pox on the King, and we'll not surrender to the hangman."

I saw that Matt from Gomshall, a sword thrust from his stomach to his throat, lay dead across a fallen tree. Apart from Harry and me, everyone else had vanished.

More horsemen pounded across the heath, but this time it was our men, some of them with pistols. Harry and I retreated deeper into the darkness of the woods, to let the soldiers recover their three dead or wounded men. We did not want to force the King's men into a do-or-die decision. Likewise, our riders from Peaslake, sensing the mood, stood off in the forest, on the other side of the open heath land. They did not whoop and shout defiance, but let the troop of King's men withdraw with their wounded comrades slung across the back of their horses. It was not a time to humiliate the soldiery. Eventual military retribution, even in the bastion of the Hurtwood, could be terrible.

It took three hours for all the stragglers finally to reach the New Inn. Matt's body was laid out in the barn and his family summoned from Gomshall, but only after Harry had put his dagger to the landlord's throat to find out who had betrayed us.

"Ask the miller, Harry," he said deliberately, with little fear in his voice. "Why should I betray thee? I live off our free trade and I never heard of soldiers so near the Hurtwood – ever. I did tell thee that a Revenue man had been beaten in the White Horse and his companion tarred and feathered. But they weren't badly beaten – a few bruises here and there, no real broken bones, or so I'm told. But that was just two days ago."

Harry pulled the dagger away from the man as he lay stretched across one of his own tables. The big man asked, "After we left?"

"Yes, Harry." The landlord was beginning to breathe a little more normally now. "After thee be gone."

"But thee still signalled that all was well from the windmill."

"Aye, Pop Rowland did that. He reads the beacon from across the Sussex down, which your cousin's men lit. And he puts the sails into the X, 'cos we had no problems here."

"But there was a troop of bleedin' Dragoons waiting for us."

"They weren't in the Hurtwood, Harry. They would never dare come in here. A revolution that would cause, and the King don't want revolutions here in England – what with all the trouble with France."

"They must have come up secretly from Guildford by night," I said. "Either a chance patrol, or perhaps to punish someone for booting the Revenue men out of Shere."

"What were the Revenue men doing there in the first place?" Harry asked of no one in particular – as he sat back on a chair.

The landlord gave Harry and me a good hornful of brandy each, and then answered in his own time, "People say they got lost. Honest to God. On their way to Godalming, and took a false turn from Dorking. Walked into a den of thieves, didn't know it. And like asses told the landlord of the house they wuz Revenue men, and then it was all bedlam there. It was an accident and nobody got sorely hurt. Yet I don't comprehend how the Dragoons could move so quick."

"Maybe they were trying out the new fashion in ballooning," I said to ease the tension.

"Unless someone was out to git after us in the first place," Harry said, ignoring my light remark. "Anyway, where the hell is the miller?"

Jenny, the landlord's pretty young wife who was sporting blubber,[8] spoke up for the first time. "Hiding he is, Harry. Knows thou woudst blame him. But he's a good man, and an old gen'leman. Don't hurt him – he's been with us free traders all his life. He ain't got no purpose in betrayin' us. Please don't go huntin' him now. Let me cook thee a meal, get a clean shirt and then let me find Pop Rowlands and I'll bring him to thee when thy temper's cooled and he can explain."

Harry nodded and gave half a smile. He could never resist a pretty face or ample bosom. "And don't be letting down[9] my ale."

Jenny knew it was in jest. She turned her dark gypsy eyes to me, and said, "And, Rich, let me cook something for thee, too – on the house."

From a drawer, she pulled out my accounts, a hazel stick with notches, and threw it in the fire. She did the same with Black Harry's stick. "On the house, as I said. And, Rich, I'll do thy choicest meal: salt pork and peas pudding, then cheese an' bread." She smiled so temptingly.

I sat with Harry. I relaxed a little now, glad that Little Will was safe and so was my trunk. But it seemed as though someone had betrayed us. I wanted to know who it was.

Ten

We Peaslake men felt better for the rest, a wash and the food. Harry stayed at the New Inn, to supervise the shipment to the White Horse in the morning, while the rest of us went home. Sad we were, because of the killing of Matt. But the drink had fortified the survivors.

Little Will was tipsy – he fell over on the walk back down the Pitch Hill. I picked him up and said, "Brave lad – you did us and your Da proud. And there is some money for Ma, and some brandy for her."

In Peaslake, Nance was waiting for us with soup, but I was full enough from the salt pork so I took my leave, eager to be in my bed. My responsibility was discharged.

Ma Nye was also waiting up for me, and with some food. I partook of a little so as not to offend her and told her briefly of our battle with the Light Dragoons.

She listened in awe. Her first question was, "Will they come after thee and Black Harry here?"

"I doubt it, Ma. But they might have recognized Harry and perhaps even me. It might be time to be away in London for a while. I was planning on it, anyways."

"Thee'll be away a while, Rich?"

"Aye, a while, Ma. I will be back, and I'll leave some of my goods, and pay my usual rent. And I will leave Diamond here.

Little Will can ride him when he wants."

She looked hurt.

"I will return. The Hurtwood is my home."

"Rich, thou didst most of thy growing here, I knows, but thee be like thy old partner Jake – partly a London man. Wouldst thee be joining him there?"

"Perhaps, Ma. He's not one for writing, is he?"

She laughed, but left well alone.

⋞⋟∞⋞⋟

I slept well and spent most of the daylight hours preparing for London. I was also going to indulge myself. I'd had enough of the long journeys with pack-horses. This time I would go in one of the fancy coaches to London.

And I would dress the part. I was wearing the new longer, tight-fitting riding breeches, which touched my riding boots. It was the fashionable custom to wear light colours in the day and dark at night when sporting breeches. My dark blue frock coat was well cutaway with the tails behind. I had a clean linen shirt and a matching linen cravat, but not too fussy. I could brook no lace or fills on my collar or cuffs. My concession to London fashion was a dark red, brocaded, double-breasted waistcoat. It was cut high and square above my waist – I had no flopping belly to hide. As ever, I eschewed a wig and wore a conventional dark blue tricorne hat. It was respectable attire for a gentleman in the country but I would have to see if I cut a dash in London town.

The next morning at dawn, Ma Nye was up early to say a tearful goodbye. "A gentleman, thou be Rich – looking every inch a London dandy – a real Maccaroni,[10]" she said, giving me a playful push, while wiping a tear away at the same time.

Even Little Will was at the gate of the farmyard to wish me well.

"Look after Diamond for me, would you? You'll be a man, soon – so ready you are to tend to my horse."

"Oh, thank'ee," he said, and he gave me the biggest smile I have ever seen.

"And here be some more shillings for you, lad. I want you to walk to Godalming in mid-afternoon, and bring Diamond and the cart back from the stables of the King's Arms. I will tell the landlord to expect your coming. Tell him you are taking Mr Durrant's horse."

"Yes, sir," the lad said, as he stood to attention and saluted me.

"Don't be mockin' the King's men. Treat them serious. Look out for they."

I mounted up and put Diamond into a trot, but I looked back to check my two trunks tied to the cart and saw Ma Nye with her arm around the lad's shoulder. They both waved me off. I felt sad – they were the closest I had to family. I also felt excited, and a little nervous about the silver I was carrying. Bills I had – good forgeries made out by Samuel Horsley. The vicar in Albury had a fine hand, and was a craftsman, nay an alchemist, in transforming contraband into honest goods. The Reverend Horsley always told us to put the money in the collection tray, but there never was a single member of his congregation present to ensure that the money didn't go straight into the money belt under his surplice. That was money for the Reverend, not God.

Thunder pillars[11] were rising in the sky, as I led Diamond through the Hurtwood tracks. Luckily, however, it remained dry and the going was smooth, through the woods across the common at Farley Green, past the mound where it was said a Roman temple had been, keeping up a fast trot to the river where I stopped to let the bay enjoy a leisurely drink. Then we took the smuggler's short cut through the marshes, until we quickly reached the bridge near the church on the outskirts of Godalming. We went up the High Street bold as an emperor and Diamond walked proudly into the big stable yard of the large plain three-storied brick building which was the King's Arms.

I gave instructions to the ostler for the horse to be stabled for the day. He helped me to carry my two trunks into the bar. We pushed them under the table in the corner, and I ordered an early lunch. The clock said eleven a.m. The London coach, the "Accommodation" it was called, was due at two p.m. I had time to relax. After I had spoken to the landlord, paid him for my fare and the stabling and told him that a young lad would call for my horse and the cart, I sat in a recess and smoked my pipe.

I had a good view of the High Street from the nearest window. And I could also see the door into the yard.

It was quiet for an hour or more. I had a book – *Gulliver's Travels* – but my reading was slow and sometimes the words gave me a headache. Instead, I examined the coconuts on the shelf behind me. Many a sailor from Portsmouth must have traded a drink or two for these keepsakes. I marvelled at the curious devices carved on them such as a crown, a fish and ornate zigzag patterns.

Suddenly, much clatter erupted in the yard, as the London coach arrived, full of noise, horses panting and snorting and men shouting. The gates to the yard were quickly shut. I felt a little alarmed and eyed the front door onto the street. I would abandon my trunks to save my liberty but it would be a bitter blow after all that I had suffered for the silver in them.

I walked cautiously to the back door, however, and saw that armed guards had been posted. I felt my stomach heave.

Only for a second. The coach was carrying convicts to Portsmouth and their guards were allowing them a short time to rest, eat and use the privy.

My coach was coming up from Portsmouth and, for the half-guinea I had paid, I expected more than this rough road wagon.

I recognized one of the convicts, a free trader I had once known, but had not seen for many a long summer. He looked bedraggled and thin and I pitied his chains, but I removed myself rapidly and went back into my recess. He had not seen me, may not have remembered my face, and, even if he had, he would not have hailed me, but I was being a cautious man. For his fate might also beckon to me… I did not want to dwell on such melancholic thoughts. I was now dressed like a gentleman, right down to my kid gloves. I needed to act as though I were a gentleman. I summoned the barman and asked him for a port. I wanted to drink it down in one, though I sipped it genteelly.

I asked about the convicts.

The barman said, "They are bound for the convict hulks, and for transportation. Poor beggars. Not sendin' they to America no more of course, but to Africa or to Botany Bay. Ne'er to see old England again, I'll warrant – that's if they survive the voyage. What justice – some of these men steal a few shillin' – or be wrongly accused of thieving."

"Botany Bay? Captain Cook done well to make those travels, but not to send good Englishmen there for hard labour. I have no more desire to try the air of Botany Bay than to see the inside of Newgate," says I.

The barman nodded in agreement and said, "I've given 'em some of the rough cider, not the best, but better than the Adam's Ale they'll be havin' for rations for long whiles, I reckon."

He went back to his work. I pondered on their fate, which could be mine too, except that our fight with the Dragoons would bring a hanging not a journey on the high seas – if I were caught.

I passed the next half-hour looking out the window onto the High Street, admiring the array of transport. After the forests, this seemed so busy – though I knew it was a backwater compared with London town. I admired a yellow fish-cart from the coast, drawn by four strong horses. For shorter hauls, I counted two dog-carts each led by four Newfoundlands which could carry a mountain of fish as well as the driver. They went as fast as coaches did these dog-carts. I remembered my last visit to Godalming when I had bought three oysters for a penny from one of the carts.

Now I was watching the world from my seat in the King's Arms. The convict coach had left and I felt more at peace, until I saw just a glimpse of an albino in a hood drawn over his eyes, but the covering moved up as he walked and for a second I could discern the frightened and yet also frightening big eyes. He passed by the window, and he had drawn his hood over his face again, yet I could see that it was deathly white. I thought of the man who had appeared in Peaselake, then I dashed it from my thoughts.

I had been shaken by the sight of the convicts and the guards, and I was fretting about my trunks. Strange that I had crossed through forests at night with my silver: free-trading with honest ruffians, then fought and killed a man after the first trunk, and two days before battled alongside Black Harry in the forest against the Dragoons. Now I was travelling on the King's highway in broad daylight, being the dandy with kid gloves and fancy new breeches.

Nonetheless, I was mighty pleased to hear the post horn which announced the arrival of my coach on its way into the yard of the King's Arms. I watched the guard with his red uniform dismount from the front seat. He was well-armed – with a blunderbuss, a brace of pistols and a cutlass. I was glad he was on my side and protecting my contraband.

Within ten minutes the horses were changed, my trunks strapped on the rear and I was sitting inside with a man accompanied by persons I assumed were his two daughters.

After polite introductions, we were on our way to the Talbot Inn in Ripley to pick up our final two passengers for London town. Despite myself, I scanned the High Street and the road out of Godalming for the albino. Perhaps I had imagined it.

I was glad to be leaving the ghosts of my past in the Hurtwood.

After our complement was increased to six in Ripley, we made good speed, about twelve miles per hour, to our next stage: Kingston. The going was improved by the new steel leaf springs of the coach.

The conversation was sparse, except for a ten-minute monologue by an overdressed lady who joined our company in Ripley. She proceeded to tell her female companion – perhaps for the tenth time as the story seemed practised – about her recent visit to Vauxhall Pleasure Gardens. She poured forth a detailed description of the music, by Handel, the fireworks and how she was "almost struck blind" by the illuminations. She then listed the menu of lobsters, anchovies and potted pigeon. All this could have been diverting except for the oh-so-dreary monotone of her speech. Presumably she had achieved her ambition of over-awing her travel companions, who did not respond in grateful appreciation or even mild curiosity. Whereupon she fell silent. Thereafter, despite the constant jolts, two of my companions managed to sleep.

I remained alert – especially after the guard fired a shot into the undergrowth about five miles before Kingston. My concern must have been obvious, because the father of the two women said, "Don't be afeared, sir – 'tis Jim's sport – he takes pot-shots at rabbit and the like. His company don't trouble him for it – shows that's he's ready to take on the gen'lemen of the road."

"I'm grateful for that," I said politely.

The two female passengers from Ripley looked unconcerned – obviously Jim's sharp-shooting was well-known to them.

It was seven-thirty p.m. on the town hall clock when we pulled up alongside Cook Row in Kingston. We all alighted outside the Wheatsheaf Inn. A coach stopped alongside, full of rowdy seamen waving flags. Six were sprawled inside the coach and three on top, obviously flush with booze, after being paid off in Portsmouth, I assumed. As I looked up, one of the more sober Tars shouted at me and said, "Sirrah, we lost two on the way. Too sodden with rum. Now they have to walk. Do 'em good – get their land-legs and…" But his voice was drowned by the raucous singing of his shipmates.

I busied myself with supervising the detachment of my trunks. The other passengers in my coach would continue to Piccadilly, but I intended to travel directly to Southwark in one of the flying wagons that ran into the George Inn on the Borough High Street.

It was usually about two or three hours' journey to Southwark in the slower and less comfortable wagons. Although I managed to get one quickly, I was placed on the first seat under the cover and I had to pay an extra six pence to take my trunks inside, after some disputation with the wagon-master.

Within a few minutes the whole wagon was crammed with over twelve passengers of all ages, condition and stations in life. We stopped more than fifteen times on the road, with passengers arguing with the driver over the fare, and where they should stop. People were up and down and generally creating bedlam. Even the most lady-like of the young women were exposing more than their ankles in the act of getting in and out, tearing and muddying their petticoats. A drunken fiddler on board managed to whistle every time he saw exposed female flesh, and once, when we stopped for a few minutes, played and sang a bawdy song to celebrate. He stopped when one of the older women pushed him under the cover to silence him. It all took an immense time – I have never seen anything so chaotic. I thought that if the King's ministers made us free traders legal, we could make the transport and passengers run much better than the crooks who ran these travelling madhouses.

Eventually, we arrived in Borough High Street, after ten pm. All the inns were well lit, though they glowed through the fog like ships lost at sea. After the wagon crossed King's Street, the covers were thrown open – people wanted to see the sights, and cared not a jot for the dust. The smell of the breweries and tanneries swept over my senses like a summer storm. Link-boys, young urchins with flaming torches of pitch and tow, were busy escorting respectable couples through the fog.

It had been a long while but I looked on with fondness at all the inns, not because I was much of drinking man – I wasn't – but because it brought back memories of my younger self. I could remember the names so well, even when I couldn't see the signs properly – the Nag's Head, Spur Inn, White Hart, King's Head, the Tabard and the George, where the wagon came to spine-wrenching halt. The elderly woman next to me had been standing and she fell right on top of me.

"Beggin' your pardon, sir. My first time to London town."

I took my hat off to her and said, "Then welcome, Madam." I spoke as if I owned the place; I did feel confident, almost happy for the first time in a year or more.

I dismounted and hired one of the waiting stable lads to help me carry my trunks to the Spur Inn, just a few minutes' slow lugging walk from the George. A washerwoman shouted to me from the balcony of the George.

"Sir, fine rooms here…and some extras for a handsome fellow like yourself," she said with her Cockney cheek.

"Thank'ee, Madam, but tonight I am spoken for."

I doffed my hat again – I was enjoying being the gentleman from the country.

Southwark was full of merchants and shopkeepers, but it was not the most fashionable district of London. The High Street was adjacent to several prisons and those who circulated around were small traders, wagoners, porters and people looking for cheap fares to the villages and ports of the south.

Bawds with fine bonnets and no doubt endearing names of Mother this or Mother that were gossiping in groups, all waiting to entice young country girls into their schools of Venus. Sad it was that an innocent's cherished virginity could be sold for the grand sum of 150 guineas. Satan's harvest indeed.

A pretty young harlot, not more than fifteen, tugged at my arm and said boldly, "Your love would make me happy."

I declined with a forced smile.

It was dark and I had valuable cargo; not the time or place to be diverted. I led the stable boy into the coffee room of the Spur. I thanked him and paid him two pence for his trouble. It was a generous tip for a few minutes' work.

We stowed one trunk behind the cake stall in the corner, in my sight. And I sat on the other one.

"Before you leave, lad, if I tip the Meg,[12] would you find a friend of mine, who has a shop nearby?"

"Yes, sir. What is your friend's name?"

"Solly Jacobson. He has the dolly shop,[13] around the corner in King's Street. His trade will be closed, but aside the shop there is a green door. Knock on it, and when he comes, tell him that Mr Rich awaits his pleasure in this coffee shop. The extra half-penny on your coming back. A bargain?"

The lad nodded and ran out, and came back within minutes, even before I had lifted the cup to my lips.

"Sir, Mr Jacobson says he will attend you shortly and he bids you welcome to London."

I gave him the half-penny, took a large sip of the strong black sweet coffee, and felt that with my old friend Solly en route a new adventure was about to begin.

I was a world away from the rustic style of the Hurtwood, and I did not feel the countryman here. Unlike all the other institutions in England, rank and birth had no place in a coffee shop. I perused the free copies of the day's London newspapers. My sense of happiness was heightened, yet I was on my guard until I had handed over my boxes to someone I could trust.

It was ten minutes before Solly shuffled in. He looked older than his sixty years and he was scruffy and dressed all in black as usual, but his eyes lit up and he straightened his back when he saw me.

"Reeech, Reeech – my dear dear boy," he said in his high-pitched voice, as he hugged me and I put both my arms around him. The way he spoke my name – like a long stroke of the bow across a slightly-out-of-tune violin – always made me chuckle.

"I've missed you, Solly, and all your roguish manners."

"And I be missing you like you vuz my son. And you not be ordering me a coffee?" but he said it like "Kaffey", with his strong German accent.

"Of course, Solly." I raised my arm and a serving girl came to us for our order. "A coffee for my best friend," I said with a flourish. And I meant it. I loved old Solly, not least because he made me laugh. He had an amazing way of speaking – Cockney, Yiddish and German. I understood him well enough, even when he mixed up expressions from his various languages.

"Now, I knows you fink I be an *alter kocker*, but I vant that you stay with me – no beggar's operas for you. Until you have put your *shtickel* there" – he looked at my trunk – "somewheres where no thief can go and *yentz* it from you. Den all your cows vill come home to roost."

I had to wait a few seconds for my brain to translate, but I got the gist and raised my coffee. "To you, Solly, and some good business for us."

Solly gulped down his coffee and belched. "Oy, I do like

this kaffey, but it do give me the *greps*. But Reeech we must be off – don't want to stay for the *shiksa* who runs dis shop. She's a bleedy rum customer when she gets lushy. Come on, let's get dese trunks from here…"

"Solly, I'll get some help…"

"It is no time yet for my *kaddish*. I carry with you your trunks. It's a short walk. *Genug!*"

Solly – despite his years – yanked up the handles of the trunks with ease and we both led them out of the side entrance.

A man with a donkey cart blocked our way, and Solly asked him politely to move.

The man told Solly to put his head up his arse.

Solly said loudly to me, "Who put a turd in that *boychick's* mouth?"

I laughed and led the trunks around the cart. It was just a few hundred yards and we were in the side lane which led into Solly's house which backed on to his shop.

"Reeech, I vant that we move these things of yours tonight. But I vill deal with two *menshen* – a goy and a Cohen – and both I can trust. I don't vant to put all my apples in vun basket. Dat be gut?"

"I trust you with my life, and my fortune, Sol."

"Aye, as you did ven you were just a little *zhlub* – and you lived with me. And now you are a genle'man, Reeech."

Aye, a gentleman in London town. A new life and no more free-trading, I thought to myself.

Eleven

*S*olly had put me in one of his back rooms, with blue panelling, and – strangely – a picture of the Christ hung on the wall. Maybe it was the room for Christian visitors. I had never been in it before. I remember it was always locked. When I was a young lad, I had shared a room downstairs with one of Solly's sons. His only daughter, Tamar, much younger than me, had been a shy young thing then. Tonight she had escorted me to my bedroom with a candle. She had been very pleased to see me and had greeted me warmly in Yiddish, as though I were one of the family. Perhaps I was – almost.

"Rich, there is bread and cheese for you, and some ginger ale on the table there," she said in perfect English now but with a strong Cockney accent. "I know Papa would have preferred for you to have a meal with us all, but you came late. He is so pleased to have you with us again."

I chanced my arm, "Are you pleased to see me too, Tamar? You have grown into a beautiful young woman."

She blushed, and her father shouted for her from downstairs before she had time to answer. She excused herself and left quickly.

"Goodnight, Tamar," I shouted after her, but no reply came back. I was certainly drawn to this buxom, reserved girl, with long dark hair only partly concealed by her cap.

I ate quickly and fell asleep – fully dressed – almost as soon as I finished the remaining piece of bread, and gulped down the last of the ginger ale. My final waking thought was not relief at a safe journey but of the picture of the Christ. Odd that, as I wasn't a religious man. Perhaps it was just the strangeness of the Christian symbol in an orthodox Jewish house.

I awoke late, and desperately needed the privy. I ignored the wash-bowl and towel set for me, and rushed to the landing, knocking over a chair on which someone had put my spare clothes from one of my trunks. The whole family was sitting in the kitchen, and I excused myself as I rushed out into the backyard to use the privy. They all laughed when I said a hasty good morning.

After I had washed and changed my shirt, I joined them.

Solly's wife, Rachel, kissed me, and Jakob, one of the boys who was still at home, solemnly shook my hand. Solly gestured to me to join them for breakfast.

"Papa says you must give me your shirt to wash," Tamar said straightaway.

I thought she was trying to indicate some sort of right over me. I didn't object.

Solly was equally direct: "De trunks hef gone off for business, Reeech. I took your fings out for you, as you said to do."

I thanked him.

"And we must fink of some new business for you. I hef a frénd who is a real *nudnik*, but who has already some merchandise for you. It is not *shmatta*. He vill call later. You vill become a proper trader, Reeech – you be no more a free-trader. Oy, you vill be a honest gen'leman…"

Solly's son Jakob said something – possibly irreverent, but I didn't understand the Yiddish.

Solly, quick as a fox, knocked his hat off and said, "*Shtoom, nebbish.*" Jakob looked just a touch disconcerted, but immediately relaxed when Solly burst out laughing. I had forgotten how lively and noisy a Jewish household could be.

❦

After a hearty breakfast of cold beef, bread and some of the tea, which I had also brought in my trunk, Solly took me into the back room of his shop to talk business. It was dank – I had forgotten how close we were to the Thames.

But the room also had a wonderful aroma: Rachel had really spoiled us –already coffee was waiting for us.

I was intending to indulge in small talk about family and then the business, but Solly came straight to the point.

"Reeech, the silver set and the extra plate vill bring us more than 200 guineas. I vill take for my troubles – ah, I vould from some udder *shlemiel* take eighty guineas – but for you, Reeech...you are like my son Jakob. So forty guineas...is good?"

I nodded and shook his hand.

"To fink that a whore earns just a shilling for all dat..." It was a Yiddish vulgarity that I didn't know, but Solly's hand gestures left no room for misunderstanding. "I can give you half of your 160 guineas now, the rest will take a vhile. I vill keep it for you. And I will use some of it, if you vant, to buy some of the lace, linen and other stuff that you vill need if you are going to be a proper trader."

"It makes sense, Solly What did you always tell me? *Saychel* – common sense."

"Ah, vee will make a good Yiddishe b*oychick* out of you. Especially if you hef such feelings for my Tamar. I saw how you looked at her, Reeech. Vee might have to make you a proper member of our *schule*.[14] I voud prefer you to a Sephardi any day of the calendar."

I laughed, but not so much that it seemed a rejection. "Solly, I remember your reputation as a matchmaker. She is a lovely girl – far too good for the likes of me. I would convert – just to be your son, not your son-in-law."

"Ah, you are pulling my ankle…and vee are being too schmaltzy, Reeech – but I am so happy that you are back again under my roof – even if I hef to vatch out for my Tamar." And he struck me quite hard on my back, surprisingly hard for an old man.

Since Solly had brought up religion, I asked him why a picture of the Christ was hanging in my room.

"It vas dere when I took de house, years ago, and I jes left it dere. I am a Jew in a Christian country, so I fink – dis is my compromise, my vay of saying, 'Live and let live.' Ah, but sometimes de Englanders do not fink the same as me. But it vas vorse in de *shtetl* back home…"

I cast my mind back to some of the graffiti I had already seen in my brief time in London. Amidst the "Christ is God", "No Coach Tax" and "Damn Pitt", I had seen the inscription "Murder Jews" and I had noticed how one of the men in the coffee house had made an obscene gesture when I embraced Solly on his arrival – the stranger had jerked his thumb over his left shoulder. Under other circumstances I might have challenged the swine, but I did not want to spoil my reunion with Solly.

Solly had become suddenly sad. He was very intuitive and I worried that he had perhaps been reading my mind. So I changed the subject and talked about our times past. Often good times. We reminisced over the coffee about how I came to live in his household. About how my father, a sea-faring man with free-trading connections, had settled reluctantly in Southwark when he married my mother, a seamstress, who was a Londoner. My mother died when I was three, and my father used to pay Rachel to look after me when he worked long hours on the tug and coal boats along the Thames. Rachel had two boys nearly my age and I had no brothers or sisters, and Solly's family lived just a few doors away in King's Street.

Solly soon brightened up and added his usual banter to our enjoyable recollections. "Ah, Reeech, I remember the night when vee gott dat note that your vater left when he went off to the seaside…"

"Off to sea," I interrupted and corrected him, just like I used to.

"Yah, Yah, such a kvetch you are. Yah, like I vas saying, when your Papa left, with just a note saying that vee should send you to his family in de forests – all highvaymen dere – but he did leave dose guineas for me to look after you – he did not just run avay – he said he vould come back for you. But, ah, he did not…"

"Perhaps, Solly, he died."

"Ah, if Gott vanted him."

"And you used to joke with me that you would sell me into slavery with the Moors on the Barbary Coast."

"Oy, and I needed anudder vun in the family like a *loch in kop*.[15] But you became a part of our family, Reeech. And you stayed vit us for – how long vas it? – four years before dat cousin of yours came to take you back to de Hurtvood. But dis is a *megillah*…"

"I've forgotten some of your Yiddishe expressions, Solly."

"A *megillah* – ah, a long story."

"But one with a happy ending," I said. "I would never have learned to read and write but for you. I always felt like I was your, er landsman – someone from your own people."

"Perhaps, Reeech…" – and Solly laughed and his chest and beard shook in tandem – "that is vhy you became a real *landsman*, taking all the geld from the sailors down sout' dere in Shoreham."

I smiled at his joke.

"But you came back too little to see us, Reeech."

"Solly, to come to London town – on the roads there are too many bad men in the forests – highwaymen and smugglers."

Solly slapped my knees and laughed again. "Talking of smugglers, I must be about my business, Reeech. Please, my home is your home."

I spent much of the rest of the day talking to Rachel and Jakob and they too had fond memories of my time with them. Sadly, Tamar had been sent out for the day to look after an elderly Jewish lady who lived across the river in Spitalfields. People came and went whom I did not know, but generally an atmosphere of relaxed and busy hospitality embraced the big kitchen. It was one of the best Sundays I had enjoyed in a long time. Despite being a Jewish household, I remembered that Solly liked to enjoy both the Jewish Shabbat and the Christian Sabbath as two separate days of not working.

Tamar and Solly came back together around six-thirty in the evening and we had another family meal. Unorthodox though Solly was in his orthodox Jewishness, never was any alcohol allowed in his house. I had been used to liveliness in the Hurtwood and I realized it had all been based on booze. It was refreshing to enjoy so much warmth and lively conversation on just tea, coffee and ginger ale.

After the meal, Solly took me back into his private room at the back of the shop and we talked a little business, mainly consisting of his advice on how to trade legally. Solly was wise in both sides of the legal divide and the conversation turned from a mutual chat into a long, but fascinating, monologue by him.

It was disturbed by a tap on the door. Tamar came in demurely and said, "Papa, you asked me to tell you when it was eleven o'clock."

Tamar tried not to catch my eyes, but she failed and blushed again.

Solly missed this – he was too busy tapping his pocket watch.

"Mushuggeneh hint dat I am, mad to buy from that nudnik dis vatch."

"An important meeting? And at this time of night," I asked.

"No, I want that we hef an early time to bed. I am up early in the morning and you are coming vit me. I vant dat you come to see a ceremony."

"A ceremony?"

"A burning!"

"Burning what?"

"Who — you should say."

"I thought that they had stopped that."

"No…Miss Christianne Bowman is going to meet her Gott."

"I'd rather not, Solly."

"I vould rather not too."

"It might be a lesson for us. You say you vant to give up free-trading, then be vitness to this, and it reminds me too that I might be sent to Botany Bay or vorse. And I vould not hef my family or a *Seder* dere, Reeech."

"Are you becoming a veritable *alter kocker*, Solly. Repenting at your age?"

"Perhaps I am tired of all dis. I sometimes vonder if we could all go back to Prussia, but dat is impossible. My children are grow'd here."

He scratched his long beard and adjusted his skull cap — a gesture to buy time that I recognized so well.

I spoke for him: "We do need to be careful. Remember the old saying — the one you taught me: 'Pride comes before a fall.'"

Solly started to bustle to prepare for bed. "I vill see you at six in the morning," he said firmly.

At six-fifteen on a chilly late September morning we walked together down Borough High Street, past the old market and across London Bridge, where Kentish men were driving their flocks of sheep. Remnants of the previous night's fog hung like a pestilential vapour. Despite the early hour, lots of little shops were already open and street traders were busy selling oranges, onions, herrings and watercress. Many of the men were haggard, with uncombed hair, and children ran around dressed in rags, sometimes chased by wolfish-looking dogs.

We went through the rookeries of Cheapside, everywhere people were loitering – women with short pipes and men with bloated faces. Boys chased along the streets whipping their tops. People were up and about earlier than usual – a public execution was treated almost like a public holiday in this town.

The houses were dark and gloomy, and streets were strewn with mud, horse manure and dead cats, and in some places small lakes of stagnant water had formed. I had forgotten how ugly and unhealthy London could be. We crossed in front of St Paul's Cathedral, all blackened – justice that was, as it was built with a tax on sea coal. When we came to Newgate Street, it was like a grimy version of a country fair: knife-grinders, women selling vegetables, bird dealers, shoemakers and hawkers selling prints, and so many traders in herrings. The busiest were the traders brandishing pamphlets, a penny a time, catchpennies telling the story of the sad Christianne Bowman – dramatized accounts, as I discovered later, of how she had been a master counterfeiter, though some of the pamphlets implied she had also murdered her husband.

"It is quite a walk to Tyburn," I said to Solly.

"No more Tyburn," explained my mentor, "the crowds were getting too big and causing de riots, it is now near the Newgate prison."

We were being pushed and crammed by a mass of people. The smell and noise were awful. Booze seemed to be sweating out of their pores; many must have been drinking all night in the gin shops. I felt almost as if I could not breathe.

Carriages and wagons were rushing into the crowds, with the screech of iron wheels on cobbles, horses' metal-shod hooves clattering, wooden axles squeaking, with the citizens flying out of their way, children screaming, street vendors barking out their wares, musicians playing out of tune…

Luckily, Solly led me down a quiet back alley that twisted and turned until we reached a blocked end, but then I spied a tiny door, upon which he knocked twice, very deliberately. It was opened to us by a garishly-dressed dwarf, in whose hand Solly placed some coins. We squeezed through the door and made our way in the gloom to a second-floor room with a large open window. Five men – merchants by their dress – were seated on five stools; we had to stand and watch the square around Newgate prison. No one spoke, except the dwarf to offer us gin, which everyone declined. The merchants were too engrossed in the spectacle in front of us.

The street below was completely filled with people, held back by wooden barriers and soldiers. On the right stood platforms for notables. The crowd was howling and shouting. Then all fell quiet as the sheriff, a big serious man with a pockmarked face and chest adorned with the golden chain of his office, emerged from the main gate of the prison. He walked solemnly to a small dais in front of the platform for the lords and ladies. He read a brief declaration which we could not hear above the roar of the crowd, some members of which were cheering and others booing.

A church bell rang. It was eight o'clock.

A woman, perhaps aged thirty, very haggard but obviously once possessed of fine features, was led out of the Debtor's Gate of the prison, alone except for two guards. She wore a simple white dress and her matted long dark hair was tied back with a white ribbon.

As she walked the short distance to her fate, I heard a collective shout –"Hats off" and then "Down in front", as though they were in a theatre. Some of the people in front of the crowd, kneeled or stooped to aid the views of those behind. All of us in our room also took off our hats.

As the trembling woman in white was led to the gallows-cum-stake, the crowd continued to shout, boo and hiss. They tried to press forward, but a large number of militiamen held them back. The two guards led her to the stake, which was about twelve feet high, fixed firmly in the ground. Near its apex was an inverted curve made of iron, to one end of which was tied a rope halter. The guards told her to kneel before the stake. As soon as she had done this, a cleric came from behind the militia and kneeled in devotion with her for a few minutes. The woman was utterly pale and clearly and understandably terrified, even from the distance of our vantage point.

The two guards placed her on a low stool and, while one held her, shaking, in place, the other mounted a small platform which he used to place the halter around her neck. The cleric stepped close, and seemed to whisper something to her, and then stood back. The sheriff now joined the sad party and read a brief statement from a large book.

Until now the woman had been struck dumb by what she was about to endure, but then I saw her open her mouth to speak to the crowd. I could hear nothing but the roar of the mob as one of the guards snatched the stool away.

Christianne jerked a little and her legs swung around, though her arms flopped to her side. Her feet dangled just twelve inches above the ground. Her face went blue and some blood shot from her nose, and her white dress was clearly marked by other expulsions from her body. The crowd kept shouting and one section started to sing, although I did not recognize what the song was. The silence in our attic room — we macabre voyeurs —emphasized the contrast with the savage clamour of the mob. I saw that Solly looked as uncomfortable as I felt. I wanted to leave, but something more than respect for Solly's wishes made me stay. I had to admit to a grotesque fascination to see the next part of the proceedings.

Five or six minutes after the stool had been removed, three people – two middle-aged women and a young man – were allowed by the soldiers to pass through the barriers and to approach the dangling figure. They knelt on the ground, and pulled her legs hard to help her expire more quickly and indeed to ensure that she had died before the next part of the ordeal. I wondered who these three people were. The young man – her brother, her lover? One of the two women was old enough to be Christianne's mother.

After a few minutes, soldiers led the three away. Other militiamen pushed a cartload of faggots into our view and the wood was placed around her and set on fire. The fire soon reached the halter and she sank a few inches, but did not fall because I realized that she was also supported by an iron chain that had been passed over her chest and fixed to the stake. I had not noticed this attachment when the men had placed the wood around her. The fire burned for an hour, or so I was later told. I had to leave after ten minutes and Solly accepted my urgings to quit this room with such a tragic prospect. I knew that the crowd would scavenge for human remains, hot, burnt and blackened as they were – such was the superstitious magic associated with these tawdry relics.

The dwarf let us out, with a salute, and we went back down the lane. Solly led us in to a turning in an opposite direction from the prison, yet the smell of burning flesh was still stronger than even the collective sweat and grime of the massed citizenry in the square behind us.

Solly and I walked quickly back over London Bridge and did not speak until we were back on the south side of the river, Alsatia it was nicknamed – somehow safer, even saner, territory, and once a medieval sanctuary from justice. I was much relieved to be away from Newgate.

"She murdered her husband, the pamphlets said. And what sort of man was he, I vonder. The pamphlets say he vas an adulterer, a thief and dat he beat her nearly every night. Though the trud be that she was clipping, that she vere a part of a counterfeiting gang. Taking bits of metal for making de new coins."

"Aye, Sol, and people are executed or transported for stealing a few shillings, or maybe putrid meat to feed starving children. And England is — what do they call it? — the 'bastion of liberty' compared with the despots in Europe. You know, you came from Germany, but it makes me angry...the laws are there to protect the bloody rich. I can see why the Americans rose up, and recently the French, and why even the Irish cry out in anger. The Grim Reaper seems to be harvesting only the poor."

"Who vill rise up, Reeech? You saw de people enjoying her misery. Dey hef to be the ones to rise up, not cheer on dese bad laws."

"Aye, they say we are savages living in the forests, while these fine gentlemen and ladies of London lord it over us. From what I saw then, I know who are the savages. I feel sick. It is strange, Sol — the refined ladies and gentlemen are amused by these spectacles, yet it is we criminals who show a good heart, a tenderness for that poor Christianne."

We were now almost outside Solly's house in King's Street.

"Rachel vill make us some good kaffey — dat will raise your spirits. And I vant dat you give up your smuggling. Jakob and his brudder Abe and my Tamar don't hef nudding to do with my business, and after today, nor vill you — you who are like my son. I am too old to change, but you are not. How you say? You can't teach an old donkey new tricks..."

"An old dog, Solly."

"Ah, vatever. Dog, donkey — same fing. I vill help you become a good trader, and it vill mean you visit us more often. Gut!"

I hoped that Solly was right: I did want to change my life. The brutal execution I had witnessed made me even more determined to hate the government, yet avoid its damned punishments. My excitement at being in London had turned utterly sour.

Twelve

wo weeks passed. I occasionally had the opportunity to talk to Tamar and a little to Jakob, who was apprenticed to a jeweller. Solly had introduced me to the *"nudnik"* who was a cloth merchant. David was his name – somehow the surname was always omitted. But if Solly trusted him, so would I. David supplied me with a trunk full of initially small items – short rolls of silk and lace goods, enough to start up my trade. And he gave me formal receipts. Other materials would be delivered to Guildford once a month. Once a year, David said, I should come to London and he would help me deal with the bigger importers once I attained more knowledge.

Rachel was kind enough to take me to a few of the better shops on the Strand and talk to me about the fashions displayed there. I had some idea of cloth from my days as a free-trader, but ladies' fashion was a mystery, though I bought her a fine shawl which had taken her fancy. It was but a small token of the gratitude I felt to her and Solly.

She then led me around the piazza of Covent Garden. The area was full of young blades and painted ladies. We walked past the Bedford Head coffee house and then Tom's coffee house in Russell Street. As we returned up the same street, and re-entered the square, she put her arm firmly in mine, and increased our pace as we passed the Hummums Hotel and the Bedford Arms.

"Stay out of these places, Rich. They be only for the deep pits of strange women, and in a moment or two you will dancing the horn-pipe[16]. And then off to the physician for the pox from the low brimstones[17]..."

I thanked her for her kind advice. I wondered whether she was protecting my virtue possibly on behalf of her daughter, or simply returning to her former role of replacement mother. It also struck me that it was strange for an orthodox Jewish lady to know so much about the demi-monde. Perhaps my country life had sheltered me from the stews of the city. It was rather me who was ignorant not that Rachel was so wise about the dark side of London town.

She did, however, suggest that we take coffee in Tom and Moll King's establishment. "This is the better sort of place," she said confidentially to me. She was right, most of the clientele seemed of more marked refinement. As we sipped our capuchin milky coffees, Rachel continued her social education of this backwoodsman. She talked of the moral decline of the capital and of "the molly houses where men do 'marry' other men, and of the upstairs rooms, where even ladies of class and society would indulge in the Game of Flatts".[18]

I thanked Rachel for her kindness, but asked whether Solly's determination that I visit the execution and now her gentle warnings about the wages of sin were attempts to redeem my criminal past.

"Perhaps, Rich. We want our children to stay out of the Old Bailey, and we care for you too. I often said to Solly that sending you to the bad men in the hills was a mistake. That is why we want to help you now."

I thanked Rachel again and told her that I was grateful for my upbringing and education, and was still eager to learn from the best-hearted woman I knew.

We also took a stroll in St James's park. Even here, in a royal park, I could not help but notice the splendid Madames who could charge perhaps fifty guineas a night, a contrast to the young girls with threadbare white stockings who tramped along the Strand prepared to resign their honour for a pint of wine and, if they were lucky, a shilling too. I felt embarrassed for Rachel but she appeared to, or pretended to, not notice these ladies.

It was clear to even my jaded sensibility that the wealth of London and all the fine architecture were built on sex as much as regular commerce.

That evening, after our excursion to the fashionable shops, a message came from a kitchen boy at the coffee house which Solly and I frequented. The boy had told Rachel that "a gentleman awaited Mr Durrant's company as soon as was convenient". I was concerned and curious, for no one outside the Hurtwood knew this alias of mine.

I left immediately I received the message, although I approached the coffee shop with some caution, and tried to discern the customers from outside, through the soot-besmirched windows. The candles threw so many shadows that it was impossible to see all the inmates of the place. I had my dagger with me. In the town no one carried swords, though it was still the custom for many in the countryside.

I prepared myself and entered. Immediately, a big arm jerked me almost off my feet. Before I could try to turn to face my attacker, I felt a strong hand covering my dagger. Damn it, the man knew exactly where I carried it. My foe was very powerful... and he had a deep laugh – which I immediately recognised: Black Harry.

"You bastard, Harry. I could have killed thee."

"Not with that knife you couldn't. Aren't you going to greet a fellow forester, old Harry? I saw you scouting outside. You should have know'd I'd be behind one of the doors. Out of sight and ready to go quick. You have lost the knowledge, Rich."

I had recovered enough to sit down, and demand that he pay for a big pot of best coffee as recompense for his silly jape; which he did with grace.

"So to what do I owe this great pleasure of your esteemed company?"

Harry became serious. "Well, I told you I was planning on things in London, said I would I would 'pike to start'. And I was intendin' to search you out but that ain't the reason for my coming so quick. I'll tell you straight, Rich: Ma Nye has come down bad with something. She's been leeched an' all, but I'm told she's dying, and askin' after her beloved Rich. Nance is looking after her...and her boy is doing good with tending Diamond. So you owe me one. And remember that when I want to trade a bit with London."

"Thank'ee, Harry. I do owe you now. I will go back on the morrow. And I owe it to Ma...to say goodbye."

I fell quiet for a while, and Harry said nothing.

"How long will you be staying in London?" I asked, trying to be courteous to my old companion-in-arms.

"Oh, a few nights, visit a few bawdy houses. Maybe you can be helping me there? You wuz always a cunning fox with the ladies."

"I can't help you with bawds, Jack, but I can recommend the George – just up the street. Good lodgings and victuals, and the chambermaids are buxom and willing, or so I do hear."

On cue, a very pretty serving girl brought us coffee and cakes. Harry smiled his lascivious best, but she ignored him.

"Lordy, Rich, are they all so high and mighty aroun' here?"

"Aye, some are – it's the country accent. Be the gentleman a bit more and polish up your speech. You have to talk more flash."

"Ah, that's easy for Sir Rich. I remembers that you spent time in London. That's how you got the airs and graces – at least for us humble folk in the woods." Harry doffed his hat in mock respect.

I ignored his whimsy. "How goes it in the Hurtwood? Have the Dragoons come back?"

"No, a fuss was made in Guildford. The magistrates put out warrants and promised hell and damnation. None of the soldier boys wuz killed, but the one I shot won't be soldiering again, or so I do hear. If we had killed one of them, they would have been forced to come strong into the woods. But no one wants to stir up too much – the magistrates don't want the district judges coming down from London and telling 'em what to do. But yeomen patrols have been busy near the Hurtwood and I hear that the Dragoons would like to come back and give us a mighty pounding. We ain't done no runs since our fight, Rich. And our dear landlord at the New Inn ain't happy, but he knows it ain't safe at present. So I would say: abide here a while, but I knows you will go back for Ma Nye. Tender-hearted you are, Rich. You don't have the killer about you."

My guilt made me think that this was going to be a shifty cue for Harry to ask about my deceased partner, but he kept silent on that matter. But my troubled heart, tempered with caution, did prompt me to ask about the mysterious hooded stranger whom I had seen in Godalming, and who had been prowling in Peaslake.

"No, Rich, ain't no news of the ghost. Though Nance has said he might have been an albino. Didn't like the light when he came into her place that night and she said he rolled his eyes like a sick cow."

I dropped the matter, and asked of more news of Ma Nye.

After Harry had paid the reckoning for our refreshments, I led him to the George and bade him well, promising to see him in the Hurtwood in a few days.

I went home – for that is what it felt like – to bring my sad tidings to Solly. Tamar was there sitting with her father in the kitchen and I could see that she was distressed that I was leaving. Her open face and the fact that she could not hide her inner feelings made me warm to her even more.

Solly, as ever, was direct. "Aye, Reeech. Gut that you care for your Ma Nye. I met her vonce when I took you to the Hurtwood when you vas a lad, do you remember?"

I shook my head.

"Rachel vill make you some food for your journey. And I will give you a light trunk for your goods, Ah, vee vill make a merchant of you. But I want that vee see you soon. I will hef dat geld for you when you come back. So I know dat you come back."

"Solly, you know that I don't need money to come back. You're the *kvetch* now." And I hugged him. As I withdrew from his embrace, I looked at Tamar, and I didn't care that Solly saw me looking at her. Quickly, she left the room, crying I fear.

I thanked my hosts and made my preparations to leave early the next morning.

I had changed my profession and restored a friendship with the gentle Tamar. But I understood that it could never be more than friendship. And it was not religion that was dividing us, that I knew. Something deep inside my very being told me not to dabble with Tamar, not just because I could not do justice to her or her family, but because I knew, yes knew absolutely, that I would be drawn by destiny to someone I had not met. Instinctively, I felt I would instantly recognize this predestined woman.

For my business plans, I had done good work for a few weeks in London. My heart was too heavy, however, to celebrate my new circumstances.

Thirteen

In the darkened room, illuminated by just one fading rush light, I could just make out Ma Nye's pale, lined and pained face. She was rasping for breath. Nance was there, holding a mug to her shaking lips, helping her to drink some tea.

"Good it be to see thee," Nance whispered. "Black Harry dun well in finding thy good self. Ma won't last much longer. I do believe she was hanging on for thee alone…"

Ma groaned, and Nance propped up her head on a pillow, and gave her more tea. But Ma coughed when she tried to drink it.

"What's wrong, Ma?"

"I know not," she said feebly. "But I am very middling[19]… that I do know."

Nance spoke for her. "A fever it is. That is what the apothecary said from Cranleigh…and he has bled her."

"Damn the leech-mongers," said I. "We must fetch a doctor from Guildford. In this minute…"

"I will send Little Will tomorrow… A doctor will not come to these woods at night."

I knew that was the truth. I said, "And with a guinea from me, to hasten his coming."

Both Nance and I knew that tomorrow would be too late.

Ma seemed to gain some strength in her voice, and she

managed to pull herself up a little. "Rich, we must talk a little...Jes thee and me."

Nance did not need to be asked. She went downstairs to make some broth for Ma.

"Rich, thank'ee for comin' all the way from London town just for old Ma Nye. Glad to see thy face..."

Her voice was fading so I leaned close to her.

"Since my Edward went to heaven, there's been little in my life except my house and lookin' after thee. I wants thee to keep this place. It is all paid for, by my Edward."

"No, Ma. You've done too much for me already."

"Rich, there be no one else – in this den of thieves. And thou hast a good heart."

"Thank'ee, Ma. I am very grateful for your kindness."

"No, it is also guilt. Some things I must say now, before it's too late."

I leaned more closely.

"Thy father...he died on the high seas. He was a distant cousin to me...I never told thee of that. I believed thou might be angry with me, because thou be angry with his leaving thee a tiny child in London...and thou might blame me..."

"No, no, Ma. There's no need to chastise yourself..."

"No time, Rich...let me finish. Thou didst have a cousin when thou came from London..."

"Yes, I recollect him well, Jimmy. He died five years ago in Farnham."

"Yes, but there be closer kin to thee, Rich."

"Who?" I asked, with more urgency than I intended.

"Jake...Jake Whapshot."

I swallowed hard. "How is he my kin?"

"This father of your'n had a wife before he met thy Ma in London. Mary was her name and she was my cousin. And they had a son – Jake. Mary died bringing him into this sad world... He kept his mother's name. Jake thou knows well, but there be more. Jake fathered a son, out of wedlock. And he was abandoned. The babe was not whole, not quite right, or so I heard. Didn't know what the trouble be, nor does I know his name. Heard tell the boy grew up with his ma in Farnham, but he was mightily teased, and they went to London. Not to an honest living, I do believe…"

She was struggling to find words now. "Jake didn't know thee and he be half-brothers, though there were times when I saw yous both in Peaslake and thought to meself how alike even yous both did walk…Now I ain't be no scholar but I thinks that his lad knows…"

She coughed. "I am not sure. But it is time to speak of this to thy brother, Rich. It is time…"

"Ma, why didn't you tell me this before?"

Ma seemed not to hear, as though a burden had been lifted from her and that now she could go to her Maker in peace.

She closed her eyes.

"Ma, please tell me." I was in tears now – overwhelmed by my grief for Ma and by my guilt, for killing my own brother.

She opened her eyes and seemed surprised to see me. She looked lost for a minute.

"Tell me, Ma. Why didn't you tell me?"

"It was for thy da to tell thee, not me."

"But he went off when I were but five or six."

"It was his secret, and I put off telling thee. Forgive me."

"There is nothing to forgive…I want just to understand."

"Speak to Jake, find him in London…Thou spake of him being there. And find his son. Family be important, especially when approaching the time to meet our God. My kin are all gone…A punishment for living too long... Hold my hand, Rich. Thee be like kin to me. Take the house…there be a will in the green box in my room…and promise me …find thy brother and nephew and make thy peace with they. I fear that thou and Jake fell to arguing…"

I held her hand, and squeezed but it seemed cold. Just as Nance came back into her bedroom, Ma gave out a slight groan and her head fell to the side of the pillow. Nance lifted her eyelids and felt the pulse on her neck.

"She be dead, Rich. Thou came in time to say goodbye. Ma wanted that very much. I think she died in peace and in God's grace."

I heard myself say, "Amen."

Fourteen

With so much to ponder upon, I slept badly the night that Ma Nye died, despite my exhausting journey back from London. I was grieving at Ma's passing. True, Rachel had been a second mother to me in London when I was a lad, but my grown-up years had been spent in the Hurtwood, being a much-spoiled paying guest at Ma's run-down farmhouse. I regretted that I hadn't done more on its upkeep, for her sake, but for also mine, for I was now its owner.

At daylight, I would rise early and ride to Ewhurst to search out Reverend Robert Mathews, to ask him to come to St Mark's, the decrepit wooden church in Peaslake, to conduct a funeral. Most ministers were wary of venturing into the heart of the Hurtwood, especially Peaslake, but Reverend Mathews was a regular recipient of our smuggled brandy. He would feel safe even in our den of thieves and would be happy to officiate in a church that was largely neglected.

The following Saturday, Ma would be buried with full Christian rites, according to the Church of England, though I suspect deep down she may have had Catholic leanings, but she never spoke of them. So I felt St Mark's could be used with a decent conscience.

The Reverend Roberts had said plainly, "I will come to bury your Ma Nye, but I will need some spiritual fortification afterwards." That would mean not only an extra cask for him, but also an invitation to the wake. Nance said she would hold the wake in her home which doubled as a public house anyway. There would be no shortage of good spirit in a stronghold of free-traders.

And I spoke to Nance about her renting, cheaply, my new farm. I couldn't sell it so soon after Ma gave it to me. That would seem ungrateful. But I couldn't live any longer right in the Hurtwood. I intended to become more respectable. A cloth merchant couldn't live in a smuggler's den. I didn't want to move too far, and certainly not to London. Albury was respectable and not so distant – six or seven miles. Gomshall was possible. I wanted my own house, in a less lawless village, but I needed to be close enough to the Hurtwood, just in case I did need a refuge from the same law whose protection I was now seeking. It was a gamble, but one I felt I had to take.

The hill men in the Hurtwood on its clean sandy soil used to speak of their neighbours on the clay weald to the south as "down in the dirt". It was not meant to be disrespectful; it was just a description of the different soil. We used so many different words for earth. For example, the earth was called "mould" if it were laying in the garden, but it would be called "dirt" if it were to be moved around. I was becoming more aware of the closeness to nature that I had once taken for granted, but my brief sojourn in Southwark had made me all too aware of my needing to live in rhythm with the seasons – that I was a countryman at heart.

I had also become newly aware of the different speech of Londoners. Yes, Solly was unique – with his German, Cockney and Yiddish, but the people around him spoke a very different kind of English from my neighbours in the Hurtwood. And even the men of Peaslake and Ewhurst spoke quite differently from the people down in the valley to the north, the Tillingbourne, or to the lands south of the Surrey ridge in the clay wealds leading to the Sussex downs. I had taken all this for granted. I wasn't trying to lord it over anybody. It was just that I was more aware somehow, and I had learned a lot from what Solly had told me about moving up in my new trade by aping the manners of my betters.

I decided to live in Gomshall. To the London eye, it would be a mere hamlet set in undrained marshes, with ill-kept roads, but busy in summer for the route from Dorking to Guildford following the tracks along the Tillingbourne River. The hedges were untrimmed and many of the farm buildings were rickety and run-down, partly because the farms were let on yearly leases. Depending on the direction of the wind, the vapours from its tannery laced the air, but if I bought on the other side of the river, the scent of apricots warming in the morning sun – in the garden I planned – would drive away the heavy acid smell of leather-making.

If I bought a cottage or small farmhouse off the main track, I could still make it a fine dwelling. I had the means, the money from Solly and my small rent from Nance, to purchase and maintain my first home. There was some business in Gomshall, fishponds with carp, watercress cultivation and a prosperous mill. I knew of a small farm for sale, near the mill. The main track ran to the north of the mill's main timbered and thatched house, to the south next to the house was the waterwheel, and then adjacent was a brew house. In front of the buildings was a large pond where the Tillingbourne collected after running through the wheel. The farm I had in mind was a short walk from the mill, and handy for flour and beer for my provisions.

In a light cart, in summer, I could also trade with Dorking, or Guildford or Godalming, as well as the fine manor houses around Chilworth, Albury and Shere. I would not frequent my old haunts, not the New Inn nor the White Horse in Shere, and I felt the need to attend church. I would worship at St

James's in the square at Shere; not just to create a veneer of a polite trade, but because I wanted to. Some of the churchmen I had met in my line of business had been over-indulgent to us free-traders, but I didn't think the less of them. Christ, I believed, wanted to save sinners, not saints.

Even now, I am not sure whether it was the guilt of manslaughter, killing my own half-brother, albeit in self-defence, or perhaps the image of Christianne Bowman hanging and burning to death. What stuck most in my memory was her kin hurrying her death by pulling on her legs. I had no real kin, but in my imagination I could not bear the thought of perhaps Tamar, Solly or Nance tugging at my bare feet to speed my death.

I was afraid, for the first time in my life. Perhaps it was because for the first time I had something to lose – my new fortune, an aspiring reputation and, yes, a yearning to make a mark, something beyond the dangers and adventures of smuggling. There had to be a better way than the constant conniving of even my dearest friends in Southwark or the Hurtwood. Maybe I was becoming the very *alter kocker* that I had teased Solly about. And, yes, I was afraid of being transported, if I were lucky. If I were tried in the courts for smuggling and murder I could swing from a gibbet outside Newgate. It was no comfort that the King's ministers had declared that the sad Christianne was to be the last public burning. For me, the gibbet was more than enough.

The wake was to be my last involvement in my smuggling past. The Reverend Roberts delivered a fine oration, despite the occasional slurring, for he had started with a vengeance on his "spiritual fortification". Even Samuel Horsley was there to assist him. Dr Horsley was entirely sober, as befitted a master forger with an ever-keen eye for detail. I was even pleased to see Black Harry there, not a man for sentiment, but never one to miss the chance for a bounty of booze.

During the wake at Nance's he sidled up in that shifty way

of his. "How be your London business going, Mr Merchant Rich?" he asked with some disdain. "Joining your Yiddishe friends, I'm told."

"I told you, Harry, that I intend to trade, but not free-trade."

"I ne'er thought I'd be seeing the day when a Peaslake man – even a half-bred one like thyself, no offence meant – was wanting to pay taxes to the King."

"Better taxes than the gibbet," I said involuntarily, after a goodly number of brandies. It was not wise to show fear to Harry.

Surprisingly, he replied thus: "Aye, Rich. There's some sense in that. Provided you can afford the taxes, and no one squeals to the beak about your past."

"Your past is blacker than mine, Harry. Better we help each other to trade open and fair."

"That I agree to, Rich. And will you be letting me meet some of your'n traders in London?"

"That I will, Harry. I'll be returning there before the year is out."

"That's settled then. I have one or two more runs to do, then I intend to wave farewell to pack horses and night marches. Except that Black Harry will probably have to retire to London. Too well known am I here as a brigand and thief. So to London goes I and I don't know the town as well as you."

We shook hands. An agreement I didn't want, but felt obliged. I accepted that it would be hard to leave my past entirely behind. But I would try my damned best.

Nance interrupted us by asking, "Rich, is it time for the fiddlers yet?"

"Nance, this is your house. Bring on the fiddlers at your leisure."

"Well, now then Rich. Ma Nye liked a good fiddler. Here's a drink to her, wherever she may be."

And Nance looked up. I raised my glass and she did the

same. She waved to the two fiddlers and they started to play with gusto. Within minutes the hard men of the forest were doing a variety of jigs together, dancing like fairies with leaden boots.

Little Will came up and said, "Mr Rich, may I still ride Diamond?"

"Aye, lad, as much as you like for I am planning to purchase a fine new stallion for myself. I will need Diamond only for my cart."

The lad beamed at me, and rushed off to join in the jig.

Nance had seen the boy smiling and she walked unsteadily over to me; she put her hand on my arm. "Thou be a good man, Rich. Thank'ee for being so kind to my boy."

"I'm not a good man, Nance, but I want to be a better one. And I like the lad. He's steadfast and reliable, when I ask something of him. I measure a man by how much he does what he says he will do. And he's ne'er disappointed me."

"I trust he ne'er will. He looks up to thee – with no father of his own."

"Yes, Nance, I understand. Truly I do."

I was slurring now, and getting maudlin. I should have been the last to stay to honour Ma Nye, but I needed my bed.

I had done what I had to do. In the morrow I would start my life again – if I were given a decent chance.

Fifteen

It was a splendid old farmhouse, albeit rather worn and tired, and the roof needed care, but it was now mine. I had had a nodding acquaintanceship with its former owner, the uncle of the landlord of the White Horse. The farm, a rare freehold in Gomshall, had worn the old man down, and he was going to retire to live with his son in Dorking. Most of the farm-land had already been sold off to help the son's business, so just 160 rods survived, what they might call an acre or so in London. It was a good day's work for one fit man to reap an acre. Extraordinary human effort had been expended on the cold, begrudging soil in the small undrained fields around the Tillingbourne. The sandy soil gave up its bounty but rarely and there had been little livestock to keep the old man busy.

I loved the woodland, even in the valley bottom, just a few hundred yards from the Gomshall corn-mill. The oak, birch, ash and new Scotch fir woods were not as thick as in the Hurtwood, but I felt at home. I would not farm straightaway although I might keep a few chickens and smaller livestock – perhaps a few pigs. I could take on more land if I needed it. But I knew how hard the farming was here, how many barns were half-full even after the harvest and how many farms kept too many hands just so they got some food – sometimes. It was no accident that so many of the local folk felt driven to smuggling; otherwise they would have starved.

I was going to do the opposite – move from smuggling to try a little farming.

The farmhouse was two-storeys, made of brick noggin, a framing of oak filled in with brick, with tile hung on the upper roof. The hedges needed rozzling to restore the wattle fences on the hedge bank. The two stables were dry. The barn was empty except for rusty ploughs and similar ancient implements. And like most farms it had a small lime kiln. The soil hereabouts was full of what the alchemists called acid so the lime had to be applied every five or six years when the land had to lay fallow for a season. My kiln was built of stone, about eighteen feet high and shaped like a round tower. Dirt had been heaped on one side to make a ramp so that the kiln could be fed from the top. The lime-burner would rake with a long pole the furze or wood fire every twenty minutes or so during the three days of the job. It was hard work and it was not surprising that the kiln was now empty – it had been too much for the old man. I remembered how often we had hid contraband in empty kilns, but I cast those thoughts aside.

I liked the kitchen garden. The old man had tended to this with obvious love. The onset of autumn had taken the bloom from the roses but the hips glowed in the fading light. A honeysuckle, with its downy seed-heads, scrambled over the door. The herb garden had evidence of rosemary, lavender, mint and sage. And traces of southernwood remained. I remembered how we used to put bergamot in our hair-grease when we were young lads in the forests – the girls loved the smell. Everlasting peas guarded the front door and the garden was bordered by China asters, which we in the Hurtwood called "chaney oysters".

The garden also boasted a straw beehive. By local custom a wandering swarm became the property of where it settled. I remembered well what I was taught as a young lad that – when the first swarms started to come in May – beating an old ploughshare with a heavy door key would make them come to your hive. If it worked, and it often did, a productive swarm was worth eight to ten shillings to its owner for that season's honey.

The kitchen attracted me most. Now the new owner, I dragged my boots against the iron door scraper by the kitchen door and went in. It looked lived in, because I had a few pieces already from Ma Nye's – especially the French clock – but I had also bought much of the old man's furniture and goods. It was easier for me, and I appreciated the simple country style he had imposed, or rather his long-dead wife had. Downstairs consisted of a living room and main kitchen, and there was a back kitchen with a brick oven and the usual hooks for hanging ham. But the front kitchen was so comfortable. It had a seven-foot oak table with a bench fitted against the wall and one long loose bench in the well of the room. The table had a date – 1603 – carved on it. So it was nigh on 200 years old. In addition the room boasted a carved linen hutch, though I would have to learn to call it a chest in London. A fine oak cofen[20] stood between the wall and the stairs to the two rooms on the first floor. On the hutch stood a Bible box. I opened it, but found it empty. I was a little disappointed, but I had no right to another family's Bible. Near the big inglenook fireplace hung a salt-box, hinged with leather. I had noticed that in the damper London no one seemed to bother to put the salt-box near the fire so as to keep it drier; perhaps because salt was cheaper in town. In the Hurtwood and here in the valley people could survive on just local produce – except salt. That's why it was so carefully hoarded.

In the back kitchen I was pleased to see that the old man had left his coffee mill. That was fair as he had included it in his list of contents for sale. I presumed his son had drawn it up, because – as with nearly all the local inhabitants – he had no reading or writing. "I be'ant no schlard," he had confessed to me, meaning that he was illiterate. The mill would need a bit of cleaning but soon I would have the fulsome aroma of coffee filling my house. Nance had sent her son with the cart to buy some provisions for me from Guildford. She would soon arrive with them and inspect my house, and no doubt provide welcome female advice. Because, despite its charm, it had the utilitarian hardness of a man's home. An old man's home. I wanted to make it more my own and the place for a younger man, a man about to enter at least the edges of polite society.

I was displaced from my reverie by a knock on the door. I assumed it was Nance and shouted, "Come in."

"'Tis a stranger, sir. I would not disturve you by walking into your home without your knowing me."

It was a local accent – the "b" in disturb was softened into a "v", the locals said disturve not disturb – but breeding was in his voice too.

"A moment, sir. I will attend the door presently."

Why I needed him to wait I do not know. I was behaving suspiciously, like the veteran free-trader I was. I looked out the window, not really expecting a troop of militia…and there was none. I felt foolish. I moved to the door and opened it wide – it was broad daylight.

"Apologies, sir, for disturbing you. My name is David Harris and I own the Gomshall mill, adjoining your new property. The mill's been here since before the Domesday Book, before those Normans came over from France…Ah, God forbid the Frenchies come again." He scratched his cheek as if embarrassed by his historical whimsy. "Ah, sir, but I came to welcome you, not teach you history. And I see that you are indeed a gentleman. Old Mister Talbot told me he was joining his son in Dorking and had sold the farmhouse to a Mr Durrant. Do I have the pleasure of meeting the same?"

"You do, sir," and charmed by his manners, I made a slight bow and gestured for him to come in. "I have little in the way of refreshments, as I have not stocked my larder yet."

"Thank'ee, Mr Durrant, I will not impose on your hospitality at this inconvenient time. But I trust we'll be good neighbours."

"I trust so too."

"Then I shall wish you 'Good-day'." He had turned to walk back down the path before I summoned the wit to say thank you.

He waved back at me from the garden gate.

A few miles from the Hurtwood and I had ensconced myself next to a cultured gentleman, yet I had instinctively behaved like a ruffian, a peasant afraid of the magistrates. Although I had to be ever-cautious, I would have to throw off the mantle of my old free-trading ways.

⋘∞⋙

I busied myself tidying the house as I awaited Nance. She was some years my senior, and no hint of amour existed, but I felt I needed her presence, almost as a benediction. It would have been nice if Ma Nye could have seen my new house, but she was gone, passed on to join the great smugglers of the past. Many of them were good people, driven by want, a sense of injustice at the King's insane tax laws and some impelled by a sense of freedom, adventure or principle. They didn't all deserve Hell. I was wrestling again with my conscience. I had to curb my inner turmoil.

I busied myself in my new kitchen, for I truly loved it. I could smell the charred wood remains in the grate, and the damp smell of leaves which came through the open shutters of the window which contrasted with the slightly dry smell of the stones around the fireplace. A strange tempting succulence – perhaps from the garden – conjured up ghosts of many family gatherings here. This was a happy place – I knew it in my soul.

The best feature of the whole house was here – the fireplace. I can see every detail in my mind's eye, even now. A wooden chair with a rush-woven seat stood next to the inglenook and, with courtly flourish, I placed myself on it to admire my new domain. The fireplace had two small wooden benches built into the alcoves at each end. On the one end a brass bellows stood waiting for me. On the other an old hourglass and a wicker bird cage paraded themselves. The latter empty, thank goodness – I had no truck with penning flying creatures, perhaps because I was a creature of the forest myself. I wondered whether my purchasing of this house was a cage for me. Once more, I was angered by my own dark thoughts.

I cleared the wood remains from the grate and was surprised to discover that they covered a keystone, which, once I levered it up, revealed an iron vault of about eighteen inches square. It was a common decoy to hide small but valuable smuggled goods in such as space and then build a roaring fire above it, if the Revenue men were expected to pay a visit. Keystones also used to disguise hiding places in a stable, where the most aggressive horse would be left, to kick any Preventer who was too inquisitive. It was rare, though, for such hidey holes to be built in the valley. Maybe the previous owner had a legacy like mine. I had planned to escape not engage my past.

I wanted Nance to come, to shake me out of my reverie.

I concentrated on taking mental stock of my new chattels. I observed the copper frying pan with the three-foot handle hanging next to an iron rack with four hoops which I could hang my clay pipes on. When pipes – although I had but two left unbroken – became foul with use we used to lay them in a rack and put them in the fire. After a time they would come out perfectly white and clean. The effects of that little ritual always used to please me. I looked forward to lighting my first fire soon and enjoying a pipe in its glow.

I noticed the small brass tongs for picking up an ember and lighting a pipe. It made me want to smoke but I remembered that Nance was bringing some recently smuggled tobacco with her. I thought of food instead as I regarded the standing toasting fork.

I got up and checked the round tinder-box which had a candle socket on the top. Inside it – and in good order – was a flint stone and a tiny bag of gunpowder to help if the spark for the tinder was sluggish. I remembered how Tamar had shown off the new-fangled Lucifer matches from France. She called them "Congreves". In the countryside I was happy with the old ways – I liked working for my fire.

I raised my eyes to the wooden mantle shelf. It was guarded by a pair of Toby jugs. I traced my hands around the matching farmers with their smart breeches, three-cornered hats and frilled shirt bands. Aye, a gentleman farmer – that's what I would be.

Above the mantle hung a mirror. The glass had a bluish tint and it was much spotted and blurred so, when I looked into it, I too seemed mottled and withered. I blamed the mirror, but thought perhaps I should grow a goatee beard. It seemed fashionable among some of the young blades I had seen in London. It would mark my new life.

I wandered into the outer kitchen, to see what I could find. On a low wooden bench I spied a wooden tea caddy with brass lion's claw feet, some stoneware mugs, three leather bottles and a red earthenware pitcher. On the window-sill lay a harvest bottle. I snatched at it with relish. I had always wanted one when I was a young boy. This little blue barrel was hooped firmly with iron. It was just ten inches high, but it could hold almost a gallon. Made of oak, it had a projecting mouth-piece and above it a small hole for the vent peg. The vent peg and the cork were tied to the rope handle so they couldn't get lost in the fields. I put the harvest bottle back and sighed. Beneath the sill was an old spinning wheel. It looked unusable, and I wondered whether I could repair it. What for? I didn't spin and I had no woman in my life.

I wandered out through the back door into the yard, past the water pump and the privy to the barn. I found a rusty scythe and a reaping hook. The barn also possessed two wooden ploughs, and a mildewed wooden cider press. Next to the barn was a rip[21]; empty, but that could soon be put right.

"Rich, Rich?"

I was startled out of these strange melancholic, yet also elated, thoughts by Nance calling for me.

She marched up to me as I stood awkwardly defending my discoveries in the barn.

"I likes thy new home, Rich, but it needs a good woman to tend it…and thee," she said forcefully, with her hands on her hips.

I smiled flirtatiously.

"'T'aint being me, thee rapscallion. I am a little too old. A young wench, ripe for plucking and babies. Be the making of thee, Rich."

I smiled and asked, "What provisions are there in the cart? And where's Little Will? He's in charge of Diamond."

"He'll be unloading the victuals. And before he puts they away, I need to be a'cleanin' some of the place…You ain't got Ma Nye fussin' o'er thee now. As I was saying, this house has needs of a good woman."

I thought that perhaps she was right. I sensed a black hole inside me. I also sensed that Tamar probably could not fill this space, but I grasped at the possibility that someone could, soon. Someone who would sit in front of my inglenook with me.

I laughed at my foolishness, gave Nance my arm and escorted her like a duchess through the back door of my new castle.

Sixteen

*A*nd then I saw her. She was walking alongside the Tillingbourne River, coming from St James's Church, and going in the direction of Albury. I was ambling past her, the wrong way; it was obvious that I had not attended the service that chilly Sunday morning, although I had my new frock coat on and my best hat. She wore her Sunday bonnet, black, drawn and corded in a neat bow. A close-fitting muslin cap showed inside the bonnet. Beneath her long navy-blue serge dress, I noticed that she was wearing pattens, wooden clogs with a leather toe-piece and bands of leather that tied with a short lace over the instep. She was demurely dressed, as a better sort of working person would be – except for the clogs. I thought it strange that she didn't wear her best boots to match her bonnet for her Sunday best. Perhaps they were being repaired, or she was too poor…

But why am I prattling on about her dress and her boots? It was her face, radiant yet foreign, that drew me. Beautiful, but the lines under her eyes revealed her inner pain. My heart felt a jab, almost as strong as a punch to my chest. I thought I knew her and was about to prepare to stop for conversation. But, no, no… I did not know her, yet I had somehow met her before. I was in a mad panic. I could not accost a strange woman on the pathway; that would be highly irregular. When she passed me, I raised my hat and said "Good morning" in common courtesy. She nodded and modestly lowered her eyes and head, as she passed.

Other members of her congregation were approaching me along the path so I could not just stand and stare at her retreating figure, but I had to see more of her. I kneeled on the frosty ground and made as though I were repairing the heel of my boot. I looked back as decently as I could and saw that she was a carrying a prayer book and a spray of herbs – perhaps rosemary or southernwood or some other sweet-smelling herb, wrapped in a white handkerchief.

A drayman and his wife were almost upon me. I wanted to stop him and demand the name of this woman who had just attended the church. I tried to think of some pretext: "Sir, why are you wearing your red drayman's hat to church. This is not seemly, sir. I will pardon your transgression only if you tell me who that angelic creature is…"

Was I ready for bedlam? I stood up from my shoe repairs, and managed a mumbled "Good morning" to the drayman and his wife. They exchanged greetings but looked a little alarmed – I wondered whether my inner turmoil had suffused my face. Were my eyes swivelling and staring madly? My heart raced like a startled deer. Perhaps, because I was in shock. I would find out who this woman was if it were my last act on this earth.

What had I seen? That she was demure, correct, and a countrywoman. That I could guess from her dress, shoes and manner of greeting. But it was her foreignness that confused me. Aye, we had a few gypsy women in the Hurtwood, with their ornate red head-scarves and great gold earrings. They were swarthy of complexion. Yet this lady had an air of gentility. She was a princess from the Mediterranean, I mused, who had escaped from her wicked stepfather. I was already conjuring up romantic fables from my childhood – Solly had given me a children's book of stories to help me to read. In it were chivalric tales of princes, knights and dragons. Nevertheless, despite all my dalliances of the past, this was the first time that I felt I had to embark on a quest for a woman... This woman whom I knew instinctively, but had never met, would be my holy grail.

At the very least, meeting her would put me back on the path of righteousness – I would attend St James's punctually next Sunday, to be sure. Although I wanted to rush into the church and demand of the verger, "Who is this graceful creature? Tell me man, or I will knock you to the ground this instant."

Not a good introduction to a congregation that I would need – and perhaps – want – to frequent.

I would have to wait for a whole week – an agony of delay.

I stumbled home, sat on my rush chair by the fire, and wondered what I could do for the vapours that had enveloped me. I had no smelling salts, used in a fine house in London perhaps, but not in the country, and not by a strong man in his prime, or only just past it. I wanted to ride up to Nance's on my new horse, Champion, play the knight errant and beg her to explain the mysteries of love. She would have laughed at me; and been right to do so.

I made up a fire instead and busied myself with two lamb chops on my brass frying pan. One hunger was assuaged, but not the other that gnawed inside me.

I devised a plan that might prevent a week of waiting. It had been a month or so since I had moved into my farmhouse in Gomshall and I had visited with my wares a number of the manor houses in the valley, as well as a few tradesmen and private homes in Dorking and Guildford. But I had not paid proper heed to three or four big houses for the gentry in Albury Park, Weston Street and Chilworth.

She had been walking towards Albury and I guessed that she would not proceed more than a few miles unescorted, even to and from church – that would not be proper – so she must live or work close by the valley from St James's Church. But perhaps not; maybe she lived in Shere near St James's, and was paying a visit to someone. To whom? I wondered. I had assumed in my mad conjectures that she was not spoken for. Perhaps she was hurrying home to her children? No, that could not be. Perhaps it was false intuition, but I knew deep inside that she was a single woman. Or was that a mere fantasy of my fevered brain?

I had been sluggish in starting up my new trade. I had ample monies, and was kept busy in my new home, and with all the suggestions – curtains and the like – that Nance had showered me with. She had even suggested wall-paper, the new London fashion. I told her that it was my private house not a public stage. And yet somehow the traditional beaten earth floor of my kitchen seemed wrong. When I suggested a rug or two, Nance had then turned the tables and accused me of "affecting airs and graces" way above my station. She quoted the popular verse to me:

God bless the squire and his relations
And keep us in our proper stations.

I had also been occupied with purchasing my black stallion, Champion, a fine horse for a gentleman-to-be. I was a gentleman trader, but had done little trade as yet. Nor was I a gentleman farmer – I would wait till spring before I bought a little livestock to give my small farm some practical purpose.

So the long week was spent visiting the tradesmen's entrances to Netley Manor, Albury Manor and to fine houses along the eastern reaches of the valley in Shire Hammer and Wootton. I met discourtesy from servants who had overreached themselves and the occasional kindness and bread and cheese in the parlours of more kindly housekeepers, senior maids and butlers. Some lace and linen I had sold, but I did not chance upon my Mediterranean beauty. Although I had determined to avoid the inns and taverns in case I came upon old comrades-in-arms, I bestowed some pennies on the George in

Albury Park, and nearby the Running Horse, and even that friendly den of drunkards and frivolity, the William IV, on the edge of the Hurtwood.

I kept away from the White Horse in Shere, however. It was not fitting that I should attend church there and tarnish my new image by frequenting the pub on the same square as the church and risk the moral pollution of my former allies in contraband. Besides, I was now trading as Richard Durrant, Esquire – that's what it said on the fancy calling cards I had printed – and did not want to be hailed by my real name. It was not uncommon for us rascals of the Hurtwood to live with a pot-full of aliases, but I did not want to risk tainting my courtship…was I crazed? I had not even spoken to this lady. I had to meet her soon, or I would be driven to insanity and ruin, bedlam or poor-house.

All I could think of when I sat by my fire in the dark cold nights of early winter was how lonely I was. Oh, if only she could be sitting near me by the fire. I had even moved the second rush-woven chair to stand to attention around the fire, to match the two Toby jugs which would, please God, portend us two – my dark lady and me – together roasting chestnuts…

Ah, it was now Saturday night, and I had polished my boots three times. My hat had been brushed as many times. I had considered riding Champion, but a new member of the congregation should enter modestly, not prance by on a charger. It was a largely sleepless night, and I had not imbibed a single bottle of beer beforehand. I felt as though I were a knight abstaining before a sacred task, a pilgrim preparing for the long journey to Jerusalem. I even attempted a short prayer for God's speed to my task. I had slept but little, yet awoke with energy surging through my body.

I dressed carefully, but could not eat. I marched from

Gomshall to Shere as though the trade winds were filling my sails. Reaching the church, I entered and sat quietly in the corner in one of the pews that had been recently built there, though the seats were not as grand as the small section reserved for the Bray family, who owned so much of the land and property in the nearby parishes. I always expected to stand, but now seats were available for nearly everyone; even the poor, for until recently you had to pay to sit down. I was very early and spent my time reading – or pretending to read – a prayer book that had been placed on a table for the more zealous members of the congregation.

Slowly the church filled and I became anxious that I would not follow the correct practice of worship. I was not a regular churchgoer, and I was never sure when to kneel, stand or pray. I tried to keep my head down, to appear as inconspicuous as a church mouse in the rafters, but I kept sneaking my eyes to the left, to the aisle, to see if she had come. I worried in case I would not recognize her bonnet from the rear.

As the church grew full, amid the bustle I could not see all who were entering. A nearby pillar constrained my view, and many older women had entered from the side door behind me. A large number had black bonnets which – to my male eyes – looked very similar.

The bells rang for a few minutes, and then the altar-boys entered and took up their seats. The vicar – Reverend Thomas Dunscombe – entered late and somewhat flustered. Soon he composed himself and bade us all to stand in prayer. I bowed my head but kept one eye open trying to scan the congregation to find her.

I must confess I paid little heed to the sermon and prayers from the good book. My heart was churning and my head burning with frustration. I could not see her.

Finally, the service ended and the choir-boys led the procession out of the great west door. The congregation followed and I tried to be unobtrusive as the worshippers filed out.

As I walked through the main door, the Reverend Dunscombe shook my hand and said, "Welcome to our congregation. I trust you will worship here regularly, sir."

"Thank you, Reverend, that I intend to do," I said with very real fervour.

I walked slowly along the path through the graveyard, to the wall near the village square. Two old men were smoking their pipes and the smoke wreathed above their heads in the chill December air. They were both dressed in the old style: dark-grey smock-frocks with tall black hats. I asked whether I might join them, and introduced myself.

I needed to stand in company, not to be too conspicuous, and to spy out the departure route that she might take. I also scanned the departing congregation to see if there was someone I might know. One or two faces I vaguely recognized, and then finally I saw an older woman whom I knew a little better. She was kin to Nance, but a respectable, godly woman living in the valley. Tilly, Tilly, Tilly... Tilly Cooper, that was her name.

I paid scant but polite attention to my new companions, who talked of horses and their breeding, a subject which normally would hold my fullest interest. I was so anxious that I might not see her, even though my vantage point commanded a full view of both exits from the church.

Yes, yes ...it was her, but she was accompanied by a man. My first impulse was to run over and strangle this intruder.

Then I perceived that he was a very frail ancient creature she was helping to an awaiting cart. She led the old man through the south exit of the graveyard, and handed her charge to a young red-haired boy, who helped the man on to the front seat of the cart, not without some effort.

Compassionate, I thought. Perhaps it was her father or uncle. The cart, drawn by a grey horse, moved off in the direction of Albury as the old man waved her goodbye. Not kin, I presumed, or she would have travelled with them.

I bade my smoking cronies a good day, and walked toward the western exit from the churchyard.

I panicked then. What was I to say? Utter some banality about the sermon, or the weather, or comment on her bonnet? No, sir.

She was upon me as I contrived to accidentally walk parallel at the same velocity and in the same direction as her.

I raised my hat. "Good morning."

She slowed her pace, turned to me, blushed, and said, "Good morning."

"May I presume, Madam, as I am walking towards Albury to take a few minutes to share an understanding of the fine sermon? Much of it was fine, that is, but much of it I did not comprehend."

She stopped and faced me. How beautiful she was. In a French accent she said, "Sir, I am not a learned woman. You should speak to the Reverend" – she rolled the 'r's in the word – "about his sermon."

This was an obvious reply to my clumsy approach.

"Madam, I meant no harm or insult."

"No, sir, there is no insult."

And then she smiled and my whole being was suffused by that magical light.

She turned to walk away.

"Madame, I apologize for my awkward ways... I...I." I was lost for words.

"Sir, we are not introduced..."

"Beg pardon, Madame" – which I now pronounced in the French way – "*Mademoiselle?*"

She smiled again. "*Mademoiselle? Oui.*" She blushed again.

"How rude of me. My name is...Richard..." I hesitated over which name to use. How truthful to be? The integrity of our beginning would matter so much. A lie once told was so hard to retrieve...

She curtsied slightly. "Please sir, it is proper that we are introduced in the church. Please excuse me."

I managed to recover with an "*Au revoir*".

She did not turn, but I think a slight chuckle was evident in her response: "*Au revoir, Monsieur.*"

No king or emperor could have stopped me staring at her back as she disappeared into the woods where the Tillingbourne bent into the fish ponds. I noticed that she had abandoned her clogs and was now wearing good boots. Fitting for church and for the frost on the ground.

I cursed myself for my bumbling manners, but she had not rebuffed me. She had been correct and it was now my task to effect an introduction in the church, but without causing a scandal in the congregation. I was entranced by her Frenchness, and slightly pleased with myself that I had engaged her with the little of the language I had learned from my smuggling days, though I had never been to France. I hoped she thought me a man of the world. And, joy, oh joy, she had made it abundantly clear that she was a mademoiselle. I took that as a great encouragement. Then I started to fret – perhaps she thought me a clumsy country oaf, and she had to instruct me in the ways of even rural society. Perhaps she would never want to speak to me again.

I realized I had been standing on the river path for long minutes, just gazing into space and nervously edging the rim of my hat with my fingers. I collected my thoughts and decided I would walk the five miles up to Peaslake and the deep Hurtwood and visit Nance. True, she came by cart once or twice a week to clean and perform laundry tasks for me, but she considered me a little too genteel now to return too often to the farm I owned and in which she lived with her brood.

I needed to walk off my frustration, concern, anger at my own folly and, yes, I suppose I was feeling what the poets called lovesickness. And I wanted a female ear, and Nance's intercession with her kin. To ask her to talk to Tilly, who would introduce me to the mademoiselle, who would welcome the introduction, the attention, my elegant good looks and the yearning in my eyes, and then allow me to escort her to her home, and during this long walk, our souls would commune, and she would declare her love within the hour…Yes, yes, I daydreamed as lovesick fools do.

I walked through the forest, but hardly noticed my surroundings. Despite the cold air, I arrived sweating at Nance's – my inherited farmhouse, although some legal papers still needed lawyering in Guildford. Little Will was not in the yard, but a few of his younger siblings and cousins were scampering about. They greeted me warmly.

Nance immediately came out when she heard the clamour. "Rich, welcome home," she said.

"'Tis your home now, Nance."

"No, thee might tire of living with the nabobs in the valley, and I could always move back into my old den."

"That's a proper public house now, Nance, not full of nippers, but drinkers, making a good profit for you. And you look so content and happy."

"Aye, but like all mothers I'm only as happy as my saddest child."

I looked around at the children laughing and screaming. "Is one of them sickly?"

"Not at all, they are as content as I am. Rich, I knows when thee be beating about the bushes in search of a hare… acting as queer as Dick's hatband.[22] What's stirring thee? I knows a troubled brow when I sees one."

I expected to go into a long careful introduction, but I just blurted out, "I have met a woman I love."

Nance didn't laugh out loud as I had expected. She gently took my arm and led me into the farmhouse, where she offered me some cider. She told her children to play out of doors and gave me her entire attention. She knew that I was a man, and could not listen and talk while children played at her feet.

"What is the lady's name?"

"I do not know."

I waited for a pained expression on her face. None came.

"How long have you known her?"

"A week."

"A week and thee not be knowing what she's called?" Now the pained expression began to show its marks on her forehead.

"I spoke to her only today – for the first time."

"Today?"

And now Nance laughed. Loudly. And so did I.

Seventeen

*N*ance was to make a special trip to see her cousin Tilly who lived in a farm labourer's cottage outside Shere, a little way from the end of Middle Street.

I had begged Nance to be diplomatic. "Fool enough I am about this lady; please don't worsen my plight," I had pleaded.

Nance came back to Gomshall to help with my housekeeping and she informed me, "All had been arranged for the young Mr Romeo."

I entreated her to tell me all the details.

"She doth know her Christian name. 'Tis Cecile. She is a Frenchie. But she knows not her family name."

"And what does she know of her?" I asked with some urgency in my voice.

"That she is an honest woman. Keeps house for a good family up on Albury ridge. She's been worshipping at St James's – regular – for nigh on three years. They do nod and pass the time of day, but that's it, Rich. Says she will – if it be fittin' – attempt to bring you lovebirds together, to shake hands. But don't promise nothin'. Church ain't like a county fair."

"Is Tilly a gossip?"

"No, I says to her, 'Keep this close, and get them pair ashakin' hands and Mister Rich will be presentin' thee with a fine new shawl.' That's fair."

I nodded. "And what are you askin' for, Nance?" I said with a smile on my face.

"Thou knows that, Rich. To find a little bit of happiness for thee. That I wish with all my poor old heart."

I kissed her on the cheek.

Nance carried on with household tasks and put bread in the oven. The whole house soon smelled of warm barm,[23] just how a house should smell in winter. I banked the fire and drew on my pipe. I was beginning to feel half-content.

Now I knew whereabouts Cecile lived – there were only two houses on the ridge where the tally of servants would fit. I would not prejudice my hopes by calling with my wares. I would have to count the days – to be truthful, the hours – until the next Sunday. I did consider attending one of the evensong services in the week. Cecile, though, would be unlikely to be free from her domestic duties to attend church then. I trusted that this godly woman would be there in the congregation the following Sunday.

Nance teased me for my growing apprehension when she paid a visit on the Wednesday to return shirts she had taken home to starch and press.

Despite the muddy tracks, I tried to keep myself busy on Thursday and Friday by riding out to Dorking to visit shopkeepers and a few respectable homes. I knew that some high-born exiles from the revolution had settled in Dorking, including, it was said, the Comte d'Artois himself, a member of the French royal family. I wanted to immerse myself in all things French, and perchance, just perchance, Cecile might have had cause to be connected with them, even possibly pay a visit to one of the households.

My mind was not on my new business. It had been conquered entirely by thoughts of Cecile.

Saturday night I slept as though I were strapped on the lower deck of a man o' war in a storm. My stomach heaved with nervousness. I chided myself that I had fought and killed and yet here I was helpless like a new-born kitten tossed into the sea.

Again, on Sunday morning I could not break my fast, except to drink some water. I put on my Sunday suit, and cape, for my dreams had been of storms and now the heavens had conspired to match my fantasies by bestowing heavy rains. I fretted that Cecile – my Cecile – would not attend in this storm. But, no, I told myself, she was no fair-weather Christian. Together we would brave the storms to meet in St James's church. Climate and mood marched together as I dreaded rejection, and yet I counted every second until I could meet this gift from heaven.

I stopped dead, even in the rain and wind, and told myself, "Control yourself – rein in these wild horses which are running away with your brains, sir."

I looked at my pocket watch, a trinket I had purchased for myself in London, with Solly's advice, and realized that again I would be early. I was sorely tempted to bang on the door of the White Horse and demand a brandy to fortify my sagging constitution. This was a policy of despair and foolishness. I could not meet Cecile smelling of "Jack". Instead, I took shelter under the church porch, shook off the rain from my clothes, brushed down my hat with my sleeve, and hung my wet cape on the wooden pegs to the right of the west door, next to the marble font.

I sat in the same place, to the back and to the right, and again adopted a pose of piety by reading the prayer book that waited on the back table. The verger greeted me as he fussed about his preparations, but otherwise the church was empty. In trying to be inconspicuous this early bird has become a spectacle. Slowly the church filled up.

When it was nearly full and five minutes before the service was to start, I saw her. I had to swallow hard.

She came in from the west door, and I swear I could smell her fragrant entrance – was it jasmine? – even before I saw her.

Sadly, she did not see me, and sat to the left of the main aisle, diagonally across from the section reserved for the Bray family. The lord of the manor and his family always filled their specially carved seats. But, even if Cecile had spotted me, why should she risk scandal by sitting next to me? I had put the prayer book to my left and thus secured a seat which no one had taken up. I picked up the book and soon the seat was taken by a fat rank-smelling labouring fellow, truly a sad substitute for the sweet Cecile.

I scanned the congregation for Tilly, my go-between. I could not see her. When the Reverend began I tried to concentrate on his words, in case I had to debate them later with Cecile. But what niggled me was the non-appearance of Tilly. Perhaps she was late, although I could not see her among those standing against the wall in the back of the church. I started to fret − I could not accost Cecile directly again. She had − quite properly − pointed out my breach of etiquette. I did not take it as a rebuff, especially from a Frenchwoman. They were famed for their style and good manners.

I listened to God's word with half an ear, as the blood pounded in my heart. Where was that damn woman Tilly − what right had she to spoil my life? I checked myself mentally. I had hardly spoken more than a few words to Cecile and yet I was being driven half-mad by my longing for her.

The service finished, and I followed the procession out of the main door. I managed to avoid the Reverend's farewell handshake and I eased out behind the thronging people, who were preparing their outdoor clothing against the rain. Again I positioned myself not too far from the gate onto the square, although my horse-fanciers in grey smocks had abandoned their posts of the previous week. I fumbled with my time-piece as though I were expecting to meet someone other than Cecile. I felt so utterly helpless as I became convinced that Tilly had deserted her mission. I tried to observe both doors, especially the south exit where carts and wagons had been corralled to take the infirm.

Then Cecile was in my sight — yes, it was her, in bonnet, and coat. The Reverend Dunscomble tarried in conversation with her. And I was utterly jealous that he was so privileged, so blessed, to speak to her at his will.

I stood as if chained to the ground as she walked towards the gate where I was standing, just outside the church wall, on the edge of the square. She could not miss me. But I would have to wait for her to speak. Just as she came to the entrance, huddled in the collars of her coat, and when she was about to pass near me, a female voice screeched, "Cecile, wait for me."

I prayed that it was Tilly, but no, no, no — it was a stranger, a woman severely dressed all in black and in her late, and stout, forties.

"Wait for me, please," the woman said breathlessly as she hurried to catch up Cecile on the path through the graveyard. Cecile turned to her right and I was standing like a mute pillar to her left. In the rain, and among the congregation hurrying from the church, my Cecile, distracted, rushed on past me, arm in arm with her female companion. I stood there marooned in an ocean of frustration, still anchored to the ground in utter helplessness and foolishness. And rancid despair.

I wanted to rush after her, to declare my love. I was mad but not yet a complete fool. Instead, I walked slowly towards the White Horse and then waited under the eaves of the overhanging roof of its stables as Cecile charged away from me along the Tillingbourne path. In anger at myself and Tilly, I slipped into the back door of the tavern, a door used only on Sundays, to avoid the criticism of the pious — though a number of my fellow congregants had already taken seats near the bar. I ordered a Jack, slugged it back quickly and, in a foul mood, walked home in the growling storm.

When the storm cleared I intended to ride up to see Nance to find out what had happened to our plot. Not long after the sky had cleared a little, I heard the cart clatter into the yard. Little Will had escorted his mother to tell me her news.

Both sat around the fire which I was trying to start with the bellows. As they began to dry out, Nance told me what had befallen Tilly.

"Rough music – that was the damned cause of it."

"What rough music?" I said, barely hiding my anger.

"Her husband, Malachi, is known for his harsh ways. He'd been warned, though." Nance touched my knee as though she sought confirmation.

"Don't know the damn fellow," I said peevishly.

"Well, he used to beat Tilly, though she never dares utter a peep. But many a time I did see her face all black and blue. Then one night someone laid a chain of chaff from the track up to her cottage door.

"Yes, yes, I know – it means that thrashing be going on there. But why did that detain her from church?"

"Hold thy horses, Mr Impatient. Let me tell thee the story in my own good time."

I got up and poked the fire, to raise some heat; part atonement, because Nance was still shivering from the drowning she got coming down to see me. "Sorry, Nance. I'm severely disappointed at not speaking to my Cecile."

"I knows that, Rich, so let me tell thee what befell my poor cousin... Will, go and see that Diamond is happy in the stable..."

"Aye, and would you be feeding Champion for me?"

Little Will trotted faithfully out to the yard and left Nance and me alone.

"Well, Malachi was furious at the insult to his house and name. But instead of being shamed into better ways, he hit her hard again with her broom as she was sweeping out the yard. But this time the neighbours saw Malachi in the deed. No denying it, now.

"A few days ago, some of the men and boys of Shere went

at night with kettles and pans and fire-irons and gave that damn batterer some rough music. The whole village heard the din, and were all a-chatterin' about poor Tilly."

Nance was into her stride now: "Malachi — damn him — is a stubborn man. I heard on Saturday that Tilly got a big hitting, and her vile husband has kept her indoors. So I guesses that she was too afeared even to venture to the church, perhaps she was too bruised and shamed to even seek the Reverend Dunscombe's sanctuary."

"I'll go and horsewhip that pig Malachi myself. Tell me where he lives!" I stood up as though I would rush out that minute.

Nance was alarmed. "No, Rich, thee don't want to be in a scandal, now that thou be livin' as a gentleman, and tryin' to court a lady. Tilly has kin, some of our people in the Hurtwood. They'll be payin' court to Malachi, but it won't be bowing' and scrapin' and lovebirds' bundling. He'll be getting more than music, I'll warrant."

I sat down in my rush chair, feeling defeated. "How long will she be jailed in her own home?"

"God only knows the answer to that, albeit I can visit my kin when Malachi is at work. She needs some comfort. As do thee, Rich."

She got up and touched me on the shoulder.

"And there's thee ponderin' on courtship — and that leads often to wedlock — and poor Tilly be chained to that beast in a loveless union. Thou knows the saying: love be blind, but marriage be verily an eye-opener. Maybe worse is not getting married, especially if a child is on the way. How does it go? 'Married on the carpet and banns go up the chimney.' And me? I loved my husband, but God took him away from me so early…"

It was now my turn to try to comfort Nance. I offered her some of my best tea, and not a bit was adulterated with rose leaves.

When it was brewed and she started to sip, her countenance brightened. "So what is the next scheme we can be devising?" she said.

"I have two choices, Nance. Either I try to see Cecile by calling with my trade or I just wait and hope that she will speak to me outside church – if there's no storm and if she thinks it fitting that we speak without the formalities...so many damn ifs."

"Go up and see her, man. Thou wuz once a bold free-trader. Go and be a bold honest trader."

"Aye, my boldness might make her disdain me, but I will abide by your female judgement, Nance. Thank'ee for coming in the storm. There's some cold beef so Little Will and you must eat here."

"Aye, I'll be doing that for you."

"No, Nance, you're always fussing after me. My turn."

"Well and good. I'll sit back like Lady Bountiful and enjoy another cup of tea. China cups these are. Better than the old mugs, eh? Or perhaps thee be tied to bachelor ways. Perhaps it's too late for Cecile to save thee?"

I laughed and threw a napkin over her head.

"No more chattering away like a magpie, woman, or I'll be asking that beast Malachi to visit thee."

"And we'll be bangin' kettles at thy door, Mr Durrant. And then there'll be no Mrs Durrant teaching thee how to be a Frenchie."

"Away with you, Nance. It's just a proper introduction I'm after."

"Ah, Rich, know thyself...I see something strong in that heart of your'n. There's destiny afoot here."

I looked at her and did not want to gainsay her with whimsy or mock admonitions. I wanted it to be true.

"Remember, I do have the sight, as did my mother and her mother too. Some things are meant to be," Nance said. I'd never seen her look so serious.

"Nance, I'm not given to these things. I believe we can make things happen… if God wills it."

"Aye, but maybe God plans it thus. But give the Almighty a helping hand. Christmas is nigh on us, go up to Albury and see if that household be wantin' some lace trifles for the festivities."

I had thought little of Christmas. "It's not a time to be alone, is it?"

Eighteen

It was a truly chilly December morning. The mist was slow in leaving the bottom of the valley, as shafts of brownish-yellow light cut through the dank air. It would be months before the nightingales sang to greet the warmth of the sun. In my valley they were to be heard earlier, and later, in the year than in any other part of England. Now, however, the sodden ground of the previous day had been frozen by the frost and I pondered whether to saddle up Champion for the journey to Albury, about three miles away. I wanted to cut a dash for Cecile, but it was not good practice to trade from such a fine horse. My customers would wonder at the prices I charged to be able to afford such a fine mount. To hell with it, I decided: I would play the gentleman.

I brushed Champion down, saddled him and then washed the smell of horse from my hands. It was not fitting to wear my Sunday best for trade, but I donned my second best and put on my best shirt and cravat. Nance would have scolded me for mixing my apparel, but I fiddled in the mirror and brushed my hair twice and wondered whether I should ask her to trim my hair soon. I thought of the powdered wigs worn by many in London, and was glad that it was not the custom in the country, at least for us more ordinary folk. I detested the things. Perhaps if I were bald. But I had a good strong head of brown hair, just greying a little at the temples. And I had most of my teeth left. I prayed that Cecile would not think me a grotesque. I was a healthy man just in to my forties, and I believed that Cecile was not too much my junior, perhaps ten years or so. Not too big a difference, I hoped.

So it was time for my adventure. Champion and I trotted out at eleven a.m. according to my watch. I crossed the small packhorse bridge and then travelled along the southern river track most of the way, until I had to take a small detour around the Duke's land and then into Albury. I rode up the ridge to the left of the river and on to the grand houses just short of the Chilworth paper mill. Two Palladian-style homes had been built here, not long after the American war. Rumour had it that they were constructed by two loyalist brothers who had fled the revolution against the King and settled in Surrey. They must have left with buckets of sovereigns for most of the land was held by the Duke in these parts and few would build such a home without purchasing the freehold – at a large price.

I rode up the grand drive of the first mansion, which said Virginia Lodge on a board at the entrance. I dismounted and enquired of a gardener where the tradesman's entrance was. He asked my business and, upon showing him some of my samples in my two saddle bags, he led me to the rear of the house. I tied my horse to a rail, and waited as the gardener sought the housekeeper.

Would it be her, I wondered. Would she think me dangerously bold or perhaps consider it a charming coincidence?

I waited for five minutes or more.

Then the door opened just a few inches.

"What be thy trade, sir?" It was the voice of an ancient woman.

"Madam, I am trading in fine goods – silks, linen and wool shawls. Some finished goods – lace handkerchiefs, and sample rolls of cloth." I added, "Some from France, Madam." I trusted that she might seek the advice of a Frenchwoman, if Cecile worked in this house.

"What is thy name and trading house?"

"Madam, I am called Richard Durrant and I am newly appointed as a single trader. I live in Gomshall and trade in Guildford, Dorking and London."

"Then for such a travelling man, it will be no trouble to thyself to return tomorrow at the same hour. I will speak to the lady of the house. Yes?"

"Yes, thank'ee, Madam. I will return tomorrow and wait on you then. Good morning to you."

I cursed as I led Champion to the edge of the drive and felt so dejected that I used the convenient mounting block to bestride my horse. All the spirit had fled my body. I almost decided to return home.

No, I would try the neighbouring mansion. I felt angry that I had not asked the cantankerous old crow in the last house as to the name of the owner of the nearby dwelling.

At the gate on to the roadway, the gardener was waiting to make sure I left the premises properly.

"Sir, who be the master of that fine house there?" I pointed.

"It is the brother of the master of this house, but they don't speak…not since they left America these fifteen long years."

"And the name of these brothers, sir?"

"Cruikshank. And thee be riding a fine horse, sir."

"Thank'ee on both scores. Good day to you."

I trotted the few hundred yards and dismounted at the open gate.

I led my horse up the wide path to the house and waited for a servant to attend. None did so, and I made my way to the side, whereupon a rather flustered and dishevelled manservant rushed out to greet me.

"You'll be wanting Mr Cruikshank, but you have come to the servants' entry."

"Good morning, I am not attending Mr Cruikshank. I am a humble tradesman…"

"…With such a fine horse. Your trade must be a good one, sir."

"It is a new trade, Mr…er?"

"Jonathan Duggan I am."

"And you, sir?"

"Richard Durrant, a trader in silks, fine woollens and lace and suchlike."

"Have ye come by appointment?"

"No, Mr Duggan, but I should like to arrange such an appointment."

"Ah, stuff and poppycock, man. No fiddle faddle here. Tie up your horse, and come into our back parlour. I will summon the female servants who may decide to call the lady of the house."

"Mrs Cruikshank?"

"Aye, she's the one. Do ye know her?"

"No, but I visited her brother-in-law's home within this hour and so learned the name."

He tapped his nose. "Best not speak of a visit there. The Cruikshanks are not what ye might call a close family."

I had tied up Champion in an enclosed yard leading into the stable area, and Mr Duggan kindly ushered me into his parlour.

My arrival had caused a stir for a stout middle-aged lady wearing a very severe white cap tied very closely under her chin. Mr Duggan introduced Mrs Smith to me.

"Sir, Sir, we'll not be getting too many tradesmen here," she said. "Welcome, ah, but I am running away with meself. Would ye take some tea, sir? We even 'ave some coffee in this back parlour of ours. Coffee, sir?"

"Tea or coffee would be most kind, Madam."

She was still flustered. "Oh, please excuse me manners, sir. I am most perturbed…ah, sit down."

Mr Duggan finally took command. "Mr Durrant is a trader in silks and the like. I have invited him in to show us his wares."

I took my cue. "And to any other ladies of the house."

"Ah, the lady of the house don't come in here very often. But we have a cook and a maid, and of course Cecile."

My eyes almost rocketed out of their sockets.

"Do you know her, sir?" Mr Duggan enquired.

I coughed as I prepared to dissemble. "I am unsure, Mr Duggan. I have a cousin Celia, and a friend with a similar name in London, but…"

"I shall call them, while Mrs Smith summons her coven."

The housekeeper gave Mr Duggan a sharp look.

"My little joke, Mr Durrant. No offence meant. And they don't burn witches in these parts no more."

"No, sir." I had no idea where this was leading.

A young red-haired girl with freckles, about seventeen, rushed into the parlour, and stopped when she saw me.

Mr Duggan reproached her: "Don't run around as though thou wast at a fair."

"Sorry, sir."

I thought: he must say that a dozen times a week.

Then a woman backed into the parlour carrying a tray of china. A she turned to put it down on the white scrubbed table, she looked up and saw me… and dropped the tray.

Luckily, it was only an inch off the table.

It was her – Cecile. Thank God. At least she had remembered me.

I pretended to be startled by the crashing of the tray rather than her arrival.

Mrs Smith had witnessed the commotion from the door-way.

"Are you two acquainted?" she asked.

I had to say something quickly before all this became a Punch and Judy show. I said boldly, "I have seen the lady in church, but I have not been introduced."

Mr Duggan took charge again – God bless him. "Cecile Leclerc, this is Mr Durrant."

It was good that he had been proper in using both our surnames.

I shook hands, gave a slight bow, and she curtsied with a just a hint of an embarrassed smile on her face.

I had also to be gallant to the scolded maid. "And who is this young lady?"

"And this is Janey," Mr Duggan said politely.

I shook hands, bowed a little again as she curtsied with an obviously excited flourish.

"Well, well, all the formalities done. May we see the samples you are carrying, Mr Durrant?" Mr Duggan said.

"Yes, yes," Mrs Smith said with excitement in her voice.

"But I forget, let Mr Durrant have his coffee first," Mr Duggan countermanded.

So we all sat drinking coffee, except for Janey who waited upon us. We sat politely and stiffly discussing the weather while I tried desperately not to look at Cecile. I was waiting for her to speak so I could look at her without creating suspicion.

Finally, after a few minutes of small talk, Mrs Smith could contain herself no longer.

"Sir, let us now behold the frankincense and myrrh...and what was the other?"

Cecile spoke for the first time: "Gold."

I looked into her eyes and it truly was a golden moment. I noticed for the first time – but how could I have missed it? – that she had one brown eye and one green, set in a serene face of olive complexion. Compared with the wan winter faces of the others in the parlour, she radiated an exotic and healthy otherness.

We both stared into each other's eyes for what seemed minutes, but must have been seconds. Though Mr Duggan, I perceived, felt that he had to harrumph and say, "Now then no gold from one of our three kings, but silk I trust."

I unfolded my wares from the saddle-bags and laid them carefully on the table. The women cooed and chattered over the silks and shawls, while I was asked to join Mr Duggan in a pipe by the small iron wood-stove.

Mr Duggan talked horses and hunting, while I tried occasionally to steal a surreptitious glance at Cecile.

I noticed that she was carefully perusing a pure silk handkerchief.

"That is from France, no?" she asked rather quietly.

"Yes, Mademoiselle," I said, although I desperately wanted to address her as "Cecile". That would have been a faux pas. "I traded it in London, but it came from Paris."

"It is beautiful. May I ask the price, Mr Durrant?"

The way she pronounced my name — the sensual roll of the r's — sent shivers down my neck.

I wanted to say, "You can have all in my bags for free...and indeed all I possess. Please take my horse, my farm...anything to be alone with you..."

"Ah, Mademoiselle Cecile, for you, it is but three pence."

The ladies looked at me as though I were mad.

"But, sir, that price is far too low. I know how much such a silk handkerchief would cost in Guildford."

"Mademoiselle, it is Christmas soon and a time to thank God for his gifts to us poor pilgrims on this earth." I heard myself saying this, and thinking – Rich, don't overdo the piety.

I knew that Mrs Smith would pounce. "And this shawl, Mr Durrant?"

It would have been more than the real price of the handkerchief but I still cut the price drastically. I wanted to be invited back again and again even if it bankrupted me.

"Mrs Smith, as a thank you for your kind hospitality, it will be specially for you but one shilling and six pence."

"That's more than fair, sir. Yes, I will have it."

Mr Duggan obviously thought I was mad.

"Have ye any gifts for us gentlemen?"

"Yes, sir, I have some pocket knives of excellent quality." I fished them out of the side-pockets of the saddle-bags.

"The small one with the fine pearl handle is – for you, sir – but one shilling and three pence, and the bigger one, because it is rougher, is but one shilling.

"And I am happy to leave the goods with you on approval, if it be better that ye all pay me next month. It would be a pleasure to return to such a hospitable household. And perhaps the lady of the house may wish to see some of my other goods when I return, if an appointment be made."

I was trying to disguise my largesse with a suggestion that method lurked in my madness, although mad with love I truly was. And now, oh thank you God, I could speak to her in and outside church…unless she reproached me for my calling. I could not lie and say it was all by chance. But she seemed not displeased by the visit.

Cecile insisted on paying her three pence, and Mr Duggan and Mrs Smith paid me half and promised that I could return in the first week after Christmas, when they would pay me the remaining debt and perhaps Mrs Cruikshank – "if she be herself, she is a delicate woman, and often retired to her bed" – would also join us.

To avoid leaving Janey out of the proceedings, I gave her a small cloth which she could use to embroider a sampler. She rushed up and kissed me on the cheek. Such was the general merriment that Mr Duggan did not scold her, but laughed instead.

I made to pack up my goods, and Mr Duggan said, "You are welcome here. When ye come on the Wednesday after the mass of Christ then there will be a Jack for the cold. I hope that will not offend you, sir?"

I was Mr Pious again. "Sir, I do drink but seldom and that seldom is around the festivities. Thank you, I will join you then in a brandy."

I thanked and bowed to the ladies. Cecile's eyes caught

mine. I could not but marvel again at her green and brown eyes.

"And Cecile Leclerc, I trust I will see you in St James's soon," I said with more confidence than I felt inside.

"Yes, Mr Durrant, I attend every Sunday."

She did not stress the "I", although I deserved such a rebuff for my mock piety. But I would have become a Mussulman for her.

Mr Duggan led me out and shook my hand warmly, while laying his great hand on my left shoulder.

A flurry of snow began to fall from the dark sky.

"Best be home soonest, Mr Durrant. This'll be a big snowfall, I knows it."

I thanked him again as I mounted Champion with an athletic swing of my legs and rode off with a wave, feeling as though I were reborn, as though my whole life on this earth had been destined for this past hour and communion with this wonderful woman, created by God just for me.

Nineteen

The next day I had to return to Cecile's neighbouring house to keep the appointment I had made with the old crow. I walked my horse slowly past Cecile's employer's home in the hope that perchance she would be in the garden, but it was cold and small snow-drifts had formed around the bases of the trees. I ached to call in again on that warm, friendly, topsy-turvy parlour as though they had become kin. It would not have been right. With heavy heart I walked past and made my way to the adjacent house. The crone greeted me slightly more warmly and ushered me in to her cold back kitchen. Perhaps because my heart was not in the trade that day, she gave my goods a perfunctory examination and sent me on my way. I cared nought. I was glad to be out of that house and walking as slowly as I decently could past the gateway of Cecile's employment. Then Champion led me home at a trot for most of the valley track.

I counted the days and hours to the next Sunday's service. I had told Nance of my progress and she insisted on making the journey early on Sunday morning to ensure that I was correctly attired.

I asked after Tilly.

Nance said, "Rough music failed, so a few of the Peaslake men – including Black Harry – went down to teach some decent manners. From what I be hearin', Black Harry told Tilly's ole man that he won't be walking agin if he as much as laid a little finger on Tilly. Her bruisin' is down and she may be going to church today."

"Then I will be thanking her myself – for trying anyways."

"Agh, thee'll be too busy with eyes bulgin' for Cecile."

"Why don't you come with me, Nance?"

"Nincompoop, I'm not dressed for church. And, besides, we don't want too many sudden converts like thyself. There must some wicked uns left up in the woods."

I had to laugh.

"Thee be dressed proper, even the hair will pass for a gen'leman's – thanks to my barbering."

"Thank'ee, Nance. Where would I be without you?"

"Well, thee won't be needin' this silly woman when Cecile becomes captain of this household."

"Don't be running in front of the hares, Nance. I hardly know her, remember."

"As I said, Rich, I knows this be serious. I sense it strong-like."

"Get away with you, and your forest ways and pagan lore."

"Don't scorn it. There are strange powers which we must not mock.

Especially today, when thee be needin' all that the gods might bring – pagan or our Christian Lord. And make the most of it – remember: the living be only on holiday from the dead." And Nance crossed herself – I had never seen her do that before.

"Right, Rich, thee must be away thyself. I will wait and do some of the chores. Us sinners can work on the Sabbath."

"You are still captain of my fate – or at least my house, Nance." I gave her a playful kiss on the cheek. And she blushed – again, I had never seen her do that before. There's no accounting for women's ways, I thought, but was wise enough not to say so aloud.

It was cold, but not raining so I decided to take my cart that Nance and Little Will seemed to use more than I did. I didn't like putting Champion in the shafts of the cart, but perhaps I could persuade Cecile to let me take her home.

I left the cart along the south wall where some of the village lads would charge a farthing or even a half-penny to tend to the horses, carts and carriages of the congregation. I told one of the urchins that Champion would whisper in my ear if he had not been cared for well. A clout or a half-penny would depend upon Champion's judgement. I gave the lad some dried oats to encourage Champion's opinion of him. I noticed that the lad, who thought me out of sight, nibbled on some of the grain himself. In my infatuation with Cecile, and my new wealth, I had not noticed the winter hunger that embraced the poor of my own valley. I felt ashamed, and selfish.

So, as I went into the main west door of St James's, a little penitence touched on my excitement at the thought of seeing my beloved Cecile.

I was not so early and a few members of the congregation were already seated. I sat to the left this time, in roughly the same place as I had last seen Cecile take her place.

And she came within the minute. Alas, she sat a little behind me, as I discerned when I risked turning around as the procession followed the vicar into the body of the church. I hardly took in a word of the service, although I felt strangely elated by the hymns; I was too embroiled in my own passions to do much more than mumble to myself as the congregation stood in praise to sing of the passions of the Christ.

When the service finally ended, I was eager to be outside the church before Cecile, but I was blocked by an aged farmer shuffling by inches on two walking sticks. I saw Cecile move ahead down the aisle and to the door. I tried to catch her in the throng, but then the Reverend Dunscombe had seized my hand and was welcoming me again. I managed to extricate myself, perhaps a little too brusquely, and reached the outer porch though I could not see her black bonnet anywhere. I prepared to hasten to the front gate of the churchyard, but I unconsciously turned to my left to ensure that Champion was still there.

I beheld a miracle: Cecile was talking to the urchin and stroking my horse's neck.

I was by her side in the flicker of an eyelid.

"Mademoiselle, so wonderful to see you," I said, as I doffed my hat. "And, see, Champion likes you too." The horse was nuzzling her shoulder as she turned to me and neglected him.

"Ah, Champion," – she pronounced it almost like "champagne" – "that is the name of your horse."

"Did you know it was mine?"

"But who could forget such a horse? ...Mr Duggan spoke of you and the horse for days."

"How is Mr Duggan?"

"He is well, Mr Durrant, and looking forward to when you wait on us again."

I wanted to say, "And do you feel the same?" but that would have been too bold.

I paid off the young lad – with a penny, enough to provide a little food.

He thanked me and ran off to join the other boys.

"Mademoiselle, may I take you home in my cart? The ground is rough with frost and snow."

"*Merci*, Mr Durrant, thank'ee, but I need to walk on the footpath to the church close by in Albury to meet Mrs Smith, who worships there."

"May I walk thus far with you? ...We have been introduced, have we not?"

"Yes, sir, but you be hardly known to me."

"It is a short walk but through the woods, and there may be brigands aplenty," I pressed, and with a firm smile.

I gazed at her lovely lowered face as doubt and perhaps fear flashed across her eyes. She frowned and then smiled too, with a little curtsey.

"Thank'ee, sir. I will accept the kind offer."

I hailed the same young lad and offered him a bonus if he would guard my horse and cart.

"Please do not think me – is aloof the right word?" She said it like it was "aluf".

"No, I understand." Although I could not then comprehend how much courage it had taken to accept my company. The reticence, I realised, was more than just shyness or perhaps decorum.

"Perhaps you do not. I lead a very quiet life. I 'ave nothing beyond my work and church."

"No kin?"

She hesitated to reply. "I did not mean to intrude on your privacy, Miss Leclerc."

Cecile still seemed reluctant to speak.

"Shall we walk then to Albury?" I wanted to give her my arm, but I refrained.

We started to walk and so many questions jostled in my head. I wanted to ask the safe ones first. "How long have you been in the household of Mr Cruikshank?"

"Oh, it is more than three years now."

"So what are your duties?"

"I suppose I am a senior maid, but I am not treated as a servant. I act partly as a 'ousekeeper, Mrs Smith is more the cook, but I 'elp her too. I also teach 'enry, Mrs Cruikshank's son, a little French when he is not away at school. They are all very kind to me."

"Yes, I knew it was a kind household by the way I was accepted into the parlour. And you are from France?"

"Of course, and proud of eet, but the Frenchies, as the English call them, are not so popular here."

I nodded. "Yes, these are bad times for our two countries.

True, a few British disdain the French, sadly, but many supported the storming of the Bastille and the call for liberty for all citizens, and certainly all my countrymen ape their fashions. If I may be so bold, I admire much about the French, and would like to learn more of the country. And where are you from in France?"

"My family came from the south, not too far from the Alps."

"And – may I ask – why leave the country of your birth?"

"I am Protestant, sir, and France is a Catholic country."

I did not want to press her. She seemed reluctant to reveal more of herself.

So I told her that I was treated a little like a foreigner, even though I had family roots in the Hurtwood, but I also had lived in London.

"You cannot be a foreigner in your own country," she said.

"Every village in these parts is a like a foreign country – not least to someone born in the next village."

"It is the same in France – in the countryside."

"Then we are both outsiders in a way," I suggested.

"Per'aps," she conceded. "I feel that you are right on that... I do not know many men, but you are different from any I have met. Oh, pardon, Mr Durrant, I do not wish to be...unbecoming."

"No, no...Thank'ee, Miss Leclerc, it is a very pleasing sentiment."

"Maybe it sounds as if I am a *paysanne*" – she pronounced it in the French way – "but I do not spend my free time with any gentlemen not of my household, so I am not, er, practised in these ways."

"Whatever your past...I feel welcome in your company... so thank'ee."

"Tell me, please, more of your business."

I tried to tell her of my past, while avoiding any direct mention of my smuggling days, though most in these parts would take it is as an honest calling.

"And, sir, you have some French?"

"Aye, some words, from my trading, but I would be mighty willing to improve my knowledge of the language," I said very obviously, before I could check myself.

All too soon I saw the Albury church rushing upon us. I wanted to say so many things, offer so many invitations, ask whether she had any free days over the coming festivities. I could see Mrs Smith standing there waving. All I could manage was: "Will you be attending the special Christmas mass five days hence?"

"I will, if I have not extra duties in the house, but if I cannot – you will be attending the 'ouse with more wares the week after Christmas, no?"

"Wild horses would not prevent me."

"Ah, but your horse seems so gentle." And she laughed. And I looked into her green and brown eyes and I knew I loved her beyond all earthly measure.

We shook hands and she sailed across the crisp frosty meadow to meet Mrs Smith.

I stood and watched as they greeted each other, and both turned and waved. I stood and stared until they were out of sight. I knew my life was about to change for ever.

Twenty

*N*ance was working in the back kitchen, preparing a meal for me.

"So all went well," she said all smiles.

"How can you tell, Nance?"

"Thy face is gleamin' like an angel's. Come on, sit by the fire and tell me all."

I did, and she sat there all attentive as though sitting at her grandmother's knee.

We ate well and she left soon afterwards to return to her brood.

And then I felt so alone, as though I were the only person on this planet. All I wanted was Cecile with me by "our" fireside.

There and then I determined that I would make this woman my wife.

But, alas, she did not attend the Christmas mass, and it nearly broke my heart. I almost went up to Reverend Dunscombe to shake him by the neck and shout, "Why didn't you command Cecile to come?"

Nance and her family helped to fill my empty Christmas as I waited out each of those five long days to return at Mr Duggan's request.

My visit, though, was a great success. They paid the money

owed, though I cared not a jot for business. We drank a little brandy. And we all laughed – Mr Duggan, Mrs Smith, Jane, Cecile and me. But, oh, how I wished Cecile and I could be alone. Cecile did at least mention that her household duties had prevented her from going to the Christmas mass.

Mr Duggan insisted that I return in a month to show my wares to the lady of the house. An appointment was made. But all I could think of was how I could convert the next Sunday's church service into a proper meeting with Cecile.

Thus it was that I attended every Sunday service for the next three months. Although she sat next to me only once, I was always allowed to walk her at least to Albury church, and on two occasions in inclement weather – when Mrs Smith was indisposed and did not leave the house – to take Cecile all the way to the Cruikshank household in my cart. I wanted to protect her day and night but I could see her but occasionally. I would have hired, or bought, a splendid carriage for her, or sported the sharpest sword to guard her, and even pray hourly that not a drop of rain should fall on her.

Cecile laughed at me when I said I would buy a new covered carriage for her. "Your cart is fit for a princess," she said.

But she did, reluctantly and of course gracefully, accept the fashionable oiled silk umbrella I bought for her in Guildford. She would not hear of my ordering her a new cape for the rains.

Cautiously, and with due gallantry, I did request that she visited my home on her half-day off duty, but she politely but firmly said that it was not right to visit my home unescorted. And, of course, I suggested she visited with Mrs Smith as chaperone. I did briefly make the same suggestion on the following visit to see them, but Mrs Cruikshank was in the parlour and it was not possible to discuss personal arrangements properly.

The talk was all of the cradle that had been given to the youngest member of the family. It had a clockwork rocking mechanism that would work for forty-three minutes. Ms Cruikshank proudly displayed the invention. But, to me, Cecile was far more fascinating than anything made by man. God had created this woman, just for me.

We did manage to spend one half-day together when I was invited to join her, along of course with Mrs Smith and Mr Duggan, on a rare visit to market day in Guildford. Despite the mud, it was a great success. We all enjoyed the brightly painted farm wagons with their well-groomed teams of horses. The carters competed in the dressing of the horses, because the brightly polished brass ornaments and the rosettes of worsted ribbon belonged to the carters, even if the horses did not. Foremost among the ornaments were the ear bells – the bells could be useful to give an early warning if other carts were travelling along narrow lanes. Or if you were walking and caught unawares. Being flattened by a cart-horse had befallen one of my free-traders who was very hard of hearing. The bells had bright plumes of black or red or yellow horsehair that followed the top strap of the headstall and buckled in just above the blinker. The face-pieces were designed in a great variety of patterns. Some had a raised crescent shape to look like Babylonian war horses. Other parts of the harness were decorated with small round brass studs and heart-shaped brasses, which were often arranged as trophies over cottage fireplaces when not on the horses.

Like me, Cecile loved horses. She also enjoyed the musical bands of the local guilds, as well as all the little market stalls. I tried hard to persuade her and Mrs Smith to let me buy them some costume jewellery, but I could induce them to each accept only an inexpensive gilded brooch in the shape of a butterfly. Our companions allowed us some freedom to talk together, but we had never been alone.

On another occasion, Mr Duggan had asked me to

accompany him to Guildford again but with him alone. In front of the ladies, he was a little vague about the purpose but any chance to visit their parlour was gratefully seized. Any chance to get closer to an important man in Cecile's household. And any, any, any opportunity to see a little more of my beloved.

I did see Cecile in the parlour for a few minutes and then Mr Duggan was dragging me to accompany him in my cart on that Saturday afternoon. I think he wanted to become better acquainted with me personally but I suspect he also wanted a partner in crime to attend the cock-pit he led me to. It was opposite the Angel Hotel in the High Street. I thought it rather a low place, but I did not reveal my true feelings to my guide. It was a circular room, with rows gradually rising, all covered with rough matting. In the centre was a pit. The cocks were well-dressed with silver heels. They often fought with surprising bitterness and determination. A few were quickly dispatched, but others fought on for half an hour. The general uproar and the noise of the betting were overwhelming. Much money circulated from hand to hand. A man who appeared from his comments to be a regular gambler had sat next to me. He asked which cock I fancied in one tournament.

I said, "Sir, I know nothing of the matter."

"Sir, I do, but you have as good a chance as anybody."

Mr Duggan laid out a small wager, but I refused politely claiming ignorance of the sport.

Mr Duggan and I also partook of some rough ale and good conversation between the fighting bouts. He was a kindly man, it seemed to me, but I could see no pity in his face, nor of any of the audience, as the creatures were mangled and torn in a most desperate manner.

Luckily, we had arrived late and so missed part of the event, for which I was grateful. Mr Duggan was obviously struck with me, which would help in my courtship. No ladies would have been invited, so Cecile was spared the cruelty, but I would ensure that she understood – without slighting Mr Duggan – that cock fighting was not an entertainment I sought willingly. And yet as a reward perhaps for my endeavours, I had the joyous experience of seeing Cecile when I returned Mr Duggan, safe and sober, to their household. We spent about half an hour in the kitchen together, and even – for a few brief minutes – we were alone.

So, over the weeks, I learned much about Cecile. Her family had been forced to flee France ten years before because of the religious abuse they had endured for far too long. They had to suffer for their Protestantism in an angry sea of Catholicism. Her parents had settled in London, but had since died, though she did have an aunt who lived just across the river from Southwark – which of course germinated a seed in my fevered brain. I was planning to return to visit Solly some time in the spring.

I could not resist saying. "I have to return for business soon in London. It would give me the utmost pleasure to escort you on your mission. Together, we will find your aunt and ensure that she is safe. And once we have ensured that, we could take a promenade along the Strand and perhaps, if it is your wish, attend the theatre performance of your choice, Mademoiselle." And I offered a deep bow. "With your aunt," I added with due politesse.

The daffodils had come out late and it was already the middle of March before they fully adorned the banks above the Tillingbourne. It was a sunny early spring day as we – Cecile and I – walked along the river-bank. No matter how slowly we walked, it was difficult to make the journey from St James's to the Albury parish church last more than twenty minutes. Nor would she allow me to escort her in the initial journey to either church; she implied that it was not yet fitting. I had to be patient with escorting her on her homeward journey, as though to an outside observer it were almost by chance.

I raised the question again of my escorting her to her aunt's.

"I have written to my aunt, but she does not reply," Cecile said.

"Perhaps we should lodge, separately, at a coaching inn in Southwark and I could help you find your aunt's address."

"Per'aps. But I will confess to you, Rich," – it had taken some two months for her to call me by my first name – "London frightens me."

"Why? It is a fine city, and I will protect you."

"I know you will, but I cannot say what grips my heart when I think of London."

"Perhaps you will tell the whole story – one day."

"I would like to, when I know you better. It is a sad story," she said sighing.

I did not want to press her. "So, let's think of a journey together. And the permission from the Cruikshank household for some free days to visit your sick aunt."

"Ah, but I do not know she is ill."

"She has not replied to the letters, so there must be something amiss, surely?"

"I hope she is still alive."

"Cecile, this is serious talk. Let's also hope that we may attend the theatre. I'm told that the whole of the city has seen the comedy *The Provoked Husband*."

"That would be wonderful; I have not been to the theatre since I was in France. Thank'ee Rich. There is some hope again in my life, since I met you."

"And may I say that you have done the same for me."

She took her arm from mine, as she always did, when we came in sight of Albury church and Mrs Smith.

I kissed her hand and bowed and she laughed as she ran off across the meadow to greet her friend.

In Gomshall, Nance was waiting for me, although I had not expected a visit from her. She dramatically presented me with a letter.

"From London," she said gravely.

"And how did you come by this, Nance?" I said a little suspiciously.

"The post brought it to the White Horse, but no official, as thee knows, will come up into the Hurtwood. James Cooper brought it to the New Inn up in Ewhurst and I sent Little Will up there."

"I trust that none of them busybodies has secretly read this."

"It is unopened, Rich. What troubles thee?"

"I know it to be bad news."

"Then read it, man."

A letter was a rare event in these parts, and Nance sat down on the bench and waited for me.

It was no use my trying to get rid of her. I had to read the damn letter there and then.

It was from Tamar. It said:

Dear Rich

I am sorry to write to you with bad news. Papa is ill and keeps asking for you. He has a fever and has been leeched well, but he is declining. Some moments he is sensible and talks to us, but at others he speaks in Yiddish or German about living in the old country. It would please Mama, I know, and me, if you could return to see him, at your earliest convenience. My father wants to complete his business with you, and say goodbye to you.

I trust that all is well with you.

Affectionately,
Tamar

Then I read the letter aloud to Nance. She could not even write her name, let alone read a letter.

"Thou must be off soonest, Rich. Solly was kind to thee as a lad. And it might be good to be away from here."

"Why, Nance?"

"I saw that albino again, the man whom I called a ghost. But I did see him in the light this time. Albino he certainly is, pale, pale, and his hood up over his head. I knows they don't like the light. And his strange rolling eyes."

"What did he want? Did you speak to him? Get his name?"

"No, Black Harry came to my front room, where some of the others were drinking. He passed the time of day with me, and then went out, and I chanced to go to the door, and I saw him greeting the albino, a little ways off, on the track to Ewhurst.

"I senses trouble there, Rich. I knows thee don't trust Black Harry, nor do I."

"So Harry speaks to an albino, that counts as no sin," I said confidently, but shared Nance's misgivings. I put them aside because I was intent on visiting Cecile as soon as I could. I could not wait another week before church. Solly might be dead by then. This was the time to visit London, and – I prayed – the chance for Cecile to come with me. Selfishly, I wanted to kill two birds with one stone.

Nance cautioned me not to be too hasty about calling on Cecile, but I would have none of it. I saddled up Champion and rode to the Cruikshank house.

Mr Duggan seemed pleased, although a little perturbed when I knocked on the parlour door. "Come in, Mr Durrant. We wuz not expectin' you, but come in and take some tea. Warm yourself by the fire there."

I was direct. "I am not trading today. And I apologize for

this intrusion, but I have an urgent summons to London to see a sick friend. A man who is like my father. I wanted to speak to you and Cecile – I understand she is planning to visit her aunt – as to whether it may be an appropriate time to be allowed to escort her to town and back."

"Yes, Mr Durrant, Cecile mentioned her request, but I know not whether this has been granted by Mrs Cruikshank. Let me find Cecile. Mrs Smith is out on some errand. I shall ask Janey to make some tea."

Janey appeared as if by magic and seemed very flustered at being left alone in the parlour with me. I struggled to make conversation with the shy young thing.

After a few minutes Cecile appeared, somewhat embarrassed, at the door.

"Mr Duggan has explained your visit."

"I apologize for my sudden arrival, Miss LeClerc" – I assumed the polite form of address – "but Solly, whom I have told you of, sent a letter – or a letter from his daughter, telling me he is dying and wishes to speak to me before he passes on. We also have some business to complete…I presume to offer my services as an escort, if you should be planning that visit to London."

"This is sudden, Mr Durrant. Mrs Cruikshank has not yet given me leave.

When are you planning to go?"

"Well, I should go on the morrow, by coach from Godalming or Ripley, but I will wait a day or two if you should wish for company on the journey. Company I should enjoy, of course."

"I will speak to Mrs Cruikshank today and send George the gardener with a message tomorrow," Cecile said decisively.

I could see she wanted to come with me, and that she sensed my alarm about dear Solly.

Mr Duggan rejoined us, and we briefly discussed coaching times and routes.

"I would much prefer to travel to London accompanied," Cecile said.

"Ah, I think that is a good scheme. Mr Durrant is a stout fellow." Mr Duggan slapped me on my back in an approving way.

I quickly drank the tea that Janey put on the scrubbed table, and took my leave.

Both Mr Duggan and Cecile waved me off enthusiastically, as though I were going to the colonies, not nearby Gomshall.

Nance, of course, was waiting for my news. I told her my story and she said, "It all depends on this George. Did thou leave him some coin to speed him on his way?"

"No, never met the fellow."

"Well, Rich, prepare for the journey – I have folded some shirts.

Will thou be needing Little Will to take thee in the cart?"

"No, Nance. I expect to be absent only three days. I'll stable the horse in Godalming."

⋘∞⋙

I sat in the King's Head in Godalming on the next Wednesday. It was eleven o'clock in the morning and I had stabled Diamond, and the cart was allowed to be left in the farrier's yard at the rear of the public house. I was very agitated.

From George the gardener's message it had been agreed that Cecile's duties would allow her liberty until Saturday evening when guests were dining in the house. Mrs Cruikshank had decided that, although she accepted Mr Duggan's recommendation that I was a gentleman suitable to escort Cecile, and that some time was spent discussing where Cecile should stay if she should not find her aunt, it was not suitable, said Mrs Cruikshank, that I should be seen to escort a single woman, without supervision, from the house. Despite their time in America, the Cruikshanks appeared eager to follow the stifling codes of English manners. Mr Duggan volunteered to take Cecile in the ancient Cruikshank carriage to Godalming, where he would hand over his charge to me, away from prying eyes of neighbours. In this case, I assumed, the hostile day-lights[24] of the rival sibling household next door.

Cecile arrived a few minutes after me, with Mr Duggan carrying her single piece of luggage. She was wearing a dark red bonnet, which I immediately commented on.

"Mrs Smith insisted that I should be fashionable for my trip to London. She lent me her new bonnet," Cecile said coyly.

I took the bag from Mr Duggan and thanked him for his help.

He shook my hand. "Despite the missions to see the infirm, I trust that ye both find time for the distractions of town. I ain't been to London – what is it now? – nigh on thirty years or more." He winked at me. "Take her to the theatre, Mr Durrant. She would love that," he said in a stage whisper.

Cecile blushed.

He took his leave, and we sat together in the side bar of the King's Head.

I asked Cecile if she wished for a drink. I could see she was in a quandry. I suggested that a small sweet sherry might be appropriate. She agreed and I asked for one from the same barman that I had seen on my last journey to London. I had a small port.

"So here we are, together at last, sitting like a lord and lady, waiting for our coach to take us to town."

"It is the first time we have been properly alone, Rich." She touched my hand briefly. I picked it up and kissed it.

"I know you are worried by Solly's health. So let us deal with our business first, and don't feel goaded by Mr Duggan into rushing off to the theatre. Ah, but I am so excited to be with you, Rich, but still afeared of London."

The bustle of the arriving coach soon interrupted us. Within a few minutes we were seated inside, and we were on our way. It was a rule that a coach should never tarry for more than twenty minutes, to change horses and collect passengers.

For a few miles the passengers joined in a debate about the Romans having left better roads than were common in Georgian England. Then silence fell, and Cecile and I just exchanged warm, knowing smiles.

We were sitting opposite each other, which I soon realized was a mistake because a fat coarse brewer – his profession he soon told us in a self-important manner – kept squeezing against her. I felt so protective of Cecile, I almost challenged the man to a duel, there and then. But I could see that his gross stomach was the fault, not any ardour, and that the thin clerk to his right was having a hard time of the bounces and jolts as well, as the brewer swayed against his personage.

It was not quite the honeymoon trip I had envisaged.

Twenty-one

The journey – for me – was much more difficult than last time. Cecile was excited and enjoyed the views, despite the rough ride, and cramped seating. But I was anxious for her, and for what might meet me at the end of the journey. I was determined that my inner fears would not spoil my special few days with her, so I put on a jovial performance.

The covered wagon leg of the journey from Richmond to Southwark was just as chaotic, but Cecile seemed to enjoy the Pilgrim's Progress of characters and numerous delays and arguments over the fares. It was called the "Flying Wagon" but it stopped more than it flew. It was well past dark when we arrived in the Talbot Inn in Southwark.

Luckily, two rooms were available. They were presentable and reasonably grand for a coaching inn situated in this part of London. It was the first time, Cecile said, that she had stayed at such a fine place. Once she felt comfortable there, and I had arranged for some food to be delivered to her room, I took my leave to visit Solly's house just a few hundreds yards away. I promised Cecile I would be back within the hour. I told her to lock her door – too many rogues were out and about in Southwark.

I walked quickly through the light fog to Solly's home, dreading that he would not be alive.

Tamar opened the door to my knocking and embraced me with tears; of relief I soon realized.

"Papa will be so pleased to see you," she said excitedly. "It's as if he has been staying alive by waiting for you."

Rachel greeted me warmly too, like a mother, and they soon led me to Solly's back room, where a small cot-bed had been prepared for him away from the bustle of the household. He looked utterly pale and drained, as though death had already placed a large deposit on his soul.

He struggled to raise himself from his bed, but I said, "Lay back, Solly, don't tire yourself."

He did put his head back, almost gratefully, and I kissed him on the cheek.

"Agh, Reeech, you are a real *zhlub*, 'til I am almost on death's gate before you visit. What kind of gratitude is dis? For a man who treated you like a son?"

I needed to laugh for his sake.

"I am so pleased that you are still your cantankerous old self."

Tamar said, "He has revived for you, Rich. By storing up some of his bad language."

The wife and daughter deliberately left us men together. I wondered if Solly had a dreadful last message about my rearing or that he would swear me to marry Tamar, and I would have to refuse. But, no, it was much simpler than that. He just wanted to say a fond goodbye to me.

He also wanted to finish our business. "Reeech, Rachel vill tell you vhere your gelt is. Then vee are straight, no? Some money is in de bank for you, and some guineas as cash. You can't always be hiding stuff in de roof, no? You vill need a bank vhen you become a big trader."

"The money is of no concern. I want you to get better."

"Don't be giving me this *dreck*. I've got maybe one day, two days, left. I vant dat you keep de eyes on my family…"

"Keep *an* eye…" I anticipated and corrected his English for old time's sake.

"Don't be giving me dat *shmo* act. I vill never hev time to learn better English now. But I vant dat you keep an eye on de family. My boys are good boys, but they vill never be de man dat you are, Reeech. And if dat you spend more time in London, you must come to our house often…promise?"

"Of course, Solly."

"And I know dat Tamar has a liking for you. Be kind to her."

"I will love her like a sister."

"A sister? Huh!" He said simply but with a wistful sigh. He pressed on by changing the subject. Solly was in a hurry to use up the last hours of his life as effectively as possible: "And how is de business? You be listenin' to ole Solly on how to do it?"

"I am learning how to be an honest trader. You already taught me how to be an honest man…and to read and write."

"Yah, Yah, I want dat you have de choice of my books. Take some home vit you. My boys dey read nuddin." He groaned, and the emotions he had just shown seemed to have exhausted him utterly.

"Now I am tired. The big last tiredness of an old man. I vill sleep but I vant to say *mazel tov* for de business… and de life."

"Don't play the *schmo* with me neither, Solly. I will see you tomorrow after breakfast."

But Solly was already asleep, exhausted by his farewell. I pulled the blanket over his chest, and quietly left the room.

I conversed with Tamar and Rachel but briefly, because I was anxious to return to Cecile. I explained that I was escorting a friend on a visit to see her aunt. I could see Tamar was anxious to question me, but she did not, as she understood that I needed to leave. I said I would return in the morning.

I hastened past the coffee shop on the corner and recalled a happier time when Solly was in full health.

When I entered the courtyard of the Talbot Inn, I could see that Cecile's lantern was still on. She had not retired early.

I went up the outside stairs and on to the balcony and knocked on her door.

"It is me…Rich. I hope it is not too late to call."

She opened the door quickly. And I was surprised to see that she was fully dressed to go out.

I took the hint. "Would you, perchance, be wanting to see something of Southwark?"

"It is not too late?"

"No, we have an hour or so before the gin shops start taking their full revenge on law-abiding folk promenading on the streets. I do know a polite little coffee shop where I can take a lady such as you."

She seemed girlish in her excitement.

"Let us, though, take a little detour." And I led her through the market area, where a few farmers were still selling their cheeses, and then we came out on a small dock next to the Blue Anchor hotel.

As soon as she saw the water, she stopped dead in her steps.

"May we turn back? I do not like ships or deep water," she said almost hypnotically.

I didn't say that we were in Southwark, right on the Thames and near many ships and boats. Nor did I question her on the reasons for her fear. I pretended to make light of her all too apparent dread.

We walked back though the market and on to the High Street, where we stopped for a few minutes to watch a Punch and Judy show. Cecile laughed out loud at the antics of the puppets, so I put a half-penny in the hat pushed in front of me by a pretty little street urchin with long pigtails.

It started to drizzle and so I suggested we take some coffee.

It was warm and cosy in the coffee house, although I was irked by two women of slightly tawdry appearance, red gowns and rouged faces, which suggested they were ladies of the night. I then noticed that one had a large key hung round her neck, which removed all doubt. I did not despise them, but I felt sad that they had to shed their honour for so little as a shilling. A labouring man might earn less than that for a long day's back-breaking work. I made no judgement as to who was better.

We took a small table in the corner, where I could see the door. Old habits died hard.

"Would you like some victuals, Cecile?"

She declined: "I have eaten well enough, thank'ee."

I ordered a small pot of coffee.

She took my hand solicitously and asked, "And your friend Solly, how is he?"

I didn't feel like dressing it up. "At death's door, or death's gate as he put it. He speaks a strange mixture of Yiddish and English and he swears like a foreign sailor who has had too much brandy, but I love the old bastard...if you will forgive my language. I will miss correcting all his mistakes. But he enjoyed that really, because he made sure I could read and write properly. I owe him a lot. And I'm glad we had chance to say a brief goodbye. I know he wanted very much to do that. I'll see him briefly tomorrow, so you must pardon my absence. It will take me but a little while, and then we will find your aunt's address. I know the area a little – it is close by here, not more than a mile or so...over the bridge."

And I remembered her fear of water.

She knew what I was thinking. "Please do not think me mad. I've good reason to fear water, but I can cross a big bridge in daylight with a good man by my side," she said laughing.

But the laughter could not entirely disguise her obvious dread.

"Yes, we have many things to tell each other. We have both lived for so long without knowing each other. I hope that I can make up for that." And I kissed her hand gently.

We talked for an hour or more and yet it seemed like a few minutes. It was light conversation – her life in the Cruikshank household mainly, but she did again mention the theatre.

"Ah, we are so close to where Master Shakespeare had his Globe theatre, but now the best theatres are across the river. Southwark was once the centre for all debauchery and literature – they often run together – now this area is a little sad." I pointed as some gin-sodden revellers tottered in.

"It's time for us to go back to the inn." I paid my bill and walked Cecile around the corner to the Talbot Inn.

My room was on the bottom floor, the single ladies were often located up on the balcony. I strode boldly ahead of her up the stairs, taking a candle from a set of three in iron holders on the stairwell. I led her to her door, and held the candle aloft as she sought her key from the big pocket in her dress. When the door opened, I gave her the candle for her room.

She stood inside the doorway facing me, with the candle in her left hand and the key in her right.

She looked at me with shyness and expectation, trusting yet apprehensive at the same time.

I leaned forward and raised her right hand, and held it with my both my hands and then I turned her hand over.

"See, there is in your hand the key to my heart. It is yours to open when you see fit."

I don't know where that came from, but the words – perhaps too sentimental and not the words of the Bard, I thought afterwards – just sprang to my lips. It was what I needed to say, so I just said it.

She said nothing, but she raised my hand and kissed it, and I did the same to her hand again.

"I will bid you goodnight, my fair Cecile. You know where my room is, should there be any alarms in the night. But a stout-hearted night-watchman guards here, so none of the drunkards will come into the courtyard and bother you. I will knock on the door at eight, if that is a good time."

She nodded and said, in a small voice. "Thank'ee, Richard, for your kindness. Sleep well."

I bowed slightly and left her to close the door.

Twenty-two

I called for Cecile, as promised, at eight o'clock, and again she was ready and dressed to go out.

"Sleep well?" I asked.

"I slept well enough, Richard, *merci*, but I must confess the excitement of being here with you delayed my sleeping. And the hope of seeing my dear Aunt Suzanne. Though I do fear the worst for her – as she has not replied to my letters for these three long years."

Cecile declined breakfast, because she was so eager to set out. I had promised to visit Solly so I suggested she should wait a little while for me, while I called to see how my friend was faring. We agreed that I would call back within the hour.

I hastened to Solly's to enquire after his health.

⋐⋙⋈⋘⋓

Tamar led me into the kitchen and offered me coffee. Rachel was out on an errand, she said, hunting for a potion from the apothecary at nearby St Thomas' hospital.

"And how goes the old man?"

"I have been into his room this morning to take him soup, but he seemed too tired to want any. Some of his spirit has left him; perhaps he was exhausted by seeing you."

"I feel guilty."

"No, no, Rich, he was so desirous to see you again. He felt that it was something he had to do."

"May I speak frankly, Tamar? How long do the doctors think he will live?"

"He must be very ill to have let Dr Levi see him; you know how he hates doctors…and leeches. You should have heard him swearing in Yiddish at poor Dr Levi. He used very bad words I did not know…"

"You know what Solly is like. Should I try to see him?"

"He loves you, Rich, but I think he is too tired to see anyone now. I hope that the time for the *Kaddish* will be some weeks yet… Will you call later?"

"Of course, I am here until Saturday morning, when I return home."

"And may I ask, who is this woman you are *escorting*?"

The emphasis was slight, but it was there.

Maybe I was being a coward, perhaps I loved Tamar too much – as a sister; and I knew it was not the right time to confide my love for Cecile. Though was I denying something about my love? Because of Tamar? Because of my former philandering ways? Or genuine concern that Solly's condition was not a fit time? Surely, even deep love, like faith, must co-exist with doubt. There was no time for introspection. I said simply, "She – Cecile – is a dear friend from Albury, close by Gomshall, and I have promised to help find her aunt in London. I came of course to see Solly, but I had promised Cecile that I would help her at the same time."

It was close enough to the truth to convince me, but I could see both disbelief and hurt in Tamar's eyes, though she said nothing.

"I must leave now; Cecile is alone in the Talbot."

"You must bring her to the house; you must not leave her alone in a strange inn."

I thanked Tamar for that kindness, as she led me to the front door, where she kissed me on the cheek.

"Thank you for coming so quickly to see Papa," she said with warmth. "I worried so that my letter might not reach you."

"It did, thank God. "And I did not reply, hoping that my return would be swifter than any message."

I felt discomfited about not being entirely open with Tamar, but I cast aside the feeling by the thought of seeing Cecile, of being together for a day, a whole day, then the day after. But I could not be too happy, while my friend lay dying. I wondered why life was always like that: strong feelings – good and bad – always came together.

❖

I knocked on Cecile's door, but I could not hear any movement inside.

I knocked loudly again and there was nothing.

I felt panic. A thousand fears ran through my mind. Was God punishing me for denying Cecile to Tamar, denying her once, though not thrice like St Peter? Had she been seized by ruffians? Had she gone to search for her aunt alone? Or perhaps even felt insulted by my leaving her twice to visit Solly? Surely not. Guilt conjured up a million imagined fates.

I walked into the courtyard thinking perhaps she had gone into the barroom of the inn; perhaps, as a foreigner, she did not know that it would be deemed unthinkable for a woman of taste to enter unescorted.

"Rich, Rich." I heard her call my name.

I turned around and saw her sitting on a bench in the far corner of the large courtyard by two large tubs of flowers.

I rushed over to her and embraced her, the first time I had ever done so.

She folded into my arms.

"Rich, what is it? Your friend is…"

"No, Cecile, I was in a dread that something had happened to you because there was no one in the room…"

"Pardon, but I had wanted to smell the spring flowers that I had seen from my window. I had meant to watch for you, but I was looking at the flowers for a few minutes on this lovely day. I am sorry to have caused alarm."

I felt foolish. Perhaps I was not used to engaging with two special women in the same hour. Give me battles with Dragoons any day, I thought.

I needed a good walk in the fresh air, if one could call the smell and grit and soot of London that, even on a sunny spring day.

"So are we ready for the expedition to find your aunt?"

"That I am, sir." And she placed her arm firmly in mine.

I noticed that she had rapidly dropped some of her country accent and had slipped more into London speech, losing her "thees" and "thous" as well as some of the Surrey burr. I wondered whether subconsciously I did the same when I left the valley to come to town. She obviously had a good ear for language, though she still tended to place her emphasis sometimes on the wrong part of a word and had difficulty with the "h". But I would stop myself correcting her, and not tutor her like my dear friend Solly. She might think I was patronizing her.

We turned right towards Borough High Street, walked past Guy's Hospital for the incurables, and picked up a rapid pace. I wanted to set a good speed to distract her as we crossed London Bridge. I deliberately wanted to keep her from looking down into the Thames.

I said, "Look how mysterious St Paul's appears, even in this haze."

I noticed that her eyes were closed, but she opened them to look up and gaze across to the left at the cathedral in the distance. I kept talking to her and held her arm firmly as though I were leading a blind woman. She kept her eyes closed until I said, "We are on the north bank, Cecile."

I felt her relax the tense muscles in her arm. I understood how much courage she was showing to share this walk with me.

⋘∞⋙

She reminded me again of the address of her aunt, which, in truth, I had only a vague opinion of where it might be. For her sake, and to avoid the appearance of a bumpkin in town, I offered a hackney cab. She insisted on walking, however, in order to see the sights, she said.

We walked the two miles up Cheapside, past Newgate — where I had seen that poor woman burned — and then on past Lincoln's Inn Fields and on to the edge of Holborn. Her aunt lived in the area of St Giles-in-the-Fields, where everything seemed damp and fetid. I could see that Cecile was shocked at the dirt in the streets where people were left to die untended, and unheeded, it seemed, except by us. Then we came into a better, wider street, full of the poorer class of traders.

The hanging boards advertising their wares creaked and groaned in the light wind. Cecile wanted to stop and read them all. One board with seven dials on it said, "Here liveth a gentlewoman, the seventh daughter of a seventh daughter — divines lawsuits and pregnancies."

Next door a sign read, "We can divine which can win in Horse and Foot races."

The boards were like a flapping gallery of painted images: a small pub — the Cardinal's Hat. A goat signified a perfumer. A fruiterer had put up a picture of Adam and Eve in the Garden of Eden. An ironmonger had hoisted a painted sign of a bag of nails; and there was the common one for an apothecary – the horn of a unicorn.

The street grew wider and it was now thronging with people, through whom we had trouble passing. One portly street vendor in an old apron was shouting right next to our ears – "Live HadRich, Eeeeels alive, oh. Mack-mack-mackereeel." A hunchbacked merchant in a cape stopped us and tried to sell from the tray of shoes he was carrying. A man offering dried hake and, carrying a basket on his head, almost knocked Cecile's bonnet off her head, before I pushed him away. Cecile did not see his obscene gesture. Instantly, a young woman, pretty except for the wart on her nose, stopped to sell oranges from a basket strapped around her waist.

"Hecuse me coind sur, I take this lubbutea of latin you know these be fresh like. Buy one for your poppet?"

My poppet smiled. So I bought one for Cecile, who put it in the large purse she was carrying.

She whispered affectionately in my ear. "I understood hardly a word. What language was she speaking?"

"Cockney," I said, and she laughed out loud.

Cecile had been distracted by the orange-seller and her attendance to her purse. I was not. I had spied a ragged woman of middling age, with hands that appeared to be stiff and palsied. The woman moved alongside Cecile.

I knew the game. I shot out both my hands and tugged at the foreign hands which were transgressing against my beloved Cecile.

Cecile turned in surprise as I pulled both the woman's hands into the air: false hands, a pickpocket's stock in trade.

The thief quickly ran off into the crowd and I threw her false arms after her.

"Be off with you, you thieving witch," I shouted, though my language, and actions, would have been much harsher if I were not escorting Cecile.

Cecile threw her real arms around my neck. "Thank you,

Rich, you truly are my gallant knight on a white charger."

I held her tightly and kissed both her cheeks, and urged that we continue on our mission.

Now the pavements were even more crowded with people selling from small carts and barrows. A young Jewish man in a dark blue skullcap was offering old clothes and hare-skins. Countrywomen, in red cloaks and straw hats, were selling eggs and cheeses, while their menfolk stood by, with flowers woven in their hair. An Irishman, in the broadest accent, wanted us to buy his rabbits. A flautist followed us for more than a few steps while serenading us with his melodies. An Italian – presumably from the name on his barrow and by his speech – tried to sell us looking glasses and spectacles. Cecile asked if she could put one pair of eyeglasses on her nose to test them, as I stood very close by her to protect her against another light-fingered assailant.

The Italian waved the most flamboyant gesture of agreement.

Cecile did try the spectacles on and I burst out laughing.

And so did Cecile after she had returned the goods to the barrow.

"You were like a schoolteacher," I said.

"What is wrong with schoolteachers? I went to school for two years in France and was glad of it," she said more forcefully than I had ever heard her speak before. That was good: she was becoming more confident in our friendship.

"My schoolteacher was Solly and I learned in his kitchen."

"We must talk of the books we have discovered," she said with real enthusiasm, though I was pained to admit to myself how few I had read from cover to cover. "Better, for now, we talk of the theatre we will see – tonight, as soon as we can escape this mayhem, and find your aunt."

The trading section of the street soon gave way to cheap night lodgings, "beggar's operas" as they were called because of the drink and drama that engulfed them. Past these we came to the shabbiest nest of tall four-storey houses, rookeries with fetid yards behind them with desperate folk living in sheds. Cecile appeared anxious that her aunt should live in such a squalid part of London.

I had to ask directions from a greengrocer. He explained the location of a very narrow street, but with a warning: "I wouldn't be takin' a lady down there, friend. Nor would I be wearin' a pocket watch." He pointed at the chain extending from my waistcoat. "If I goes there, I go in as bare as a bird's arse."

I thanked him for his kind advice, and prepared to double my guard.

Cecile had said it was "Glenmore Mansion, Coronation Lane". It was a sad street indeed. Men in rags with florid faces sat on upturned carts, women in soot-streaked dresses huddled and smoked short clay pipes, while a man with no legs sat on a little trolley and begged us for money. I wanted to give him a penny, but I did not want to show we had money – although our more refined attire made us look as distinctive as invading Moors. Hungry-looking children chased a hoop down the street. One young boy bumped into me as he was looking the other way.

"I begs your pardon, Mister. Got a farthin' for me?"

After I had patted my pockets to see all was safe, I said, "I'll give you a half-penny if you can tell where Glenmore Mansion is." Few houses had names and none had numbers.

He pointed at a derelict-looking five-storey pile.

"Do people live there? It looks ready to fall down."

"No, Mister. People does still live there."

"We are looking for Mrs Suzanne Leclerc," Cecile asked.

"Dunno, missus. But that's Glenmore Mansion – joke, see, cos it's the most broken-down 'ouse in the street."

He held out his hand, and I placed a halfpenny in it.

"Anovver halfpenny, Mister, pleeese? I ain't eaten today."

Cecile looked at me and I had no choice. I gave him a second coin.

I took Cecile's hand and stepped carefully around the cesspools that almost swamped the street, and practically tiptoed to the house where the aunt lived – perhaps.

I told Cecile to stand back and to let me knock on the door. I did so with my cane.

I rapped hard twice, and waited for a minute or more before a fat bedraggled woman with an eye patch opened the door a little.

"Whatcha be wanting with us?"

"I am enquiring as to a Mrs Suzanne Leclerc," I said firmly.

"Who's askin?"

"I am a friend of her niece, who is concerned with her welfare."

"Listen, Mr Toff, I be concerned with my bleedin' welfare. My information is precious and needs to be paid for. Give us sixpence and I'll tell you all you needs to know."

"Threepence, Madam, would be fair," I said as a gentleman would although, truth be told, I felt like reverting to my old ways and grabbing her by the scruff of her filthy neck.

"Fourpence ha'penny and we're square."

I did not want to appear too mean in front of Cecile, so I put the coins into her enormous calloused hands.

"Now what is it ye be wantin' agin?"

"Does Suzanne Leclerc live here?"

"No."

"Where does she live then?"

"Nowhere."

"Don't be impertinent, woman."

"Don't ye be giving me no grief or I'll be tipping ye a volloper right across the snout, gen'leman or no gen'leman. And I don't need to be calling me old man, who's even bigger than me."

"Madam," I said through slightly clenched teeth, "I have paid what we agreed. I am merely trying to find an elderly lady, the aunt of the lady there." I gestured.

"She's a poppet...I might tell 'er."

I beckoned Cecile over. "I think this, er, lady might be more inclined to give you the information rather than to me."

"Madam, we are sorry to disturb you, but I am looking for my aunt. She wrote to me and gave me this address. I thought it was a...more substantial 'ouse."

"No airs and graces, Missus, please, especially from a bleedin' foreigner."

Cecile suddenly took the woman's hand.

"I meant no 'arm, Madam. Please, tell me, she is my only relative left alive."

"No, she ain't."

"What do ye mean?" I asked − perhaps too aggressively, because the harridan was obviously warming to Cecile.

"She's dead, that's why. These two years past."

Tears started to well in Cecile's eyes.

"What did... my aunt... die of?" Cecile asked haltingly.

"Dunno. She just died. Blessed relief for her; she was ailing for months."

"Did she leave anything − personal possessions?" I asked.

"Aye, a few things, but we sold them to pay for the rent owin'."

The Hell cat's tone softened at Cecile's obvious distress. "Look, poppet, go around to St Luke's church − it's a few streets away − that way" − she pointed − "and the priest there might tell yous more. She didn't pay the rent, but she did damn well pay her respect to God. Regular-like."

"Thank you for your help," I said reluctantly, and led Cecile away.

I wanted to take Cecile away from this slum.

"Cecile, I will find this priest tomorrow. I think it's best that we leave this area. It is unhealthy and dangerous. I know you may not be in a mood for frivolous things, but let me take you to Covent Garden, and then into the Strand. We can visit the fine shops there, and find somewhere to take refreshments. Then we can talk — I would like to hear about your aunt."

I noticed that she wiped her tears with the handkerchief she had bought from me on my first visit.

"I appreciate you being so kind, but I need to know more — now. Please," she said imploringly. "Let us find St Luke's."

"Yes, of course." I had been insensitive, but had meant well — the eternal condition of over-attentive males.

We soon found the church, it was but a few hundred yards away in a quieter area. There was even a little park, graced with two elms, at the end of the graveyard. Luckily we found the vicar in the church, a rare event outside of a Sunday for many a priest holding too many stipends in too many churches. I left Cecile kneeling and praying at the rear of the nave, and went to speak to a man who introduced himself as Reverend George Eccles.

"Sir," I said, "we were looking for a Mrs Suzanne Leclerc, a French gentlewoman who fell on hard times. Her former landlady tells me she has passed away but that she did worship here. Do you recall her?"

"As a matter of fact, I do, Mr, er?"

"Apologies. My name is Richard Durrant." And we shook hands. "You were saying, sir."

"Yes, I do remember her well. Charming old lady. I tried to offer her a room — shared just by one other woman — in our almshouse, but she politely declined."

"She was living in a terrible hovel."

"Ah, I did not know that. I could see she was infirm, but she was too proud to accept my offer, I believe."

I felt bitter. "She died in a hovel — a backyard shed, I suspect, of a house owned by someone who would rival the scarlet beast of the Book of Revelations."

"A churchman, are you?"

"No, sir, but a Christian man when I can be. What else can you tell me or can tell her niece there?"

"I can say very little except that she came here to worship, even when she could barely hobble through the door. But...let me think. Would you excuse me a minute? I recall something from two years ago...Would you ask your friend, Mrs Leclerc's niece, to join us?"

I gestured to Cecile and smiled at her. She got up from her prayers and joined us. I introduced her to the Reverend Eccles, who led us into a room near the entrance to the nave. It was a dusty sort of office and store for Bibles and prayer books. He gestured to us to sit down on two benches.

"Now let me see," he mumbled to himself. He fished around in a wooden box full of papers. "I think it's here somewhere. Ah, this may be it. No, no. Hmmm. Perhaps this is it. Ah-ha! A letter addressed to 'Cecile Leclerc'. I think, Miss, this may be for you."

He handed Cecile a large yellow envelope, with a small red seal on the back.

Cecile stood up and eagerly took the letter and then rushed to open it. She started to read and slowly the teardrops trickled down her cheeks. We two men just stood and waited. We did not want to intrude on her private grief. Eventually I had the wit to put one arm around her shoulders, and she turned and sobbed onto my chest.

After a minute or so, she said, "Pardon me. I am overcome."

I could not contain myself: "What does the letter say?"

"It is sad. But, please, read it."

She gave it to me. I thought it was strange that it was not in French. It said, in excellent English:

My dear Cecile

I believe I am nearing my last days. I want to say farewell to you, my dear niece, and to explain why I have not written. My condition in life has declined from our days in France and, when we first came to London. I did receive some of your letters, but then they were sadly lost. And some of my memory has gone and I could not recall the address from which they were sent. I have left this letter with Reverend Eccles in the hope that my neighbours – such as they are – may direct you to the church I have regularly attended in my last years.

I have so often thought of you – you were more my beloved fille rather than my niece. And you are now my only kin. I love you so much and I hope that you will find love.

I have dreamed many nights – a similar dream – of your finding a good man – albeit he is an Englishman – in the countryside where you now are. I hope this is true or will be true.

I will entrust my soul soon to my Maker. Pray for me, as I have so often prayed for you. I hope that, if I am granted entry into heaven, I will meet my beloved brother and sister-in-law, your Mama and Papa. We will embrace and look down upon you and try to guide your steps.

Adieu, Cecile, with much love

Your aunt,

Suzanne

There was almost a tear in my eye, too, as I turned and embraced Cecile.

After a good while, Reverend Eccles coughed politely. He said, "I am glad that the letter reached its rightful owner. It is very moving."

"How do you know?" I asked gently.

"I wrote it," he replied.

Twenty-three

You wrote it, sir, why?" I asked.

"I was about to ask you, Reverend, because this is not my aunt's script. And her English – her written English – was not so...so refined."

"No, no, as I said, I wrote it...because she could no longer move her hands properly. They were crippled with arthritis. She asked me if she could dictate a short letter to you and of course I agreed. I could see she was near dying – it was, sadly, her last visit to my church. At first she tried to dictate it in French, a language, alas, I have no mastery of. So she spoke the words in English and I polished them – with her agreement."

"When did she die, Reverend?

"Well, Miss Leclerc, it was nigh on two years or so."

"Please, where is she buried?" Cecile asked.

"I regret to say she has no headstone here."

I could see where this was leading and I tried to deflect the subject. "Reverend, I do thank you deeply for this final mercy to an old woman, and..."

"Where is she buried, please?" Cecile said with determination.

"I am sorry to say that she was buried in a pauper's grave, not here..."

"But where then?"

"Cecile," I insisted, "I will explain later. Meanwhile we must thank the Reverend and take our leave." We both shook his hand.

Cecile started crying but quietly this time, as I led her out of the church.

Just outside the entrance, I glimpsed a pale figure, who disappeared around a street corner. I thought of the albino in the Hurtwood and Godalming, but I dismissed it as a figment of my imagination. Even if real, this was not the time to chase after the phantom.

Cecile and I walked in silence on to the street and then eventually to Drury Lane and down to the Strand. Not far from Somerset House I noticed a small but better class of public house which had a covered terrace where some ladies and gentlemen were dining. I led her to a table and took the liberty of ordering for her. She was in no condition for decisions.

First, though, I ordered her a big glass of port, half of which she drank very quickly.

I tried to cheer her up. "This is terrible news, but it is perhaps better than not knowing. Your aunt obviously loved you so much and her last thoughts were of her dear niece."

"But she died alone," Cecile said, "in pain and poverty, and is buried in a hole somewhere – a pauper's grave. And we were such a respectable family in France, before we were driven away from our 'omes. The Catholics did this to us…we were such God-fearing people – worshipping the same Christian God. Why could we not live side by side…let the lion lie down with the lamb, as the Bible promises?"

I reached out across the table and held her trembling hand.

"To think that she lived in that...that den...with that awful woman," Cecile continued. "If I had known her condition, I would have asked Mrs Cruikshank to help me find her somewhere to live near Albury. I would have worked every night and day to provide for her. I did not know...I did not know." She started sobbing again.

She finished the port in one final gulp.

"I had two letters from her and they did not mention her condition."

"She was too proud," I ventured.

"Yes, she was proud. We were a proud family...before we came 'ere. No, no, I do not wish to blame England...we were refugees here. And we started again..."

She collected herself. "I will tell you about my life at another time. Your patience is being tried, I fear."

I tried a little levity: "Ah, I will be more patient, and help you to find the good man prophesied by Aunt Suzanne."

She smiled and squeezed my hand: "I do not think I will have to search too far."

I dined well, and Cecile ate some of her food.

"What would you be wanting to do this sunny afternoon?" I asked more cheerfully than we both felt.

"Forgive me, Richard, but I do not want to go to the theatre later."

"No, no, it would not be fitting, as you are in mourning."

"I shall not mourn now, in public. In my room and in my 'eart and in my prayers, I will remember my aunt. And you are worrying about Solly. We must have a pact..."

"To enjoy the day, but with quiet respect for those we care about..."

"*Exactement,*" she said, with a smile. "It is our special time, too. Life is so cruel so often that we must not let it steal all the precious hours…"

"Cecile, I had intended to wait for a better time, but I must confess now…that I have fallen so in love with you. I want to be here for you now, and for ever."

"Richard, please stop…"

"Have I offended you? Then let the devil rip out my tongue…"

"No, no…please. Ah, I too was waiting for…*Quel dommage!*…when I am emotional…I think in French…I cannot find the right words…so I will say in bad English… per'aps I should not. I am so afraid…but my aunt's words…she had the gift of seeing into the future…she must have talked of you, Richard."

She paused, as I savoured again how she rolled both the "r"s in my full name. I did not want her to use "Rich".

She took a deep breathe and confessed, "There has never really been a man in my life…not one, until now… *Merde…*"

She took both my hands firmly and looked me straight in the eye. Boldly, not with the shyness she had worn for all the time I had known her.

"Richard, I love you, with all my 'eart. There, I 'ave said it…and let the 'eavens fall if it be a lie."

⧁⟡⧀

I leaned over and kissed her gently on the lips for the first time. She responded with tenderness and passion.

It is a pity we are in public place, the hunter in me thought. I saw two old ladies at a nearby table stare in disapproval even at such a brief kiss.

"So what shall we two lovers do on this lovely spring day?"

"If not to the theatre, then let's walk down the Strand and to Westminster Bridge, and walk past a few fashion emporia and, perhaps, if you should take a fancy, we will go in and look."

She smiled, and some of the colour came back to her cheeks.

I paid the account, and gave her my arm, and like a dandy I escorted my lady down the Strand. We stopped in one or two drapers' shops, where I displayed a little of my new-found knowledge. A few items attracted her interest, and I promised that I would provide them later…at a much better price, although my heart told me that I could never charge her for anything in my whole life.

I could see she was now looking tired, and I suggested we find a short-stage wagon or a hackney to take us back to the Talbot.

"No, no, they use the carriages here like cannons, all fighting with each other. It is too dangerous," she said.

"They call it 'hunting the squirrel', Cecile. The hackney carriages try to get as close as possible but without touching wheels. They treat it as a sport, like hunting."

So again Cecile insisted on walking back, although this time we crossed over Westminster Bridge. As we were leaving the steps descending from the bridge, a sedan chair almost knocked her over. We had not heard the "By your leave, sir" shouted at us.

We came through the rougher streets of Southwark to reach our accommodation. We stopped once to very briefly observe a cock-fight, though I led her around a crowd gathered to watch female prize fighters.

When we reached the Talbot Inn, she said that she wanted to rest and to change.

"I would wear all black for mourning, but I do not have suitable attire," she said sighing.

"We can buy such, if there be the need."

"No, no. We have a pact: to enjoy our time together…"

"That smacks of impermanence," I said anxiously.

Again she looked me straight in the eyes in the courtyard of the Talbot and she said slowly and clearly: "I will love you for ever, for as long as I live, but I say once more – lives can be cruel and short…"

"Though I am not in the first bloom of youth, we are healthy, Cecile…and I will make sure that our lives together will be comfortable. So tonight, what will be your fancy?"

"Just to be with you, Richard…but I am happy to walk somewhere close by. Per'aps that coffee house."

"That would be very agreeable. How long will you be resting?"

"Would two hours suit?"

"Of course…I will visit Solly again and I will call for you at seven o'clock."

I could see that she was slightly embarrassed…

"I 'ave no watch. I had one when I was a child – Papa gave me one – but it was stolen when we came to England."

"Please take my pocket-watch for now, and I will ask Solly to find me a small lady's timepiece, a gold fob-watch, for you."

"I could not accept such a rare gift."

"Please, let me just display it to you, and see if you approve and then we can discuss it."

I kissed her on the cheek and waited as she walked up to her room off the balcony. She looked down at me and waved before she entered.

⋘∞⋙

Jakob answered the door and let me into the kitchen. I was pleased to see the son who was so like his father in looks, if not in ways. He was a gentle soul, despite his large muscle-bound frame, and he was quietly spoken. I had never heard him utter a profanity, at least in English.

"How is the old man?" I asked straightaway.

"Dr Levi is with him now. He sleeps a lot and swears but little."

"Not swearing is not a good sign," I said. "Where are the womenfolk?"

"At market. That's why I am here – to tend to my father when the doctor leaves."

We waited a long time for Dr Levi to come out of Solly's room. When he came out, he shook my hand and greeted me warmly although I had not seen him for years.

"How is he, Dr Levi?"

"He will sleep now. I have given him a tincture with opium. That will ease the pain."

"What ails him?" I asked directly.

"It's consumption. It's been with him for a long time. He has fought it, but he can not for much longer, I fear."

"Is there any hope?" Jakob asked.

"There is always hope, but from my experience I think he will not be long in this world. And he knows it. He has asked for Rabbi Kaufman."

I was surprised: Solly was not a man for rabbis.

Jakob escorted the doctor out of the house.

When he came back we talked of our younger days together and of Tamar.

Eventually I said I would have to go.

"Will you eat here tonight? Mama is preparing some borsht. You used to like that. And she will make a blintz for you, I'm sure."

"Thank you, Jakob…very tempting, but I will be going to the coffee shop nearby, with the lady I have escorted from the country."

"Yes, Tamar mentioned her. And that she had invited you both to visit."

"I cherish your sister and I think she might be hurt if I brought another woman into this house."

"She does think of you more than a sister would of a brother. Certainly more than she thinks of me," he said with a grin.

I changed the subject and asked him whether there were any small pocket watches in Solly's big safe.

He went to look and came back in a few minutes with three gold watches on chains.

The smallest one looked the best. I picked it up and examined it.

"It's French, I think," Jakob said.

"That decides it then. How much for this?"

"Ah, you must speak to Solly. Is it for the lady you are…escorting?"

"Yes, I said I would find a time-piece for her. She has never owned one since she was given one as a child, but I suppose few ladies do have them. But she deserves one, not least because she has suffered – or rather discovered – a bereavement today. Her aunt."

"I am sorry to hear that. Death is hiding around every corner, it seems. Then, please, take the watch on approval to see if she likes it."

"That I will do, Jakob. Thank you."

Then I took my leave.

⋖⋗⋈⋖⋗

Cecile had changed her dress and I thought how lovely the dark yellow looked and how it complemented her brown and green eyes, and Mediterranean complexion. No bawdy women plagued the coffee house; the company was genteel and merry. After such a large lunch, we had a simple meal of cheese and bread, with a little wine which was rough and no doubt too sweet, but Cecile was too polite to criticize the English way with wine. Then we took some excellent coffee – "just sailed in from Brazil," said the young woman serving us.

Cecile talked of her aunt and a little of her time when they all lived in France. She explained that she had learned to play the harpsichord and had loved to dance the Boulanger. She painted an idyllic picture except for insults from the Catholics, a few whispers at first, then public taunts but which led eventually to the burning of their house. Then they left for the freedom of Switzerland and finally they came to London. That was her story, but I sensed she was keeping back from me something more tragic. I did not question her; I listened as best as I could amid the growing hubbub of the inmates of the coffee shop.

I was enthralled to share so much of my Cecile's past. I was off-guard. And I had my back to the door. So I did not see a big man, over six foot three inches, with a grizzly beard, enter the coffee shop.

But I immediately recognized his voice when it boomed in my ear:

"So I have fucking found thee at last."

I spun around to face Black Harry.

"Harry, that's not a fair greeting for an old comrade in arms." I was wary but I had not gauged his real anger. I had confused it for his eternally brusque manner.

He soon disabused me of any doubts: "No comrade, Rich, but a traitor, methinks."

I needed to be diplomatic, especially with Cecile in my charge: "Harry, sit down and join us. This is not the time here and in the company of a lady to argue, but we will talk anon. Whatever is angering you, let me first take the lady to her rooms, and then I will attend to whatever is wrong here."

Harry lumbered onto a nearby stool, ignoring Cecile who fidgeted anxiously in her seat. "I will sit down," he said, "but I will not let thee flit off before I have said what angers me."

I could not ask Cecile to walk to the Talbot unescorted. I said to her. "This is Harry, a former business partner. Please excuse his gruffness." I was still hoping I had misread the man's rudeness. So I tried to control my anger when I offered Harry a coffee.

"Aye, I've come a long way and could do with something strong and hot."

I gestured to the waitress for some fresh coffee in a jug.

"I have no secrets from Cecile, if you must insist on confronting me here. By the way, how did you know I was in this part of London?"

"I had someone following thee."

"Why, Harry?"

"Because the Dragoons came into the Hurtwood and raided the New Inn. They took five men away, including the landlord, and they said they wuz comin' after me. And they took some of my stock which was stored there. And I wuz told that thee be party to that, that thee be leadin' 'em into the Hurtwood. Now that thee be all so respectable. Maybe buying thy freedom with turning us in, eh? Filthy informer, eh? So I comes to London, lying low, so to speak, and needin' to have a word with thee."

"Harry, that's bloody stupid. I have been in London, with Cecile and seeing my dear friend, Solly."

I now sensed that Harry was being devious about the reasons for the Dragoons, that this accusation against me was a feint. I suspected deep down that he might be accusing me of informing to cover his own parleying with the Revenue men.

"Maybe not, then," he said lowering his voice and perhaps his temper, "but the Dragoons have been, and it's a long time since we bashed 'em."

I looked at Cecile, but she did not seem shocked by the reference to a battle with Dragoons. She would certainly have heard of it, but not of my involvement.

"But I have something else to talk about...Jake."

I felt sick in my stomach. "What about Jake?"

"What happened to him, Rich?"

"And you are his keeper, his brother?"

"Ah, but I knows he was thy brother, Rich And thee should have been his keeper, not his..."

"Harry, I would care to talk about this, but not here."

"I bet thee would. And when we do I wants some share."

"Of what?"

"The silver trove."

"Not here, Harry, I warn you."

"Warns, me, Hah, 'cos thee be afeared of this lady learnin' about thy wicked ways. Don't worry about what she thinks. I knows about her too: she's a bloody French whore…"

It took far less than a second for a searing red mist to cover my eyes, clear and then for me to get up and punch Harry so hard on the nose that he shot back from his stool and lay both dazed and amazed on the floor. Blood poured from his nose.

I heard Cecile scream and, as I half-turned around – reluctant to take my eyes off Harry who was getting to his feet – I saw her throw the jug of hot fresh coffee over someone.

I had diverted my attention from Harry for a second more than was safe. From the corner of my eye, I saw a bottle raised above my head. Before I could swing my arm up to take the blow it crashed into the side of my face. I managed, I think, to land a second blow on Harry's bleeding face.

Then, as a black cloud started to envelop me, I saw a strange figure in front of me. An albino in a black hood. The last thing I remembered was seeing the knife in his hand.

Twenty-four

Slowly the blackness cleared and spots of light intruded into the shadows as they moved from darkness to grey, and gradually I looked down, not on beaten earth or cobbles, but on a carpet. I was lying face down, but I could move my eyes gradually outwards to see a wall-to-wall dark green carpet running to join a white baseboard.

Where was I?

I staggered to my feet and looked around. This was a strange room, full of unusual yet familiar objects. I saw a brown leather armchair and fell into it, as my head spun around.

This room belonged to me.

But who is me? I asked myself.

My head was full of a man named Rich, and his longing for this creature of light and love, yet I was now someone else. I tried to fight it off, but I could not blank out the realization that I was someone else, somewhere else now – and I did not want to be this person and not in this time and place.

I felt utterly sick, and I thought I was going to vomit, but gradually the nausea subsided. I felt my head and it was sore, very sore. And I noticed that my coffee table had been knocked over. In my self-hypnosis, had I struck out, stumbled and knocked my head against sharp corner of the table? It was possible, and even logical, but I wasn't doing much with logic at that moment.

A massive wave of anger overwhelmed me as I fully understood that I was Dr Thomas J Martin, an American living in London in the twenty-first century. I did not want to be this man – I was being torn from my life and my love.

I shouted aloud, "I am an Englishman, not some bloody Yank."

I remember almost screaming, "My time is then, under Mad King George, not, not, not in America, or England, for that matter, ruled by mad George Bush and his poodle Tony Blair.

Worse, far worse, and I hated myself for it: I had left the love of my life alone with angry blood-thirsty men. What would Black Harry do to her? Would he drag her off and violate her? The woman I was sworn to protect. All my friends in Southwark and the Hurtwood, what were they doing? Were they all dead now, dust in the earth?

I saw a bottle of brandy and carefully sniffed it before pouring myself a glass. Slowly, I recovered my persona and current memory, yet amazingly I could recall nearly all of my previous life, one that had ended a few minutes before.

I saw the tape recorder and switched it on.

Yes, yes, it was all there. I could hear myself arguing with Jake, fighting for my life. I could hear me, but where was bloody Jake? Silences intruded where he should have been…I played it on and on, and listened to long periods of silence. The tape ran out just after I heard myself urging on my horse. Where could I put a horse in central London? I asked myself.

The scientist in me struggled to rationalize what had happened. I had lived a lifetime – in how long? I looked at my clock on the mantelpiece. I had been under hypnosis for what – less than an hour? Yet I could write, and indeed I am now writing, a whole book on my experiences in the 1790s.

I played the tape again and heard someone speaking in a south Surrey dialect. It was almost my voice, a different timbre perhaps, but definitely not my speech patterns.

Had I gone from hypnosis into a deep dream state?

Had I imagined all this, or had I indeed entered fully – too fully – into a past-life experience? Was this what the experts called "trance logic" which dispelled all scientific incongruities?

I needed to think. And I needed to talk it over with someone.

Jane. A doctor. My woman, but that sounded very wrong. Yes, I would ring her.

But no – she would think I had become demented.

Because I would tell her that all I wanted to do was go back to Cecile, a woman and a love I could feel as though she inhabited my very being. I could imagine that Jane would not be very sympathetic. I wasn't that mad.

Or was I? Was Cecile some sort of idealised Jane? Had I created one from the other, in some Frankenstein metamorphosis?

Perhaps this feeling would wear off? Otherwise I could go literally insane – if I was not already.

I would need more than a few hours to sort myself out. Yes, above all, I needed to buy myself some time.

Impulsively, I rang up my secretary, Mary. It was still only nine-thirty p.m., not too late.

Mary answered straightaway.

"Dr Martin, what can I do for you?"

"Mary, I never pull sickies, do I? And in truth I am feeling pretty weird. Would you do two things for me please? Reschedule my private appointments for this Friday and Saturday morning, and would you ring the hospital for me? I have nothing really earth-shattering to do there and I need three or four days off."

"What's wrong with you, Tom?"

She sounded very concerned, because I never cancelled anything except for the very occasional wedding or funeral.

"I'm not sure. I've had a very strange experience and I need to understand it, Mary. I've actually been doing a serious experiment, some field research if you like. I've had, er, curious results, and I need to work on it. But tell my patients and the hospital I've got a terrible stomach bug."

Mary said that of course she would help, and I rang off. I suspect that she thought my behaviour very odd. I wondered whether I had inadvertently slipped in some old Surrey dialect in my attempt to switch back to the twenty-first century

I next phoned Jane, now just a little more confident that I could perhaps communicate effectively in the modern era and without going into too much detail about the trip in my self-created time machine. Besides, I didn't want her to get me sectioned before I did more work on this machine.

Jane's answer phone came on. I was relieved that I didn't actually have to talk to her...I left what I thought was a short chatty message – please ring me back, I concluded, but was nervous about replying to her, or anyone, on these strange talking machines. Afterwards I wondered whether I had accidentally called her Cecile. It was possible. Anything was possible now.

I sat down and tried to work out what had happened. It was very rare for anybody under such hypnosis to remember so much, and I seemed to have almost total recall of what happened. When I felt better I promised myself I would check on some of the historical details, perhaps visit some of the places, to see how they matched my...what? Vision, dream...it was like some trip on LSD, as some of my more daring, or foolish, college friends had told me. I kept a good distance from such things. Or had I perhaps enjoyed a genuine past-life experience, a real insight into a previous existence? Certainly Rich seemed as real as Tom to me. And why not? How long would all this last? Recalling past – but unreachable – experiences for eternity?

I forced my brain to work out scientifically what had happened, but my mind drifted off to the extremes of fantasy. Was there some conspiracy? Was someone deliberately plotting to unhinge me? I was rational enough to realise that "somebody" could be me. Was I being self-destructive by indulging in self-hypnosis? Or was that bloody man Crozier behind all this? I asked myself almost deliriously.

Then my mind snapped back to Cecile, and I made a deliberate attempt to concentrate instead on Jane. I started to wonder if I could make her more like Cecile. Maybe get her to dye her hair brunette, and encourage her to grow it longer and wear it in pigtails. Maybe I could get Jane to ride horses, or I could even rub horse linament on her. The smell would be deliciously different, more like the time I craved for. That was crazy of course. Hell, I was driving myself mad, even if I wasn't already.

I suddenly felt very hungry. I looked in the fridge and saw nothing that was the least bit appetising. I remembered the Chinese take-away a short walk from my apartment. I wanted to see if the outside world was real, to check that I had not slipped into an alternative or parallel universe or was cocooned in some imaginary hologram in my own home.

I found my keys in the drawer – my twenty-first-century memory appeared intact – and nervously went out into the street. I walked uneasily, a little as though I were tipsy, even though I wasn't. The lights, the noise, the people – this was an image of hell for me. The cars were all driven by manic psychopaths, I thought. I watched them swirl with total abandon around a traffic circle.

I reached the Chinese restaurant and looked at the menu in the window. It all seemed so confusing, and also so unnecessary. I yearned for simple fare of cheese, cold beef and fresh bread. A little further down the street stood a small convenience store, next to the realtors. I managed to somehow purchase bread rolls and cheese. That would be my feast.

As I came out of the store, clutching my provisions, I accidentally bumped into a man. He turned to say the omnipresent English "Sorry" and I saw his face.

He was an albino.

In shock I dropped my goods and the man helped me to pick them up. I rushed away from the shop without apologising to him. I was completely unnerved.

As I walked home, I asked myself, "Was that a coincidence or had I imagined it? Could I no longer distinguish reality from imagination?"

I didn't have the courage to go back to the shop and ask the Asian woman behind the counter if she had just served an albino, just to satisfy myself that I wasn't imagining it all. I did stop and turn around but I just couldn't face the truth. That was not like me, but I was totally confused by what had just happened to me in the shop… and in my previous life.

Nevertheless, I felt triumphant that I had managed to scuttle back to my apartment safely. This new modern world frightened me. It was a world I did not like, want or could hardly believe in.

I sipped another brandy and wolfed down the bread and cheese.

There and then I resolved to write down as much as I could, as quickly as I could. It was Wednesday evening and I wasn't now due back to work until the following Monday. I had been a fast typist when I was a student. I needed to get the chronicle recorded on my laptop. I could use a tape recorder to rapidly dictate some of the story, if I felt it slipping from me. It was my best connection with the world I wanted with every fibre of my being, longing and soul.

The phone rang. It took me a few seconds to realize what the sound was – my thoughts were so engrossed in a long-ago reverie.

"Hi," she said breezily, "hope it's not too late. How's things? Still overworking?"

"Actually, Jane, I'm, er, feeling a bit under the weather. I'm taking a few days off."

"This is sudden. You were fine on Sunday."

Jane sounded very anxious. Perhaps Mary had ratted on me. Unlike her, though. Mary must have been worried sick about me. So was I.

Jane must have guessed my mood. She switched into a matter-of-fact medical tone: "Not like you to go sick. Will you be OK for dinner tomorrow? You said you would cook for me – on Valentine's Day."

I had forgotten but I said, "Um, come around for seven."

I controlled myself, stopped myself from saying my only love could ever, ever, ever be Cecile.

"Are you sure you're well enough?"

"Sure I'm sure."

"See you tomorrow – I've got to dash. I'm working later tonight. Bye."

The truncated conversation of today seemed so different from the more stately language of yesteryear, I thought.

I felt famished again – my body chemistry was going haywire. This time I found some almost-out-of-date ham at the back of the fridge and made myself doorstep sandwiches.

Then I wanted desperately to talk to Cecile. But – my God! – I could not phone her. I wondered whether my brain cells had sprung a leak.

After my second snack and another brandy, I felt utterly exhausted. I put myself to bed, but soon found myself crying into my pillow, weeping uncontrollably for ten minutes or more. At this rate Jane would be forced to section me, or more likely send me to the Priory. I was hooked on my past, not booze or coke.

I must have fallen asleep but when I woke up, my alarm clock said ten – presumably in the morning, as it was light outside. I had expected to be in my house in Gomshall, to see the bare earth floors of my kitchen, not a carpeted, over-elaborate apartment festooned with gadgets. I wanted, with my entire essence, to wake up with Cecile in my arms. I needed her as much as I needed air, food, water and light…what kind of existence could there be without her?

I could not think of Jane – loving as she was – without instinctively thinking of the difference between life and death. Cecile was my very being.

It took me minutes to get up and accept where I was – frozen in the wrong time and in the wrong place. I prayed – literally – on my knees: "Please God, send me back to Cecile or, if this is some kind of punishment end it now, or end me, or please take the memory away of the life I had before…"

I was convinced that I had lived this Surrey life in another time. Either I was bonkers, which was possible – especially for a practising psychiatrist like me – or it was real, that I had experienced something of a past life. Intellectually, I knew that all sorts of explanations were possible, yet in my heart of hearts I knew that it was a real journey into my past. Richard Bryant – or Durrant – was closer to my reality than the pompous

American quack could ever be. I felt an imposter in my own skin.

I looked at my hands to see the calluses I had from the more physical life of my past, from riding my horses, carrying India goods or repairing the farm. I felt for the scar on my face from the recent fight in the coffee shop. There was nothing except a growing bruise on my forehead, presumably caused by a table in Kensington, not a smashed bottle in Southwark. I tried to speak aloud in the south Surrey accent of the 1790s. I could remember the dialect words, but could not pronounce them properly.

I was in dread of losing my memory of this time. I made myself a coffee and started writing on my computer, though I was half-amused to find that it took me a few minutes to feel comfortable with a laptop – I had once considered myself something of a hi-tech expert. Though now saddling a horse correctly seemed much more rewarding to me.

I was in a frenzy as I started to write – to get it all down before it disappeared from my recollection, although I wondered how I would live with those same memories if they did not fade. Yet I never wanted to forget her, her face, her eyes.

I wrote all day, stopping for coffee and the occasional snack. The phone thankfully, did not ring. Mary, I presumed, was sensible enough not to forward any urgent calls. She was like my Nance, I thought, always looking after my interests, although I didn't think she would relish the loan of a horse and trap.

It was six p.m. before I remembered that I would have to dig into the freezer to find something for dinner. The wine rack was well-stocked, however. I did not want to go out again into the traffic-crazed streets of modern London.

I defrosted some mince and prepared a quasi-Italian concoction which Jane always seemed to appreciate. And I laid the table with candles which she also thought was a nice touch. But this was so false.

How could I go through this charade? I kept asking myself.

At seven p.m. precisely the door bell rang, and I vowed I would behave as normally as possible, not that I felt in the least normal. I was enough of a doctor to understand that I was suffering from sort of minor post-traumatic stress disorder. I would tell her a little but try to keep shtoom about the zanier bits. And, yes, I reminded myself not to deploy my Yiddish vocabulary.

And I must not, not, not call her Cecile, I told myself.

"Tom, you do look a bit pale. Are you OK?" she said kissing me in a sisterly fashion.

"I'm A1, honey," I drawled in my best American, trying to be a cavalier as possible. I almost asked how her journey by coach had been, or whether we should toast to the sanity of King George. Or toast my lack of sanity.

We ate and we drank and she talked of hospital gossip. I tried to talk as little as possible. As a fellow physician I used to relish such tittle-tattle; now I had to control myself to stop talking about the corn crop this year, or the state of the King's navy, or how much I loved the French, or that the government should stop burning women at the stake, and that transportation to Australia was detested by the mass of citizenry…I just about kept a lid on my surreal sense of wafting between two lives.

We had twenty minutes of small talk, including my apology for forgetting to buy her a Valentine card or flowers, and then I had to tell her something of my strange journey. It was just a snippet. She listened carefully, almost clinically, and then began to get very angry.

"Tom, you're a doctor not some variety-show hypnotist. You've been irresponsible and medically unethical, and experimenting on yourself is the pits. Stupid. If you absolutely had to do it, you should have had somebody medically qualified with you – even me there, if you were so damn determined. You should take more than a few days off. You need a bloody good holiday in the sun."

"I take it you don't approve," I said sarcastically.

"No, I do not. You're a man of science, Tom. OK, if you were planning some kind of Jeffrey Archer-type novel, then I could understand your scribbling all day. Hell's bells, Tom, I always admired your American pragmatism. I never saw you as some kind of deranged mystic."

I eventually managed to change the subject, but the evening was spoiled.

Later, over a few drinks, I made a totally innocent reference to an historical fact – not 1790s' England – and Jane's mood became more irascible, then downright hostile.

"Not only do I think you need a break from work, you need a break from me," she said. "This must be some calculated form of escapism to piss me off. Or some bullshit pretext – you have a funny look in your eyes. If there is some bitch out there who's on heat for you, she's bloody welcome."

I had never seen her like this, but she had sensed exactly what the problem was – my eccentric approach to my patient and fellow traveller to a Surrey past, but more so that I was in love with another woman. I should have said, no, I love you, but I could not even begin to frame the words and betray Cecile, even if she was, theoretically, a phantom of my imagination. I could hardly bear to touch Jane. Cecile was too real for such hypocrisy.

Jane picked up her coat and started to walk out.

"Good night and thank you for a night at the freak show, Dr Martin. Remember that you're a doctor and a bloody brilliant one, or used to be. You should take a holiday, then consult with a trusted colleague, spend some time lying on a couch yourself, mate. Ring me when you come down to earth."

I did not protest. The doctor in me agreed with her. The romantic in me had to let her go. I was sad, but I wanted time alone, to finish the journal of my adventure.

And I had a plan: a very simple one. I would try once again.

Jane left at around nine-thirty and I'd had a few glasses of wine. It was not the perfect conditions to conduct a medical – a psychological – OK, a very personal – experiment. But Cecile's face was before my eyes and dominated my heart and my brain.

I would have to replicate my previous experiment. Cecile was – is – in grave peril, I kept telling myself. I needed to rescue her, if I could. It was the only thing I wanted in the world. And perhaps the window into my past was a brief one. Why had I phoned Mary or met Jane or even appeased my hunger? I had to get back. Now, now, now.

I set up my tape recorders and repeated my system of self-hypnosis. I prayed to God that it would work. I willed myself with all my being to return to my past, but who could say, even if worked, whether I could return to the precise moment of my exit? I had to find out…

I set down the two tape recorders, and put them on. The first had my own voice counting down. "Alpha 20, Alpha 19…Alpha 10…Alpha 1." I didn't feel especially drowsy. My disembodied voice began to count down again. "You will relax… Alpha 20… Alpha 10." The room began to drift away, and I felt a floating sensation.

Twenty-five

For a few seconds I was stunned into immobility and silence. I was lying on a bench and could smell a river. Was it the Thames? The stench was very familiar. I was afraid to open my eyes, but I did feel my clothes. They were course and I was wearing a waistcoat, something I never did in London. Of 2007. When and where was I now? I felt a little nauseous and confused, as though coming round from anaesthetic. My eyes could not focus properly.

I stood up rather unsteadily and looked across the Thames. It was a prospect I recognised, and, far more, utterly desired.

I had come home.

I looked around and realised I was in Southwark, and not too far from the coffee house where I had been forced to leave Cecile. I was intent on rushing there.

As I started to run, I soon realised that something strange had happened to me. A couple walked towards me and I instinctively moved to one side, but they suddenly changed direction and strode right towards me.

I tried to say, "Mind your way, sir." But no sound came.

Instead they seemed to walk right through me.

After they had marched on, I reached to touch the side of a pillar and my hand went through it.

Where was I now? In some limbo of purgatory?

I was moving through objects and people. Was I invisible, a ghost? A phantom of the air? How could I embrace my Cecile, or stay the hand of Black Harry?

Yet I pressed on to find her. I came to the coffee house, not more than a few hundred yards from Solly's, though I had little thought of him, or Tamar, or anyone else, except my love.

I stopped outside the window and looked in. Oh, if there be a just God, why had he done this to me? Make me whole in body, I prayed, so I can use my arms to protect my beloved Cecile!

Inside, though the grimy distorted pane, I could just make out the Richard Durrant that was me, sitting with Cecile and a clearly agitated Black Harry.

I could not contain myelf. I rushed in and shouted, "Cecile – take care, this man Harry wants to harm you!"

I shouted the same again, and nobody could hear me. The crowded room ignored me. Two or three fellows just walked through me. I was a will of the wisp. A spectre.

For a few seconds I stared in admiration of my Cecile. Her eyes, her skin, her grace…but she was in real danger. I could hear but not be heard. I could plainly discern the angry words of Black Harry.

Instinctively, I moved towards my own corporeal being, not to enfold Cecile. I knew I had to inhabit my other self. I stood and then crouched down behind the seated Richard and tried to copy his posture. Something told me to lean into his body, to merge, to somehow allow my consciousness to posses his senses: to warn him of what was coming.

I felt a comforting heat rush through me, and instantly picked up the cup of coffee in front of me. It moved easily to my lips. I had been re-united with myself… A life or death struggle was coming. But my eye-lids suddenly grew heavy like lead.

Twenty-six

I must have blacked out for a second or so. When I re-opened my eyes, the albino was standing over me. I felt warm blood trickle down my face but I staggered to my feet. He still had a knife in his hand, but it dangled by his side as he pulled his other hand to his face. The hot coffee thrown in his face had very temporarily disabled him.

The last of the people remaining in the shop had started to bolt for the door. Fighting was common entertainment, but the blood and knives had made them run outside and look in from the windows.

Through a haze of pain, I saw Harry − face splattered in blood − blundering towards me, feeling for and then pulling his dagger from his belt. I had knives at each side of me now; though the albino seemed out of the fight or waiting for Harry to finish me off. I knew how dangerous and quick he could be. Somehow I managed to get enough momentum to lunge towards him and give him the hardest kick in the groin I could muster. He fell to his knees groaning.

I shifted my heavy legs around and saw the albino, one eye closed and puffy red but advancing on me with his knife.

Suddenly his good eye pivoted left. He must be going for Cecile, I thought. But I could not see her anywhere.

I felt my strength ebbing away. I felt utterly nauseous and I knew I was about to collapse. Yet I stood my ground to face the albino...but my hands were bare. Where was my knife? I fumbled in my belt...as the albino was arching his right hand to slash me with his knife.

Suddenly he was jerked violently backwards. I saw a strong arm around his throat and the other grabbing the albino's arm holding the knife. The force of the jerk backwards and the twisting of his right hand made him drop the knife.

Then I saw a face behind the pained expression of the albino.

It was Jakob's, thank God.

Jakob picked up the knife and ordered the cowed albino to sit on a stool. Without Harry on his side, he had lost all willingness to fight.

Harry wasn't in much of a mood to fight on either. He was utterly winded, and his nose was broken, but he was more defeated by the surprise that I had stood up to him and knocked him down – twice.

Cecile was now by my side. She must have taken cover under the stairs in the corner. She started dabbing my bloodied head with her new handkerchief.

Harry had regained his feet. He faced me square on and, although I could see the aggression burning in his eyes, I knew he was not going to attack me again.

"Harry, we had better be gone from here, before the Watch is on us," I said. "But tell me what made you do this? Not some cock-and-bull story about the Dragoons. Come, man, you know I would never betray the men of the Hurtwood. What else is it?"

I stepped towards him, and to my surprise he flinched.

"Tell me, Harry what is it?"

"That albino, there. That's Jake's son."

I looked at the now pathetic figure, holding the scalded side of his face, red welt against the pale mottled skin.

"And my...nephew," I said quietly.

"Aye," said Harry.

I stared hard at my new-found kin, his good eye rolling in hurt, anger, fear, despair – I knew not.

"There's money in this, ain't there Harry?"

"Aye, Rich. I wants to know what happened to Jake, for the albino's sake, and for mine. And for a share of the money. As I told thee, I want to be a fancy business man comin' up to London too."

Jakob interrupted. "Whatever family quarrels you men have, better to fight about it later. The Watch will be here soon, and we'll all have long to lament in prison. Nobody's too much harmed."

The owner of the coffee shop now came up from behind his counter.

"Gentlemen, do not be leaving us without some payment for the refreshments and the damage."

I pulled a half-sovereign out and slapped it on the counter.

Jakob was now seriously agitated. He pushed me towards the door. "Rich, come with me," he said.

I took Cecile's hand and led her out of the coffee shop. We both followed Jakob into the night.

⋖⋧∞⋨⋗

I could hear Solly's coughing as we sat in the kitchen. Tamar had prepared a hot mustard poultice for the bad gash on the side of my head but, as she was about to apply it, a look of intense mutual understanding materialised between the two women. Tamar handed the bowl and poultice to Cecile.

It hurt a great deal as she applied it to my head. Rachel took in a deep breath which matched mine.

Jakob sat quietly watching my doctoring. Then he said, "You must not go back to the Talbot tonight."

"I agree," I said. "Though I suspect that they will crawl into some hole tonight and not bother us…for a while."

246

"I will come with you tomorrow and get your things. You must stay with us."

"Yes," insisted Rachel and Tamar in unison.

"When were you intending to return to Gomshall?" Jacob asked.

"On Saturday…but I think we should return sooner. Cecile, I do not want you to be in danger. I need to get you back to the Cruikshank household, and I need to talk to Nance about what has been happening in the Hurtwood."

Cecile did not look disappointed. "I have found out what 'appened to my aunt and I am content to return tomorrow, if that is what we must do, Richard."

"Thank'ee Cecile. I am so sorry that Black Harry has upset you by his insults. But I am happy to accept Rachel's kind offer for us to stay here tonight. We shall go back by coach in the morning. Nance, I suspect, will be able to tell me more about that albino lad… Harry didn't introduce us. So I do not even know his name."

Cecile stopped dabbing my head and said simply, "His name is Albert."

Twenty-seven

 $\mathcal{M}$ y first thought was that she had pronounced "Albert" without the "t". And, oddly, it was only the second thought that came to my dazed brain: how the hell do you know who he is?

In this kitchen it was not the time to interrogate her. It was enough to explain to my hosts, let alone myself, why an unknown nephew had tried to knife me.

I kept the explanation to them and Cecile simple: that I had only recently discovered that a free trader from the Hurtwood who had disappeared was my half-brother. Tonight I had also discovered his son.

"Not a happy family reunion," I said, "considering he had tried to put a knife into me. And this business about my betraying the free traders is nonsense."

I looked at Cecile.

"The family here – my family here – know that I was a free trader, but Solly was party to persuading me to stop and become an honest man and pay the duties on my goods. And that battle in the Hurtwood…"

Cecile interrupted: "Do not be ashamed, Richard. They talk of the 'urtwood men standing and fighting the Dragoons as though they were 'eroes." She suddenly looked as though she had spoken out of turn. "Well, that is what they said in the parlour in the 'ousehold where I work," she said, with a renewed defiance in her voice.

"I'm not sure we were heroes. We fought back against them, it is true, when they tried to take us by surprise. Now I am glad that no one was killed on their side, although we lost one man. I fought alongside Harry, as he well knows. I must get to the bottom of this mystery."

My heart felt heavy. I knew that Harry was using "Albert", or whatever his name was, to get at some of the no-doubt exaggerated fortune he thought I had in hiding. I would willingly share some with Jake's son – my albino nephew or half-nephew – once I had discovered the full story. But I would rather be lashed than hand any money over to a conniving blackmailer like Black Harry. I didn't regret hitting him hard – he'd had it coming for a long time.

That night Cecile slept in the bedroom with the picture of Jesus. I slept in a rough cot-bed in the same room as Jakob, just like when we were young lads. It gave me the chance to thank him for saving my life.

I slept well but I had troubling dreams, which were still running through my brain when I took my leave of Solly. I remember exactly his last words to me: "Trying to make a good honest man of you, getting you even to sell a better class of *shlock*, and vhat you do? You go getting my son into fights…and who is dis woman, eh?"

He winked at me. No malice was in evidence.

"My Tamar says she is *balabatish*[25], and if Tamar says she is that gut then she must be."

"Thank you for all your help, Solly."

"And stop all dis trouble in the hills vit all dese bad men. I want dat you be a big man wid a big business. And if dat happens, you can make my Jakob a partner, no?"

"I would be honoured to do so."

"Goodbye," he said, as I kissed him on the cheek.

I saw that Rachel or Tamar had put a new yarmulka on his head – that he obviously wanted to look his best for the rabbi who was visiting later. As I closed his door, I took one look back at the wizened figure huddled in the bed. I knew that I would not see dear Solly again.

⊰⊱

Our rapid departure from London was smoothly done. Jakob and two of his friends, rather large men who did undefined "heavy work for Solly", escorted us to the Talbot, and we collected our possessions and paid the account. Then they put us on the wagon to Richmond and waved us off. I hadn't expected to see Harry or the albino – they would be licking their wounds. Nor did I expect them to rush back to the Hurtwood. I needed a day or two there to get the lie of the land.

It was near impossible to talk confidentially either in the crowded wagon, or in the coach back to Godalming. I had paid a little extra to get on the next coach south. The six passengers, Cecile and myself, as well as two married couples, sat largely in silence. There was much that Cecile and I needed to talk about, but my prime concern was to get her safely back to her household.

My head throbbed, and I winced a few times when the coach jolted over potholes, despite the new cantilever springs. Cecile put her hand out to touch mine, to give me reassurance, not just for my sore head, I sensed, but also for the confessions I had made about my past. And I wondered about her. How could she know of "Albert", the relative who had tried to kill me? The events of the London adventure spun around in my head, as we made good progress to Godalming.

At the staging post of the King's Head, I removed our luggage, and retrieved my horse and cart. When that stabling account was paid, and we had set off briskly towards the encroaching dusk and Albury, it was the first chance I'd had to talk alone to Cecile.

"We must converse at length soon. I have much to tell you."

"And there are many things I must confess too," she said.

"About Albert?"

"Yes."

"First I am concerned with your safety. I need to get you back to the Cruikshanks. I don't want my lady endangered in any more knife-fights, although I think that Black Harry will leave me alone for a while."

She took a deep breath and, drawing on all her courage, said, "Richard, I am not expected back until tomorrow afternoon. We have an evening and a day when we could talk. I 'ave never been to the little farm that you oft spoke of. I would be pleased to visit now."

I was silent for a moment or two. "Aye, I would like you to see my home, and – in the unlikely event that Harry pays us a visit – I doubt whether he would be pressing me too much. He may have learned his lesson."

So we rode on past Albury and down to the track that went through Shere, and within a few minutes we arrived safely at my little home in Gomshall.

After I had stabled Diamond, I led Cecile around from the back yard to enter my home at the front. When I opened the door the last light entered with me.

I lit a rush light and Cecile had the chance to see my domain.

I was completely startled to see someone sitting in a darkened corner in the seat next to my fireplace

As I reached instinctively for my dagger, Nance spoke, just as I recognized her features in the shadows.

"Rich, didn't know thee would be back early, but I came here just in case…"

"Nance, a surprise…er, let me introduce you to Cecile."

Nance stood up and, instead of shaking hands with my guest, she embraced her.

"Ah, Rich, she is as lovely as thy stories of her."

Cecile bowed her head slightly.

I explained, too quickly I suspect: "Nance is my friend, and my part-time housekeeper."

Nance made a slight curtsey to Cecile.

"It may be too late in the year for a fire, but a chill there is in this spring night. I will light the fire. Ladies, please sit down."

As the fire flickered into life, Nance said quietly that she needed to speak to me, alone.

"You can speak freely in front of Cecile. She has recently met Black Harry and knows of my past."

I told Nance briefly what had happened.

"It is of Black Harry that I came here to tell thee. Urgent it is. That's why I waited here, to tell thee of the danger. The families of the men who were taken by the Dragoons have steel in their hands and fire in their hearts…"

"They suspect me of betraying them, as Black Harry said?"

"No, Rich. We knows that Black Harry turned informer, to get his pardon. And the Hurtwood men are chasing him. They're taking him on a French holiday…"

Cecile interrupted by gently asking what that meant.

"When smugglers turn against their own," Nance explained, "sometimes an informer who will be a witness is taken away, under strong guard, to Calais or nearby port. They don't kill 'em over there, but they spend a rough year or two contemplatin' their betrayal, and away from the courts. Our men will get Black Harry, either here or in London. He might try to get the Revenue to protect him, but that's not his way. He may have betrayed us, but he ain't no coward."

"But do you think Richard is in danger?" Cecile asked plaintively.

"Perhaps not. Besides the men the Dragoons took to Guildford jail, there are a few more names on a list. I am told Rich's name is not on it," Nance said firmly.

"So Black Harry may not have informed on me. I think he wanted me free long enough to force some money out of me. If I were in jail, he would have struggled to get his hands on my sovereigns in London."

"The news needed to be told to thee, Rich. Now I must leave the two lovebirds to coo on their own."

I asked Nance to stay for a meal, but we both understood that I needed to be alone with Cecile.

I led her to the yard and told her to take my old cart and Diamond. Will could return it in the morning. I didn't want her walking through the woods at night. I thanked her and said goodnight. Normally I would have escorted her home, but I needed my time with Cecile.

I walked briskly back in and took both Cecile's hands. We stood in front of the fireplace, and I said, "Enough of smugglers' derring-do. Welcome to my house. It is yours as much as mine."

"It is so pretty," she said. "And clean and well-ordered for a man on his own," she added, with a smile.

"I have Nance to thank for that. Please explore, as you wish."

She took me at my word and wandered around the downstairs.

"May I look upstairs too?"

"Of course." I offered her a candle.

I had two bedrooms, but only one was properly set up. There was a cot bed in the second room. I was unsure of what to do.

The fire was burning cheerfully. Cecile had come downstairs and had offered to help prepare a meal, although I had but cured ham and cheese. To drink I had only brandy. I pulled up a small table by the two rush chairs in front of the fireplace. It was what I had always wanted.

We talked of the house for a while, including my concern at the rough beaten earth floor.

"I have laid two small rugs down, but it still doesn't seem right."

"They are good rugs," she said.

We drank a little brandy, and I drank a little more, because I needed to fortify myself to tell my story. And there in front of the roaring fire, while holding her hand, I told her of my life.

She let me talk for an hour or more, although she did ask one or two questions or for me to clarify the occasional word she did not understand: a Yiddish phrase when I spoke of Solly and a dialect word about my time in the Hurtwood. I left out one major incident: my killing of Jake.

I was almost glad, though, when she cut straight to this omission when she asked about what Black Harry had said about the missing man.

"I will tell you all the story, although it grieves me to do so," I said.

Finally, I risked all by explaining how I killed the man in self-defence.

"There − I am a murderer too, although in truth it was manslaughter. He would have killed me. I doubt if you can forgive me or love me still, after that chronicle."

She got up from her seat and gently kissed me on the lips, and then walked around the room as if trying to make a decision.

She returned to the fireside and placed two hands against the mantle-shelf and looked hard into the fire.

"Did this Jake have a large scar on his face, here" − and she touched her cheek − "on the left side?"

"Yes," I said. "So you knew him, as well as his son?"

"Yes, I knew them both. Now that I have seen Albert again, there can be little doubt."

"How did you know of them, Cecile?" I said, trying to hide my fears.

"Ah, I 'ave kept so much tied inside my heart. So much 'urt. But going to London, and finding out about my aunt, and then...what 'appened in the coffee shop, and seeing the albino Albert again...and what you are saying about his father...and then the question of my love. I will relate my story though I fear you will never love me again. I am per'aps not worthy of that love. I will confess all now, because it is about Jake and it will, I 'ope, make your guilt feel less of a burden. I do know he deserved to die."

"It was self-defence, as I said."

"No, for me, it was more than that. It was God's justice...for what he did to *me*."

Twenty-eight

She pulled her chair to face mine, and she took both my hands and faced me squarely, as the firelight accentuated the glistening teardrops in her brown and green eyes. She squeezed my hands, and then took in a deep breath and exhaled heavily.

"This is my 'istory," she said. "And it is a sad tale."

Again she stopped, and it seemed as though she would break down in tears. Her lips trembled, but then her face took on a stronger look. She pursed her lips and continued, after taking a sip of the extra brandy I had given her.

"I have told you some of my travails in coming to London. My mother, father, aunt and I came to England in 1782. I was then but twenty-two years of age. My brother, Alexander, died in Switzerland, a year or so before we left for England. Although the Swiss had been kind, little work was to be found, and my father was promised employment in London. My father was a skilled man, especially in the making of watches and clocks. For two years we lived, firstly in lodgings, then we rented a small 'ouse in Chelsea, very near to the Royal Hospital. We were content that we were making a new life. My father arranged with one of his customers for me to go into domestic service. It was a very respectable 'ouse in St James's Square. I lived in, but it was not too far for me to walk out on weekends to visit my family.

"My new master was Colonel David Prendergast, a Guards officer. He was stern, but his wife – Mrs Charlotte – was generous of spirit. They had two young children, George and Caroline, whom I doted on. I was worked 'ard, but I was quite 'appy. It was a respectable 'ousehold, I had saved a little, and my parents were beginning to prosper. But I could not know what was to befall me.

"I had been with the Prendergasts for two years, and all was well. They would sometimes ask me to stay in the 'ouse over weekends, if they were to go to the countryside. Often the manservant, Mr Trotter, would stay too. But occasionally I was left on my own, with strict instructions to open the doors to no one. I was allowed to go into Colonel Prendergast's library to occupy my few free hours by educating myself. I did read some of the worthy tomes on the natural sciences, but I must confess to pouring over the romances which the madam contrived to leave for me. The colonel said such books 'corrupt the minds of young women, if they do not have the breeding and education to separate the wheat from the chaff. But for servants they fill their minds with nonsense.' I enjoyed reading them.

"Yet per'aps he was right. Perchance they did fill my head with nonsense, because I made a very terrible mistake. Occasionally, a tradesman, who called himself Bill Butcher, would call. He traded in hardware – saucepans and the like. The cook and the madam would sometimes buy from him. I had a passing knowledge of him. I answered the door to him once or twice, and I had seen him in the servants' kitchen in conversation with Mrs 'opkins, the cook, or Mr Trotter. But we had never exchanged more than a few polite words.

"Then, in the summer of 1785, the master and the madam took themselves off to Bath for a week to take the waters there. Mrs 'opkins and I were left in charge of the 'ouse, as Mr Trotter accompanied the family. Mrs 'opkins, against orders, decided to take some leisure hours with a man of her fancy who lived nearby. So it was that I was left alone one Saturday afternoon. I had finished my chores for the day, and I was reading in the servants' kitchen.

"I heard a knocking at the door. I thought perhaps it was Mrs 'opkins who had forgotten her key. I was under strict orders not to open the door, especially if I were on my own. I was afraid, though, that Mrs 'opkins would be in a fury if I left her at the door. She 'ad a fierce temper.

"The knocking continued. And so I went behind the front door and I shouted, 'Is that Mrs 'opkins?'

"Then a man's voice I heard. 'No, it's Bill Butcher, with goods ordered by the madam.'

"'Sir, I cannot let anyone in. I am under strict instructions not to do so. Would you call later, at least when Mrs 'opkins is here?'

"'Miss, I cannot. I have an urgent request for my goods this afternoon in Grosvenor Square. And your madam has exactly stated that she wanted these pans to be delivered this afternoon.'

"I did not know what to do. Either way I could cause grave distress to my mistress. And in the summer many maids are turned out of their employment, so I did not want to cause offence.

"And so I opened the door.

"Mr Butcher was standing there with a wooden crate.

"'Miss, I shall carry this heavy box into the kitchen. It is too heavy for a slip of a girl such as thee.'

"'No, sir,' I says strongly. 'I will carry it. I cannot let a stranger in while the 'ouse is empty' – foolish for me to admit it, I know.

"But he was already around the door, and walking to the kitchen.

"I closed the door, and followed him into the kitchen.

"'Sir, you must leave now,' I says...I talked in the London fashion then, not as we do here in the country. It was "you", not "thee", as is the way here.

"Anyway, I says he must leave promptly. But he dallied in the kitchen, boldly unloading some of his pans.

"Again, I says, 'Sir you must be going now, or I will lose my job. And Mr Trotter and Mrs 'opkins will be here presently, and will be upset with your presence.'"

"'Now, little French missie,' he went on. 'I knows they all be out. I saw Mrs 'opkins leave a while back on her way to meet a man, no doubt.' And if I may speak as he did – 'She likes a tipple and a toolling does that one.'"

"'Sir, please leave now. I am offended by your coarseness.'"

"'Ah, your dainty French manners,' he said."

"I said nothing."

"'In that case I will withdraw immediately.'"

"Much relieved, I felt, when he marched rapidly to the door. He got there a few yards ahead of me, and instead of leaving, he opened the door and two other brutes came in.

"I started to scream, but the three of them grabbed me and tied a cloth around my mouth, and then they dragged me to the kitchen and fastened me to a chair with rope that they had.

"I was in very great distress, especially when one of the men started to undo the top buttons of my dress. But Bill Butcher said, 'Leave her, son, we have silver to unload – no time for courting.'

"For fifteen minutes or so, I heard them run all over the house. I heard them go into the dining room, and I heard the clatter of plate. The silver, I presumed. No one paid heed to me in the kitchen. After those noisy minutes, it went all quiet.

"Richard, imagine how I felt. I had disobeyed my orders and now the 'ouse had been robbed.

"It took hours – it seemed – there was no timepiece in the kitchen – before I 'eard the key in the front door, and then the 'eavy steps of Mrs 'opkins.

"The rest now seems a nightmare.

"Mrs 'opkins undid my gag, but did not untie the ropes. She immediately suspected me of helping the criminals. She listened to my account for a few minutes and then went back out to get the Watch. Within half-hour, I had been taken to the Magistrates Office in Chelsea.

"I spent the next five days in a cell with four women, all prostitutes. They were very kind to me, especially one called Sophie, and they protected me from the constables who would have taken me to a single cell and forced themselves on me. One drunken man who came into the cell to take me off was given a mighty beating by the ladies. And I was glad that they treated me so well, even though I was French and not of their calling.

"I had explained to them that I had never known a man. That I had once been briefly walking out with a young man called Claude in our home village near Lyons. The ladies thought it amusing that I had been but kissed once or twice. They delighted in telling me all manner of things which shocked me then, but proved to be useful lessons for what was soon to come. They all proclaimed they had once been women of virtue – that's what they told me – that they had been set on a pedestal which had left them little room to move, except to fall. They warned that virtue was a poor defence; I need to be cunning, they said."

I had to interrupt: "Surely the Colonel must have stepped in to help, or the family – Aunt Suzanne, who must have been a determined woman."

"Yes, my father came to my cell as soon as he found out and brought me food and clean clothing, and I told him all.

"Later, I was told that he had gone straight to the Colonel, who refused to meet him. Mr Trotter did heed his words, and my father begged him to carry the message to the Colonel. By my own admission I had disobeyed his orders and his military mind showed no mercy for those who disobeyed orders. The Colonel, I believe, was poisoned by Mrs 'opkins's ...innuendoes – is that the right word, Richard?"

I nodded.

"I think she may have played a deliberate part in my misfortune. I will never know whether she was in with those devils who robbed us.

"After five days I was taken before the magistrate who read out a brief in…indictment – I think that is correct – and I was taken in chains to Newgate.

"I cannot even begin to describe the hell that was Newgate prison."

I poured more brandy into her glass, and she took a big swig. She stood up and walked towards my grand clock. I watched her touch it carefully and examine it.

"I think I have seen this clock before. It is so charming and distinctive. I am sure my father worked on this, or one very like this, in France when I was a young girl. Perhaps tomorrow in better light I can look at it in more detail?"

"Of course. You are intrigued by the clock and that might explain why I was always so drawn to it. Ah ha, a mystery solved, and a good portent of our life together: we have all found each other – in my humble farmhouse."

These were clumsy words to revive her spirits. I understood that she needed time to gather her strength for the rest of her harrowing tale.

Cecile walked around the room for a few seconds, then sat back in the chair and looked again into the fire. She began again and her voice took on almost a monotone of dread.

"The first thing that overcame me was the smell – a mixture of decaying bodies, dead and alive, foul air, urine – *mon Dieu*, I would need to tell you in the worst gutter French. And the noise, everybody seemed to be shouting. I had read some of Dante's *Inferno* – a French translation – and Newgate was worse, worse than I heard about the conditions in the Bastille, in Paris, Richard. It really was.

"After the smell came the fettering around the ankles, much 'eavier than the chains they had put on me in the magistrate's court. 'Ironing,' they called it.

"Because I was waiting trial for possible execution, but not yet convicted, I was not put in one of the dungeons without light. Newgate, I soon learned, 'ad more levels of rank than the old court of the French king. My father had managed to pay one of the jailors, so I was given a cell – with thirty other women – where we could pay for food and drink. It was called the Master's Side, for those who could afford the half-crown weekly rent. Only those with supportive families or 'igh-class courtesans and successful shoplifters could afford this. The other women lived in far worse conditions in the Common Side – those without means to pay for the extras. They lived on three ha'pence worth of stale bread, odd scraps and foul water per day.

"Yet even on the Master's Side, our cell had just one window on to an inner courtyard. It had no beds. Inside was a wooden ramp with a beam across the top. This served as beds – the others slept on the floor – stone slabs, full of spit and piss – please excuse my language, I am trying not to speak like a 'Newgate bird' or 'nightingales' as the women called themselves…I have tried so hard since to speak good English not the patois I learned in that jail.

"My father worked hard at keeping the jailers bribed, so I could hire a raw hemp blanket. Without 'blunt'- money – from the outside, few could survive for more than a few months.

"Everything stank. When I was led into the cell – the women all cheered, and laughed as I lifted my feet, thinking I was walking on snail shells in the garden – it was a sea of squirming lice which my feet crunched.

"The 'matron' of the cell – the head woman – shouted to the others 'How are we going to make this black dog walk?' which I later found out was: what sorts of barbaric initiation rites are we going to impose on her. 'We have to get her ready for the cheat' – that's what they called the gallows.

"I was bullied and beaten, until the matron, realizing I had money being paid by my father, took me under her wing, but for a considerable consideration. If anyone came in with money, she would take it and she would act as cell treasurer, buying food for her favourites and giving naught but scraps to those whom she disliked."

Cecile stopped and looked at me. I nodded to urge her on to continue her story.

"At seven a.m. a bell woke the prisoners – those who managed to sleep – and we then had to empty our chamber pots, be counted and then get scraps for breakfast. For the rest of the day, Newgate was given over to drinking 'hogwash' – watered-down beer; the favourites sometime could buy spirits. It kept the prisoners and jailers occupied, until the rare pardon, terminal sickness or the gallows released the inmates.

"The matron – that's what we always called her – I never learned her name – took a liking to me, not just because of the money from my father. She was very tough, a big-boned woman, who would often strike us, but she also wanted to better herself. She asked me to teach her a little French, and would stop the other women abusing me just because I came from France.

"On two occasions she took me with her – after paying the guards – to the drinking cellar. It was a dungeon without windows, but it had pyramids of candle wax, six feet high. The smoke used to go out of a flue in the stone ceiling. A male prisoner nicknamed King George sold gin there, although people called it Cock-my-Cap, Kill-Grief or Comfort. In a corner some of the women sold themselves on the damp straw without even a curtain, but matron looked after me. Except for two trips to drink gin, I did not leave my cell for over two months.

"My father and my aunt were allowed to visit me once, although it cost more than a sovereign, and they spoke to me through an iron grille on to a dark corridor, but we could talk for just a few minutes. Papa told me he hoped that someone from the Prendergast 'ousehold would speak up for me, though the Colonel would not withdraw charges, even though he knew that the missing silver amounted to far more than a capital offence. Papa tried not to cry when he visited me, but he knew I faced the gallows, although we did not speak of it. My aunt was practical – she brought me a book and some food. Matron took the food, but let me keep the book. It was a romance in French called the *Les Amours de la Tristesse* by Michelle Dubois – but that was a nom de plume. I read it five times over and then parts of it to the matron, who asked me to translate the more romantic passages.

"We saw no doctor or apothecary, though the cell was sprayed from a barrel and a foot pump. We were covered in an evil-smelling liquid, which must have had some vinegar in it by the smell of it.

"After two months I was told by a jailor I was one of those 'cast for law'. Matron explained that I would be up for the sessions at the Old Bailey soon. And one morning, very early, I was led in chains though Dead Man's Walk, a closed passageway that ended up in the High Court. I was with Mary, who was a coiner, and a mad woman, Lucy, who screamed endlessly and who was charged with stealing a silver cup. Another woman was in our procession; she had a young baby with her. Five men were also in chains with us. From what I remember, one had stolen a horse and the others were charged with 'stealing privily' – picking pockets.

"So ten of us were led into the court in the Old Bailey. It was winter but all the windows were open. I could smell the wine and vinegar which had been used to cleanse the large courtroom. Herbs were being burnt on two open braziers, the only heat in the very cold room.

"The public gallery was full of idle folk, all chewing, I think, on garlic to prevent infection from the prisoners' breath. We did look like we could infect the whole of these islands.

Dressed in brown prison serge dresses and the men in similar coloured tunics, we were filthy and lousy, although we had been told to dress our best, which was almost impossible in the cells, where open sewers ran through the middle of the floor.

"We all filed into a wooden pen. A clerk read out the names of the commissioners of the peace, the mayor, bailiffs and constables, and finally Justice Mr Frederick Makepeace entered and everyone stood up. The twelve men of the jury then came into their box, which had benches. They were all men, nearly all fat and middle-aged. Worthy citizens, no doubt. We were still standing in chains.

"Judge Makepeace gave a short speech on the glories of the English constitution, though I do not think that had anything to do with me being French. I did manage to glance behind me and see that Papa had found or bribed his way into the public gallery, I am sure the occasion would have been too distressing for Mama.

"The judge then left to go into his private chamber, to listen to the charges against us, I was told later. The witnesses were summoned before the judge, away from the public and us. My father had told me that Mr Trotter would speak on my behalf, but he had not seen any of the events, so he would, I 'ope, have spoken of my good character.

"The judge came back into the court and read out a brief summary of our offences, and we were asked to raise our hands and say how we pleaded. Half of us – including me – said we were not guilty.

"Then, oh so rapidly, Richard, throwing away lives like children throw sticks in a river" – and she got up from her chair and touched me on the shoulder – "he read out the verdicts – all guilty.

"Mine was read out last: Transportation to Parts Beyond the Seas. I would have fainted, from fear, injustice and prison fever, but we were chained together and crowded in that wooden box. I took little comfort from the fact that two of the other women and one man were sentenced to death. The others, like me, would be sent in exile to the British colonies."

⟨≋∞≋⟩

I could see that Cecile was very understandably agitated. I said, "Please take another brandy."

"No," she said firmly. "I have drunk enough – *merci.*" I sensed that her use of French implied that she could relax with me. She had obviously made great efforts to learn good English, the London style and our dialect here in Surrey, as well as the prison language, of which I had only a smattering from living with Solly in Southwark.

"Despite my trials – and the awful gin in Newgate – I drink but little," she said with a laugh. She had not lost her spirit, and I admired that beyond measure.

"Do you wish to retire to bed now? It has been a very tiring day for you. We have, God willing, many years to share and your story can be told later," I said.

"No, please, I wish to tell it now. No one has heard it all before. It has weighed so much on me. Please let me finish."

I pulled the wooden bench up to the fireside, and patted it to ask her to sit down next to me.

She did so, and I put my arm around her as we leaned towards the fire, which I had banked up with more logs.

⟨≋∞≋⟩

"So what happened after the court? Was there a reprieve, because I must assume that you were not sent to the colonies?"

"I had no reprieve. Colonel Prendergast did not relent. We went back to Newgate. And I was put in the same cell. It was almost reassuring that matron was there to ask how I had fared. But, the next morning, I was dragged to another – even worse

– cell. This had no window, just a small grating high in the wall. Nearly twenty-five women, three with children, were in this plague pit. Two women, one aged about fourteen, attempted to kill themselves during the night by stripping a piece of serge from their hems and trying to hang themselves from the top bars of the cell gate. We got them down in time – the jailors would not have cared a jot.

"I got no extra food, so perhaps my father had not been able to bribe anyone, or the officials had simply put the money in their pockets. The regime was much 'arder – one jailor in particular liked to come in and whip the women, for any kind of reason.

"In those terrible conditions, a person has to talk to someone or you become mad. A milliner was in there who had been accused of stealing a hat or perhaps two. And she knew a little about transportation. I understood so little, but anything – even the gallows – was better than trying to survive in that hell-hole.

"The milliner – I forget her name now – told me that the Americans, having fought for their republic, refused to allow any convicts to be transported there. So the British government was sending more convicts to the Caribbean. Some of the most depraved felons, she said, were being shipped to West Africa, to trading posts in swamps, where few survived and many were eaten by cannibals.

"None of this seemed attractive to me, though taking a chance with a cannibal grew increasingly more pleasing than being whipped in that disease-ridden tomb. Three women had died of prison fever in two days before the milliner shared her knowledge of geography with me. I had no idea where I was to be sent, and I was desperate to speak to my parents to wish them farewell. I could not bear to be sent away to die in some foreign part without at least a final glance of them.

"It was 'orrible then to be woken up much earlier, at five I believe, and for three of us women's names to be called out.

The milliner, another woman whom I had not spoken to, and myself were taken out. Irons were riveted around our wrists and we were roped together with five women from other cells.

"Dawn was just breaking as we were led out of Newgate. The foggy fresh air tasted as though it was the finest wine in Christendom. I shall never forget that sweet, sweet air."

I felt impelled to offer a response. "Should I open some of the shutters in this room?"

"No, no – your cottage smells so sweetly and the aroma of the fire-wood is so pleasing...But I must finish my tragic tale.

"At Blackfriars Bridge we were loaded like sacks on a lighter and were rowed down the Thames to Galleon's Reach. After the confines of the prison, the world exploded around my eyes. Even at this early hour it was marvellous to witness so much hustle and bustle, with dockers loading and unloading the tall-masted ships. Coal dust 'ung in the air, as many of the ships were colliers.

"Yet I felt so free, even though I was in chains and probably destined to be a slave in Africa. The women were all chattering about being out, out, out of the hell that was Newgate, while others lamented their forthcoming exile without a chance to bid farewell to their loved ones.

"At Galleon's Reach we were then put in a slightly larger boat and taken to a prison 'ulk on the river near Woolwich. All around the waters of Woolwich and Deptford lay worn-out shells of vessels no longer good for naval service.

"When the transportations to the American colonies stopped, more and more 'ulks had been press-ganged into use as prisons. The government expected the American rebellion to be brief. But, years after the war ended, a whole shantytown of floating prisons had formed their own convict colonies on the Thames. Some of the men had been there a decade, sleeping in fetters and working twelve hours a day in the government dockyards.

"As we were taken past them, many of the male convicts

waiting to be rowed ashore for the day's hard labour waved and shouted at us.

"'Ah, our sisters in irons. Welcome to 'ulk heaven,' one said from a boat near us. Others made very lewd suggestions, which I shall not repeat.

"We embarked on to a female convict ship called the *Resolute*, although its days as a proud fighting vessel were long gone. It was a fetid floating brothel, I soon discovered. The air was better than in Newgate. That was all that mattered for the moment. I was living not by the day, but by the hour. That was the main lesson I had learned from being a Newgate nightingale.

"After our heavy fetters were removed from our wrists, we were put in light leg irons. The captain summoned us to stand to attention. He said that this would be an overnight stay. We were told that we would be sailing to Africa in twenty-four hours on another ship. If families wanted to bid us farewell, they should be quick about it, he warned.

"How could I inform my dear parents? I would never see them again."

Twenty-nine

I was not to know that I would spend nearly two years on this ship.

"After the captain had addressed us we were locked up below decks. It was even more crowded than in Newgate and it stank almost as much. We were cooped up in the bow, chained, and the space between the decks was a foot shorter than I stand.

"The next day – we had not been fed, although some water had been given us – the manacles around our wrists were removed, although we were chained at night by light ankle fetters. We were told these would be removed once we were at sea in the ship that we were soon to embark on.

"The captain left and we were put under the command of a superintendent of convicts, a man named Philip Clark. He proved to be a poor leader, withdrawn – per'aps because he used to – ah, we would say *bégayer* in French…"

She looked at me. I could not help.

"Er, *bégayer*, yes…he 'ad a terrible stutter.

"Although our personal lives were run by another matron on our deck level – the prison rules were much the same as in Newgate – our overseer was a man named Michael Southey. Everyone called him Mad Mike, although never to his face. If my life was hell on this ship, my greatest tormentor and cause of most of my distress was this Michael Southey.

"The days became weeks on the ship. We were not let off the *Resolute* but we did spend an hour or so per day on the deck, in shifts. We scrubbed the decks and were allowed a short time for personal cleaning and laundry. Because we expected to leave at any time, the pardons, petitions, pleas for clemency because of sickness or pregnancy – 'pleading the belly' it was called – kept the ship's clerk very busy. I had no money, but I persuaded Rebecca, a counterfeiter who had befriended me, to put in a letter to my parents in one she was sending to her husband who lived close by Chelsea. She used her last pennies to bribe the prison clerk.

"Three days later my father came on board. He paid five shillings for ten minutes with me. He was so overjoyed to see me alive and still in England. He had been told I had been transported to Africa. He brought me news of my mother, although he did not then tell me how sick she was. Aunt Suzanne, he said, was hale and hearty. Papa brought me food, clothing – and, thank heaven, some books. He also secretly gave me some money, which I sewed into my dress. Because we were expecting to sail shortly, custom allowed prisoners to wear their own clothes, if they had them.

"My father promised that he would do all in his power to seek a petition, signed by Colonel Prendergast, to ask for clemency, to at least be allowed to serve out a sentence in an English jail rather than be sent to New 'olland or Africa.

"Mad Mike soon hurried my father off the ship, and then he said, 'My beauty, you'll be staying with me on board this ship. There'll be no petitions for the likes of you.'

"It was a mistake for me to wear my new dress. In dirty prison clothes I was less likely to attract male attention, but in a clean dress – which the matron allowed me to keep – the guards began to take more notice of me.

"I soon began to learn a new language – that of the sea. Few sailors were on board, but we soon came to pick up what was aft and for'ard and which was the mizzen mast and which was the main, although the ship had no sails for the masts. We became used to the feel of hard timber beneath our bare feet and the stench of the bilge, and the privies, which we learned to call 'heads'.

"The smell from the old bilge and ballast touched every part of the ship, even when the wind was up on the river, especially in the lowest levels of the ship where we were locked up. Even though the vessel smelled like one 'uge privy, the ship itself was clean. Some of the guards were retired sailors and they had us stoning down the wood, whitewashing and scrubbing with vinegar. It was in the jailors' interests to keep typhus and other diseases at bay. Yet we were still over-run with lice, fleas, cockroaches and big river rats.

"After the weeks became months, tempers grew worse, both among the jailors and the female prisoners. Two or three times we were let off the ship – in chain gangs – to help pick potatoes, strawberries and the like in nearby farms. Only small numbers were trusted to leave, even in chains and under guard. This led to many fights among the women. As in Newgate, the matrons led rival gangs. These ruled the roost when the lights went out on the bottom decks.

"Conditions became so bad that Mad Mike had one matron tied up to the main mast and he gave her one dozen lashes with the cat o' nine tails.

"Although none of the convicts wanted to leave England, the constant expectation – always dashed – that we were about to embark on a sea-going vessel caused difficulties, especially for the jailors. Some were due to sail with us – to Botany Bay we were now told. Once a ship set sail for foreign parts, the sailors – and guards – had new rights, the unofficial law of the sea. Every man, and officer, had the right to take a female mate, which made female convict ships more attractive to many sailors. And the government allowed this: they wanted more babies – new settlers for the colonies.

"Mad Mike was a cruel tyrant, though he kept the guards under control – there were few attacks to take advantage of our bodies. Slowly this rule broke down.

"Mad Mike soon made it clear that I was intended to be his mate. This terrified me, because he was a brute. He kept the other guards from beating or using me. They were as afraid of him as I was.

"He told me once, 'I've got my pride, girl. I could take you when I chooses, but I wants to be a gen'leman like. I want you to come to me when we set sail.'

"We did not set sail, and Mad Mike grew angrier.

"At first, he would regularly whip women as an example. He seemed to pick the uglier women, rather than the trouble-makers.

"He whispered in my ear, after he had been drinking, 'I don't like my lovelies to be scarred by the cat. So you'd better be behaving yourself for me, and you will not feel its lick.'

"After a year on the *Resolute*, Mad Mike truly began to deserve his nickname. He had a dog, a big bull mastiff, whom he had trained..."

⟨※⟩

Cecile stopped, and sipped a little on the brandy glass that I had topped up again.

"Richard, I am leaving so much out of my tale, for your sake as well as my own. I know that you will think me a common whore...but I will complete my story."

I put my arm tightly around her.

"Yes, Mad Mike trained this dog to...use women. Again it was the less pretty women that were so grossly attacked. Two of the matrons petitioned the superintendent, but they were ignored and Mad Mike had them whipped with twenty lashes, and left tied overnight and no one was allowed to tend their wounds.

"This was a dark time for me. It was helped by the arrival on board of Louise. She was French and, although she did not tell me directly, I think she had worked as a courtesan. It was so wonderful to speak in French. She shared a wooden bunk below mine. And we had time to whisper at nights.

"She told me a French quotation, which I have never forgotten: 'In France women are the companions in the hours of reason and conversation, but in England they are merely momentary toys of passion.' It seemed true, although of course I did not know what French prisons were like. I expect they were the same.

"To Louise, I confided my fears of what that beast Mad Mike would do to me, and she gave me much advice of a female kind. It would not be fitting to say too much beyond that she explained what was called 'an English overcoat'; that I should not become pregnant at all costs, being with child and bearing it on a long sea journey could kill me and the child, she said. She told me about other ways to prevent a child, were I forced to submit to the beast, and she also told me about the French way − *à la derriere* − which shocked me, but she kept saying that anything was better than a pregnancy, especially with such an animal as a father. The women, she told me, were always abandoned, once the voyage was over.

"Louise told me, 'If we go to Botany Bay, we should contrive to arrive as single women, and hopefully our French style and our pretty faces − if our looks survive the voyage − will catch us an officer there. We will live better, and that is a place to have a child − on dry land and with a decent man, not the scum that run this ship.'

"One day, when I was scrubbing the deck, Mad Mike sent one of the guards to summon me. The superintendent lived onshore, and the brute had taken up the captain's space − the quarterdeck. It was the most airy part of the ship, and the most comfortable.

"I knocked on the door.

"'Come in,' he shouted.

"I stepped nervously in to the cabin.

"'Look, my little French beauty,' he said, 'we bin on board this rotten heap of timber for nigh on a year, and I bin a gen'leman to you. It is now time for you to give somethin' back. I wants you now – in my berth there. Take off that dress, or I will take it off for you.'

"'No, sir,' I said. 'You have no rights of that kind until we set sail – and leave English law.'

"'Poppycock, woman, what lawyer men hae' ye bin listenin' to? It is my right now.'

"'No, sir, I will lay a complaint to the superintendent.'

"'Ha, that stuttering little pimp of a man…But, as I said, I don't want to be forcing you. We need to get on like, during a long voyage. So, please, come and lay with me in my berth.'

"'No, sir,' and I turned to leave.

"'Why, you cheeky French strumpet, I'll let my dog hae you instead.'

"'The dog, sir,' says I boldly, 'is more of a man than you.'

"Then he shouted for two guards to take me.

"They rushed in and dragged me to the main mast. Mad Mike stood there watching me, as my dress was pulled down to my waist.

"And there in front of the whole ship I was given twelve lashes for insubordination.

"He ordered thus: 'Don't whip her face lads or her fine breasts – just let her back feel the lick. I want something left of her for later.'"

❧⟊❧

Cecile took another sip of her brandy. I expected her to break down, but she did not.

"He whipped me twice more – on one occasion I had twenty lashes."

She undid some of her top buttons, enough for her to pull her dress and undergarments a little off her shoulder.

"See, the wealds there, like claw marks on the back of my shoulder. I have scars all down my sides and back."

Looking at them broke my heart. I also saw the pain in her face and the creases under her eyes that my love-sick vision had hidden from me. No matter, I loved her even more.

She saw my hurt, but she continued, "I am proud to say that I never succumbed to that animal. I could not have stood many more lashings but, a few days after my third whipping, he was suddenly transferred. I know not why, though I doubt if the superintendent had him moved. In Newgate and on board the prison ship we convicts very rarely felt that any authority cared a penny for us prisoners.

"A few months after the beast left, Louise died of fever. That was another dark time for me. At the same time, my father visited again and told me that Mama had died. He didn't say exactly what killed her, but I am sure it was a broken heart – her only child chained up in a ship, waiting to be sent across the world."

"I am sorry to hear about your mother," I said.

"I still grieve for her, and blame myself for my stupidity in causing my family so much hurt. But on the ship I had to survive, day by day, hour by hour, minute by minute. Then some better news came. Botany Bay, we were told, was not to be our destination. We were to be sent to ships in Portsmouth. I was glad – the guards on board who had been sailors told us the wreck was about to sink. It certainly was taking in water in the lower deck. Living in a foot of water in a confined space was hard for us, especially for my counterfeiting friend, Rebecca, who was pregnant. She had not been raped – she took comfort from a friendly guard who brought her – and sometimes me – fresh fruit and, on some joyous occasions, cold beef or pork.

"I was resigned to my fate – more years on a ship, but per'aps Portsmouth would be better, I hoped.

"Then, in March 1789, the ship took part in the celebrations for the King. The whole of England celebrated the official declaration that he had been cured of his illness. The common people talked about his madness, of course. The guards got drunk, barrels of gin were rowed out to the ship from nearby inns on the shore. Strangers were on board, and many of the younger females were unchained to join the party.

"Rebecca went to the festivities and I chose not to. I never saw her again. I was told in the morning that she had flirted with the sole guard on the quarterdeck, unhappy that he could not join in the drinking, managed to get him drunk, and slipped overboard. It was said that she had an accomplice, her husband, waiting in a boat. They both fled to the West Country. That's what the matron said.

"I was glad for her but I also felt hurt that Rebecca had not told me of her plans.

"After all the years in Newgate and on board the *Resolute* – four years in all – Providence smiled on me at last, Richard."

"It seemed as though Providence had taken her time."

"Yes, per'aps, but we were told that some Newgate convicts sentenced to death had been reprieved. They would serve life instead. It was all due to King George's return to health. We female convicts awaiting transportation would also be considered.

"So it was, on a sunny May day, we were all assembled in ranks on deck, when Superintendent Clark read out a decree.

"It was long and full of legal words I did not fully comprehend, but what it meant was that women who had served four years, had no previous sentence and who had behaved correctly while in prison would be pardoned.

"He said he would read out the name of ten women who were to be freed.

"He read out nine and then stopped. My name 'ad not been called.

"The superintendent referred to a second piece of paper.

"Then he said, 'Convict Cecile Leclerc will also be pardoned.'

"I fell to the floor in a swoon. Matron picked me up, and plied me with some of her hidden gin.

"For once, the authorities had shown some compassion. My father had been informed. The next morning, I was rowed to shore with the other nine women, and deposited on a wharf at Woolwich. My father was one of the crowd waiting for us.

As we landed, I swore that I would never go on water again. As you saw in London, I have a dread of water…"

I got up and raised her to me and held her firmly. I kissed her gently. She slowly released herself from my arms and sat down once more on the bench.

"My tale is not finished…My father embraced me. He had to hold me for a while, because I had hardly stood on solid ground for two years. It took me quite some time to be able to walk steadily. Ah, we spoke of so many things so quickly in French in the nearby inn, the Sailor's Tavern. I remember what we ate. My father had dressed fish and sauce − at 1/6d − and I had griskin and potatoes for a shilling. We even had some wine. It was a wonderful reunion. We stayed talking and I began to wonder why my father didn't rush me to our home in Chelsea.

"Eventually I said, 'Papa, thank you for the meal, but all I want to do is to go home.'

"He looked very sad. 'Since your mama died, and with all the expenses, your aunt and I moved out. We both have lodgings now in St Giles.'

"I knew my father was too proud to tell me that the burden of supporting me and the many bribes over the years must have broken him.

"'Papa,' I said, 'I know what it must have cost to keep me in Newgate and on the ship, but I would not have survived for even a few weeks without your help. I thank you for saving my life.'

"We went in a lighter to Blackfriars, and stepped off at the wharf where I had left from Newgate. Then we walked to his lodgings – it was close by where we tried to find my aunt's last dwelling when we were in London.

"It was a very poor house, and the room was shabby, but he had made up a little bed for me. He was ashamed, but I told him so many times that this was like a palace after all I had endured.

"I really meant my words but he was unconvinced.

"That night he told me what he had planned for me: 'Cecile, I know that my last recommendation for employment ended tragically, but I have spoken to a young American man, who is more open about your time, er, away. He has spent time in a prison, or rather a military stockade, for refusing to fight the British. He was forced to leave America and has now settled in the Surrey Hills, about thirty miles from here. He is prepared to take you into his household, even though I could not get a letter of reference from Colonel Prendergast. I wrote to the Colonel again yesterday and asked him to show some mercy, especially as you have been pardoned by the King himself. Alas, I do not anticipate a reply. I presume, my dear, that you are prepared to work again in domestic service?'

"'Father, we both know that securing employment for a fallen woman, an ex-convict, will be very 'ard. I have to marry – if anyone would have me, work on the streets or find employment. I will glad take this opportunity in ...where was it again, Papa?'

"'Albury, in the Tillingbourne valley.'

"'I would like to spend some days with you and Aunt Suzanne, but then I will be happy to be away from London. Is Albury a pretty place, like when we were in France?'

"'I have not been there, Cecile, but I am told it is very beautiful ...and peaceful.'"

"And away from water," I said.

Cecile smiled, for the first time in her story.

"It was July 1789 that I came to work for the Cruikshanks. The master and madam know of my past, but not the other servants. And no one has ever mentioned my shame.

"After a year my father died. That was the information in one of the letters I had from my aunt. Although he was broken, he stayed alive in the hope that I would be free one day. And he did all he could...and more.

"So for more than three years here in this valley I have worked so 'ard, and attended church, and led a blameless life, Richard.

"So now you know of my life. I am an ex-convict, a Newgate bird. And I have seen many terrible things, but against all the odds I kept my health and my honour, thanks be to God. And, until I met you, I avoided two things in my new life – shallow men and deep water. Truth is, I have avoided all men when possible, except for my duties in the 'ouse and in church."

"And we crossed those bridges in London together, holding hands," I said.

"Thank'ee for listening to this long drama of mine. I applaud your patience. Yet I fear that I have forfeited your love."

"How can that be, my love?"

"Most decent people would now regard me as worse than a whore, even though I am innocent. We could never marry."

"Cecile, no, no. There is no other woman that I have ever wanted to marry.

280

"And remember, I have confessed to you that I am a murderer. I am guilty of killing a man, even though I had no choice, other than to be killed myself. I too could still be for the gallows, or transportation, for my free trading, or for attacking the King's Dragoons. I am guilty of so many things. I too live by the day, by the hour…"

"That is why we must seize our hours together…"

"Yes, Cecile. I am so glad you are here with me tonight."

"I have one more part of the story to tell you."

"Albert?"

"Yes."

"He was one of the men who robbed you in the Colonel's house?"

"Yes, I could hardly mistake him."

"And knowing his name?"

"The older man who called himself Bill Butcher addressed the albino by name, Albert. When the albino boy started to undo my buttons, and Bill stopped him, I could hear some of the conversation afterwards as they went to steal the silver plate. It was clear that they were father and son. And the father had the scar you described."

"So Jake and Bill were the same man."

"I am sure of it, Richard. And you are not responsible for murder – it was justice done to a robber who caused me to rot in prison for four years, when I was innocent of nothing except …fear of my mistress…and opening that accursed door to that accursed man. Richard, as a Christian, I should not say this, but I am happy that you killed the man who brought so much torment to me and my family.

"This is no guilty secret now shared," she said. "It is an eternal bond of trust and gratitude we now share."

"For years in prison I dreamed of killing that Bill – Jake or whatever his name is. I feel some of the burden is now removed.

"I have talked so much. And we have been so serious – though I am glad that the tale has been told.

"I feel much more confident now with you, though I never doubted you. You are accepting of me... and my past.

"I have one more favour to ask. I have said to you that, although of mature years, I have never been with a man...Richard, I love you, and I fear for our future. And the past wasted in those prisons. I want to celebrate our time together.

"May I be so bold, though unbecoming of a woman, even one who is an ex-convict, as to ask whether I may share your bed, and that you understand that I know little of what is expected of me in these matters?"

I kissed her and embraced her in front of the dying embers of the fire.

"Cecile, I will cherish you for as long as I live. It is my greatest honour to share a bed with you tonight, and a marital bed as soon as arrangements can be made."

Deep inside me, fear gnawed. This was the best moment in my life. I wanted to marry this woman as soon as I could. I feared losing her. But having got what I really wanted I was desperately afraid of it being snatched from me. It wasn't so much the dread of prison or Black Harry or the albino. Something was cutting away at my insides...and it was threatening to take away all I held dear. I pushed it aside with a final swig from the brandy bottle.

Thirty

I led Cecile up to my bedroom, lit two large candles and showed her where she could wash. I also lit the bedroom's small log fire that I had rarely used even in the winter. I went back down and carried up her bag and left her to the privacy of her ablutions, while I dampened the fire downstairs. I went out and checked the stables and pulled tight the bolts on the doors and shutters of the house.

Finally, I went up the stairs full of expectation and yet nervous despite my experience with women.

I knocked on the door, hesitated and then walked in. She was sitting up in bed in a white nightdress. Her hair, before always put up in a bun, was now tied into two pig-tails. She looked so young, as though the prison years had not affected her beauty or her soul. She had her arms folded. Her green and brown eyes flashed at me. Did they betray a little fear mixed with expectation, and perhaps desire? I did not know.

She thanked me for my hospitality and for the fire, as I took off my shirt and vest and pulled my nightshirt over me. A little shyly I took off my breeches and boots and stood at the end of my own bed, rather self-consciously.

"May I join you?" I asked politely.

"You are welcome, kind sir," she said smiling.

We talked of little things while I held her hand.

And then I leaned over to kiss her cheek.

After a second or two of hesitation, she put her arms around me and pulled me towards her.

I kissed her harder and then eased her up towards me, as we sat embracing on the bed.

I gently undid the ribbons holding the front of her nightdress and tenderly kissed around her breasts and then licked her erect nipples slowly and then a little more rapidly.

She started to kiss my neck and shoulders.

Then she pulled me towards her and I held her as though I was afraid to lose her forever.

Her legs began to entwine around mine, as I rolled on my back and gently started to move the nightdress up her body.

She stopped kissing me.

"Richard, may I leave my nightdress on, at least until we are married? I am so embarrassed by my scars..."

"If that is your wish, Cecile," I said softly, "but I see in front of me the most beautiful woman I have ever beheld. Your scars mean nothing to me, except to remind me of your hurt in the past. I promise that in the future no man will ever lay a hand on you in anger or hurt."

I took off my nightshirt and she undid the rest of the bows on her nightdress. Her ample, firm breasts drew me towards her and we embraced flesh to flesh for the first time.

She started to sigh as I moved across her, holding my weight on my elbows as we pressed towards each other.

She became very passionate, as though she had waited a lifetime for this moment. I reached my hands up to her back under her nightdress and felt the scar tissue, but caressed her back as I lay on my side now.

I moved down to kiss her stomach, and then back up to her breasts as she stroked my hair.

Gradually I reached with my hand towards her thigh and moved my hands inwards as I felt her sweet liquid rejoicing in my touch. She groaned a little louder as I moved her legs apart.

She asked me, "Do you still love me, after all that I 'ave done?"

"I respect and love you even more for surviving so much while still being such a gentle person, and so beautiful…"

She pushed me back slightly and then she took off her nightdress. She held it against her breasts and stomach, while she leaned over and blew out the candle next to the bed.

She lay on her back, with her legs astride but holding the nightdress across her middle.

I leaned over and kissed her again and she held me increasingly tightly.

I could not hold back any longer.

I eased the nightdress away and lay on top of her.

Gently I placed my hands under her buttocks.

And as softly and as slowly as I could I pushed inside her.

Cecile was very quiet but responsive.

I asked, "Am I hurting you?"

She said no, but I could sense the slight pain in her voice.

Slowly, slowly, tenderly, tenderly, I pushed deeper inside her, as her nails pressed into my back.

Carefully I increased my tempo, as she released the pressure of her nails and instead she started to move her hands up and down my back to match the speed of my increasing movement.

She started to groan with pleasure, as I moved her legs gently over my chest and across each shoulder as I returned my hands to hold her buttocks.

The flickers from my bedroom fire illuminated our love-making and enabled me to see her face, wearing a serene smile. We looked in each other's eyes. And then there was a wild bewilderment in her face, soon transcended by a passionate intensity, as we started to move in a joint rhythm together.

She started to cry, and I said, "Shall I stop?"

"No, no please do not stop, *mon amour*. Ah, this is all so new to me. I want you to keep pushing inside me."

She started to take faster shorter breaths as I started to reach the beginning of my climax. I did not want to be selfish, I wanted to do everything possible to make this a celebration of love for my Cecile.

I moved faster inside her, while trying not to thrust too hard. I felt my body was on fire with love and desire as I reached my point of no return.

"I love you, Cecile. This is what I have waited for my whole life...as though it were many cycles of lives waiting for this single moment."

"I am so glad that I waited for you, too," she said.

Then in a volcano of love, I held her as passionately as I could, and then finally, finally, relaxed in her arms.

The gentlest feelings washed over me, but also the fear that it would all soon fade.

I kissed her and, after a while, we talked of all the things we would do in the future, and of the children we still might have.

Eventually, I got out of the bed, and put a small iron guard over the grate and extinguished the second candle.

Soon we were asleep in each other's arms.

I had no idea how long we had slept, but it was dark outside the shutters when I heard a horse whinny. I was instantly fully awake. Was someone trying to steal my horse, or were there friendly visitors?

I got out of bed as swiftly as I could without waking or alarming Cecile.

I moved the shutter across an inch or more and looked out into the moonlight. I could make out at least two horses, perhaps three, in a wooded area to the side of my yard.

Cecile was now awake.

"What is it, Richard?"

"I don't know, Cecile. Horsemen. Stay here – I will go and see."

I pulled on my shirt, breeches and boots, and made sure my dagger was in my belt.

I went down the stairs, grabbed the heavy poker from beside the fire and then cautiously unbolted the back door on to the courtyard. I opened the door and looked out, waiting for my eyes to get used to the darkness before I stepped out. I could hear nothing.

After listening intently for a few more minutes, and with my eyes now able to penetrate beyond the stables and shrubbery I stepped cautiously into the moonlit yard.

Suddenly, a great force dragged me backwards.

The strength was more than human. I was pulled deeper, deeper, deeper into some black hole...I dropped the poker and the dagger as I felt sucked into a massive whirlpool of air...then it was all black. Black nothingness.

Thirty-one

I was back in my accursed apartment. My head throbbed and my throat ached with dryness. Anger coursed through my entire being. What if, what if, I could not get back another time? I had been lucky, or blessed, with my second round of self-hypnosis. Now I was utterly drained. Although every ounce of my consciousness yearned for Cecile, I knew that I really had to take stock. I realised that I was severely damaging my mind and body.

And why did it end when it did? What happened to me in Gomshall that last night with Cecile? Was I attacked by Black Harry and his minions? I had a very selfish masculine thought, but it was about our love, not sex. Thank God I had made love to Cecile before I was sucked back to the present.

Oh, I so missed her. I had left so many things unsaid, so many things we wanted to do together. I loved her so much I could almost medically define an ache in my heart.

Was there something uniquely metaphysical? We had both been outsiders in the Tillingbourne valley, we both somehow felt different – though many in the Hurtwood had stood by me. She had loved me in the end, and I reciprocated. Had a cosmic chain been broken by our act of true love? Was it some kind of redemption or revenge? Had the consummated act of love made me free? Delivered me from a preordained calamity?

Although it seemed more like I had been cast down to the underworld.

I had left Cecile there, deserted her, possibly at the mercy of that ruthless swine, Black Harry. And what had happened to dear Nance, and old Solly? And my lovely Tamar? They were all like grains of sand, ashes to ashes now – if they had ever lived and breathed on this earth. It was as though I had read a borrowed copy of a mystery novel, and then I got to the final page – to find out who dunnit, and the damn page was missing.

I obviously needed to rest and restore my health, my sanity even. But I felt consumed by a sense of destiny. I had to get back to Cecile – for ever – or die in the attempt.

Once more, I set up my self-hypnosis paraphernalia.

Thirty-two

*F*irst came an impression of falling, falling, falling, and of being caught in a warm web of welcoming light, as though it were a trampoline made of candy floss, sticky, sweet, fluffy, enticing…then a sudden acceleration into pitch blackness, as though a massive hand had lifted me up, and then I was stationary, standing like a marble statue in the midst of the universe, with small pinpricks of stars…I heard an eerie whistling noise…next I heard the deepest voice imaginable, but pleasant on the ear. The voice said, "Why are you travelling here?…This is not your time. You may see things which are unimaginable, which may damage your soul…You should go back. You can if you want to…"

I understood what the voice said, although the language was not English.

Perhaps it was some sort of telepathy, the same power that knew that I did not want to go back.

I felt I was falling again. And once more I was still, standing in the midst of all creation.

I sensed love around me, and that love, I knew, was associated with my Cecile. I had been forgiven for leaving her. I had been set free.

I opened my eyes, and I was savagely disappointed not to be in the Surrey Hills I loved, before cars and before world wars, and speaking a dialect of English which I could share with Cecile, Nance, Little Will.

I looked out of the window of a modern house, and I saw a sleek red helicopter flying low. Who needed to fly in the time I loved and needed?

Yet it was a strange kind of helicopter, flying close by, but almost without a sound; a new kind of engine, I guessed.

I was curious, however, and I wanted to explore more. I tried to walk towards the window, but I could not move. My body was constricted.

I perceived that I was somehow tied to a chair, a wheelchair. I could not move my legs. I could not move my arms. Have I been constrained? Was I in an asylum? I could not see any bonds. I must be in some way disabled, I reasoned. Have I suffered a stroke, am I perhaps a paraplegic? I could move my hands, and my neck a little. Fear swept through my brain.

Darkness started to envelop me and I lost consciousness.

Thirty-three

opened my eyes with blurred vision, and a throbbing headache, as though from a monster hangover. I blinked a few times, but it took two or three minutes to force my eyes to focus properly.

I looked at the clock in my study. I had been "transported" for about ten minutes. There was at least a fit here: my recollection was a few minutes' vision into what? My future? My fate? My karma?

I had wanted with all my heart to regress to return to Cecile. But if regression was real, and I believed it was – despite all my scientific training – then, logically, progression was just as possible.

Had I really gone forwards instead of backwards?

Or was I really mad? Or had one iota of remaining rationality given me this dream, warning me not to play with my mind, my fate, my future or my past?

It certainly gave me the willies, to use one of the first English phrases I had thought was really cute when I first came to England; a country which had turned my life and brain upside-down, inside-out.

I would give my mind and body a rest. Maybe Jane was right. I missed Cecile with every fibre of my being, but the doctor in me sternly warned of tampering with my psyche any more. I still believed fervently in my past-life experience of Cecile, but I was tempted to conclude that my wheelchair episode was a result of stress, exhaustion, guilt over my argument with Jane, booze – you name it. I didn't believe in that glimpse of the future, I didn't want to believe it. I would not let go of the past, however.

Jane rang me late the next morning: "Tom, I apologize for going over the top. I over-reacted because I was – and am – so worried about you. Psychiatrists have a habit of going a bit berserk on occasions, but they are brilliant at hiding it. For quite some time, until...

"You were like Jekyll and Hyde last night. I was angry because you couldn't see it. I remember reading one of your earlier research papers, when we first went out: about cognitive dissonance. Great stuff. Can't you see that you are looking at one set of facts and yet choosing to believe something else? That's OK in religion, but not medicine, Tom.

"I can't get the next few days off, but next weekend, why don't we get back down to earth, as I suggested? The weather's not great at the moment, but why don't we go to the Yorkshire Dales?"

I didn't choose to interrupt her. She obviously had carefully prepped for this call.

"It's not that far from my parents and I have to pop in a present for my mother's birthday. We won't stay there long, but then we can go for two days walking in the Dales. Stay at a guest house or something. Just get away – you and me. Peace. You know what Wordsworth said about the countryside restoring the tranquillity of the soul. What do you say?"

I was quiet for a second or two. I was trying hard to think. "Thank you, Jane, I felt like shit after you walked out yesterday.

I hate arguing, as you know. OK, let's go see your folks and your over-sexed aunt. Next weekend."

"Good. Do you want me to come over tonight? If you want to talk about what happened, I promise to listen. I shouldn't have thrown my toys out of the pram. I wasn't behaving like a doctor either — I should have patiently listened to what my special patient had to say."

"Please come over, but I don't want to talk any more about my little, er, experiment. Let's get our relationship back on an even keel. OK?"

"Sure, see you tonight — not sure when exactly but we'll talk through the trip to Yorkshire. Are my walking boots at your place, by the way?"

"I think so — in the kitchen cupboard. I'll have a look."

"Bye then, Tom, I do love you, but I do worry about you sometimes. I suppose that's the price I have to pay for going out with a genius."

I didn't have time to protest...she was off the line.

I would take the holiday. But first I would finish my journal — this story. I would maybe wait for a day or two, get my mind more balanced. Then I would try to recreate the exact conditions of my first experiment. I needed to try just once more. I am not sure whether it was to be with Cecile for just a few more minutes. Perhaps I needed to say goodbye... Perhaps I was just fooling myself. My feelings were so intense about her. I was like a nicotine addict saying, "I'll have just one last cigarette." Being without her was like a heroin junkie having his fix snatched away in front of his or her eyes. I would say or do anything to get back to what I craved.

⋘∞⋙

I have taken a day away from this journal. And nothing has changed about my desire to see Cecile. I feel like an adulterer planning a trip with Jane, while Cecile is breathing in, on and from every pore of my body.

There are so many things I want to say, not just about Cecile, but about my feelings regarding life in the 1790s. Nothing has faded. I keep comparing the superficiality of the modern era with the reality of life then: living with the seasons, being more attuned to nature, the intensity of relationships, the meaning of community, but of course disease, dirt and danger intruded on the idyll. I keep weighing up the different ways of living. And, in the end, I would choose the 1790s, even if there were no Cecile.

I face the prospect of my existence in the twenty-first century with gloom and apprehension. Medically and intellectually I suspect, but also emotionally, I am not convinced that this mood will fade. Yet how can I face another week without Cecile? Another day? Another hour...?

I have two things I must do almost immediately. I have to face Jane and her family for a weekend. And I will try again, perhaps for the last time, at the same time of hour and the same place, to recreate my deep relaxation – though I want to call it deep regression. I do not want to float off into a fantasy of the future, the what-ifs. I need to go back to the real past. It is my past, I know it!

Jane was right about saying that I need someone medically qualified to supervise my regression, but I can hardly ask her, especially if I start ranting about my love for Cecile. Mary, my secretary, can be trusted. But, against my better medical judgement, I will repeat the experiment exactly as before, alone – that stands a better chance of replicating the regression I want.

Soon, too, I will visit Shere, Gomshall, Albury and all the places I had known in and around the Hurtwood in those days of swashbuckling and smuggling. I want to check out references in libraries, and I will perhaps talk to Jim Crozier, the patient who started all this. I wonder whether our shared experiences will enhance or undermine a future meeting between us. I realise if I talk to him he might decide to use my confession as part of an official complaint to the General Medical Council. Should I risk all? Yet he's my only living connection with my life then. Somehow, I couldn't see my colleagues in the Royal College of Psychiatrists warming to the words in my journal...if they managed to get their hands on a copy.

I don't want to be metamorphosed into some history anorak. I have to resolve this massive angst which is driving me to...who knows where.

I have to try to get back to Cecile and the mores of the eighteenth century, and yet I must practise modern medicine, co-exist with Jane, drive a car...be normal. Or what others would call normal. I passionately believe that I had been a better man in the 1790s. Was that experience intended – by whom? God? A god? – to make me more understanding in 2007 and thereafter?

Perhaps I should go to church and pray. Or spend time with my old college friend who is now a rabbi. I should read more about eastern religious concepts of reincarnation. My scepticism has flown. I believe. But I do not know where to go for help to explain my beliefs. Modern medicine – no. Professionally, I would be forced to diagnose myself as suffering from a delusional state, bordering on what used to be called schizophrenia. So far, I have not heard voices inside my head or God whispering in my ear, though my experiences have certainly made me more aware than previously of a spiritual dimension.

Apart from short breaks for snacks, some naps, my argument with Jane, and a day off, I have been writing this journal almost non-stop. I have to get this all down quickly. So far my memories of yesteryear have not faded. I need to go back and check what I have written to make sure it is as accurate as I can make it.

I will finish my story when I have tried once more to revisit my past with Cecile.

May God bless my noble endeavour.

February 2007, London...to be continued...

Thomas J Martin, MD

Editor's Postscripts

September 2007

I have tried very hard to make sense of Dr Thomas J Martin's journal. As I said in the introduction, it was given to me in May 2007. Tom Martin disappeared in February 2007. I spent three months interviewing his friends and colleagues in London, as well as visiting his family in the USA. I checked police records and there has been no confirmed sighting of him since his disappearance. Initially, Dr Jane McCarthy helped me a great deal in my research, but her former colleague, and lover, had simply disappeared from the face of this earth. I will keep searching, with an open mind. I cannot explain the final brief diary entry relating possibly to the future, although I have spoken to a number of experts on the paranormal. I encountered numerous cases of past-life experiences, regression, but little scientific evidence of progression into the future.

I can offer a number of possibilities. The most obvious is that Dr Martin became unhinged by his regression experiment and a) moved to another country or, as a committed Anglophile, has taken up a new identity somewhere in the UK; b) suffered some bizarre accident, and his body has not been found; c) he has been murdered and his body has been hidden; d) or he committed suicide, perhaps in a remote location abroad. Suicide seems unlikely as all his associates have confirmed his zest for life, and there has never been any suspicion of serious depression, although Dr McCarthy did suggest that he had become obsessed with his research into regression.

Another possibility suggested by two of the psychiatrists I interviewed is that Tom Martin, having lost his wallet and ID, has been committed to a mental home and soon got lost in the infamous NHS "system". I spent a few days ringing around various such institutions and drew a blank. They did not confirm whether a male fitting Dr Martin's description was in their care. In most cases, they refused to give me any information at all, and that's when they could be bothered to answer the phone.

Another alternative is possible, a less scientific conclusion perhaps: I would like to believe that he somehow contrived to return to the 1790s, to be with Cecile. I do not have any explanation as to how he did that. Such passion and conviction, as well as detail, suffuse his account of his past life that this is a compelling dramatic explanation, but it requires an act of faith which the rationalist in me finds hard to accept.

The strange future entry in his diary is perhaps the result of some traumatic reaction to his time under self-hypnosis. The events he described in the late-eighteenth century span a number of months, yet experts say that a period of self-hypnosis is unlikely to last more than a few hours, at the very most. There is some evidence from Tom Martin's neighbours that in a period during mid-February 2007 his flat was occupied, but that no one answered any enquiries at the door of his apartment. A postman confirmed that he had tried to deliver a parcel and registered mail, and police records show that calls were made from the flat. Dr Martin may have been preoccupied with writing his diary. Dr McCarthy did telephone him during this period, visited him and did express concern at his later not answering subsequent calls and visits, which eventually led to police forcing an entry into the flat and finding it deserted.

So if the doctor was utterly preoccupied with describing his regression, perhaps the tiredness, emotion and unsupervised experimentation led to some kind of delusional state, hence the projection into the future.

Until Dr Martin – or his body – turns up, all we can do is speculate.

I offer you what I have been given. I repeat: I have slightly edited the story for grammatical errors and occasionally shortened the narrative and introduced or amended some of the dialogue, but I have not altered anything of substance. His family and Dr McCarthy gave me formal permission to offer this story for publication in the hope that any publicity might help in the search for an able and promising psychiatrist. Perhaps he might even read it and return to his loved ones. I hope he will. Deep in my heart, however, I would like to believe that Tom Martin is somewhere where he cannot read a book published in the twenty-first century. If that is so, I hope that he and Cecile are together, and happy, in their lives in Surrey – more than 200 years ago.

December 2008

The story continued to intrigue me even after the police inquiry into Dr Martin's disappearance was completed – no final conclusion was reached and the case was left open.

I could not leave the story there.

I continued to press Dr McCarthy for more information,

but she refused to help any further once the police enquiries were completed.

On 20 October 2008, a year and a half after Tom Martin's disappearance, Dr McCarthy committed suicide using an overdose of morphine. At the time of writing, police sources indicate they have reopened the case and that they are investigating a major argument in Tom Martin's apartment on two occasions in February 2007. Police search teams, with tracker dogs, have also been investigating isolated areas of the Yorkshire dales. Police established from earlier statements by Dr McCarthy, as well as eyewitnesses, that both doctors visited the Dales on 18-19 February 2007 and stayed in a guest house. Dr McCarthy's return to London was verified but not Dr Martin's.

The more lurid elements of the popular media have suggested that Dr McCarthy murdered her former lover, and that she invented the diaries – which are published here – as a cover to suggest that he had lost his mind, and may have simply chosen to disappear. The tabloids also tried to link Dr McCarthy in a love triangle with Jim Crozier. Photographs were produced of her visiting one of Crozier's clubs some time after they first met, according to this journal, at a charity event she attended with Tom Martin.

From police sources, based upon analyses of both doctors' computers, it is clear that Tom Martin emailed his journal to his secretary Mary, perhaps for safekeeping. Parts of the diary were also emailed to Jane McCarthy. My access to police data on the journals is fragmentary but, although the essentials of the diary were almost certainly recorded on Tom's laptop, it is possible that some embellishments were made by Dr McCarthy in the version that appears here in print.

Whether she was trying to suggest that Tom Martin was deranged and perhaps took his own life will never be known. Dr McCarthy's motives will remain unclear, as she left no suicide note or diary. It may be that she changed the journal's modern section to exaggerate or perhaps minimise Dr Martin's affection for her. Or she could have exaggerated the conclusion to indicate that the doctor was losing his grip on reality. This could have been a form of self-deception for her own emotional needs, a coping mechanism after the death or disappearance of her partner. Or more sinister motives could be the reason – that she was trying to disguise her own acts.

Although police forensic experts can work out what computer produced what version of what email I suspect that the experts will not decipher who did what when and why, because, three months after Dr Martin's disappearance, the police allowed Jane McCarthy to take the laptop used by Mary Duncan, the secretary. Presumably they had examined it and found nothing suspicious, though it is possible that they did not examine it thoroughly. If they had looked at the journal, they might have assumed it was some kind of fantasy novel in progress. Even if the police had taken the journal seriously, it would imply that Dr Martin was – to say the least – suffering from emotional, if not delusional, problems. This would have enhanced the impression that he was a missing person, who had gone on some kind of deranged walkabout. If Jane McCarthy was guilty of tampering with the journal, this was perhaps her intention. The fact that Dr McCarthy was also anxious to obtain the permission of Tom Martin's family to publicize the diary may also support this view, although at the time I was convinced that her motives were genuine – that she wanted any publicity which might solve the mystery of the missing doctor. Dr McCarthy did admit to me that she had made minor changes in the diary before releasing it to me; she implied that there were one or two personal and intimate references to her that she did not wish to see published, although the two sex scenes remained. It was on that condition that the copyright was assigned to me by Dr McCarthy and Tom Martin's family.

So the provenance of this final version of the diary may in parts be questionable, but, from my own investigations and from the internal evidence of textual consistency, I believe that it accurately represents the general intentions of its named author, Dr Thomas J Martin.

Perhaps I had been too engrossed playing detective in the present day. I was so convinced of the authentic intention of Tom Martin that I partially accepted his level of analysis. I had to delve into the past. I spent many hours researching his family tree but could find no obvious connection with Surrey's history.

Next I tried Dr Jane McCarthy, and I found something interesting. On her mother's side I traced her initially disguised Jewish connections all the way back to Southwark in the late eighteenth century. The records showed Jane McCarthy could trace her ancestry back to Tamar Jacobson. I rejected any fanciful notion of revenge, thwarted love, festering in the genes through the generations. Tamar was portrayed in the diary as loving and kind, and we have no firm evidence that Dr McCarthy was in any way implicated in Tom Martin's disappearance.

Something still niggled in my brain – one question remained, which I tried to answer by investigating in the Surrey History Centre in Woking, where church records have been collated. In the open-plan office of the new building, I eventually found on microfiche what I had been hunting for. I still needed to make sure.

The History Centre was most helpful in allowing me access to the original archives in the basement. Wearing special gloves, I was allowed to open a large red leather-bound register, scuffed and sprinkled with a light coating of dust, but otherwise well preserved.

It contained information dated 19 July 1794. The place was St James's Church, Shere.

There were two lines, in impressive copperplate script, about a marriage on that day:

"Richard Durrant, Esquire, 43, tradesman, and Miss Cecile Leclerc, 33, spinster, both of this parish."

The second line read: "Witnessed on this day by Albert Whapshot Esquire.

So it appears that Richard Durrant not only married Cecile but was also reconciled with his nephew.

That record made me feel much happier about editing and publishing this book. It gave me hope that Thomas J Martin perhaps found what he was so desperately searching for – the love of his past life.

Notes

1   Two sentences were removed here, on legal advice.

2   Ugly woman.

3   Fool.

4   Informant.

5   Jane is referring to President George W. Bush

6   Editor's note: Dr Martin's few pages of handwritten notes contained a sort of dramatis personae. It appeared originally that Nance's son had been called Michael. Instead, in the typed text, the name is Will. The previous name is the same as Dr Martin's brother. Whether this was an inadvertent error or a token of affection for his brother is unknown. It may have been an artifice by an author who was reflecting on both lives, rather than faithfully chronicling the events of the late eighteenth century.

7   Colloquialism for "getting back to London".

8   Showing too much cleavage.

9   "Diluting with water".

10   Another word for dandy.

11   Thunder pillars, eighteenth-century Surrey dialect
        for cumulus clouds.

12   Tip a half-penny.

13   Pawn-shop.

14   Synagogue.

15   Hole in the head.

16   Polite slang for having sex.

17   Rough whores.

18   Sex between women.

19   Dialect for very sick.

20   Dresser.

21   Chicken coop.

22   Acting strangely, out of order.

23   Yeast.

24   Colloquialism for eyes.

25   Admirable, worthy, having fine qualities.